To: Mary
Stay Awesome

SPLIT *Ends*

MAGNOLIA SERIES: BOOK TWO

TAYLOR DAWN

To: Mary
Stay Awsom

Cover Design by ZH Designs
Edited by Wendy Garfinkle

This is a work of fiction. Names, characters, places, brands, media, and incidents are either the product of the author's imagination or are used fictitiously. Any resemblance to similarly named places or to persons living or deceased is unintentional.

ISBN: 13 – 978-1533087270

Princess Press

Split Ends is dedicated to Christina and Annelle. The two of you will just have to fight it out over who gets Cole Matthews. Good luck, ladies!

❦ Chapter One ❧

"YOU'VE GOT TO BE SHITTING me," Cole Matthews gawked at the stark white piece of paper in his right hand. His other hand flailed through the air like he was batting flies away from his face.

"Whoa, you don't look happy." Luke walked by Cole's workspace.

"Look at this shit." Cole tossed the letter to the edge of utilitarian metal desk, Luke snatching it up quickly.

This was the last thing he needed. He'd had so many life changes in the past 6 months—including moving to the FBI field office in Biloxi, Mississippi. Doing so was a leap he hadn't really thought about before he found himself knee-deep in his decision. His partner Luke

Daughtry had transferred here to be closer to his girlfriend Ava, so Cole got it in his mind he should move too. What a numbskull move.

"Am I reading this right?" Luke sat the paper back on the desk.

Cole pushed a hand through his gelled raven hair. "Yup." He blew out a frustrated breath.

"You're married?" Luke's face was one of pure shock. Cole couldn't help but think his partner had the same look a cartoon character did when someone handed them a stick of dynamite.

"Apparently so." He let out a frustrated sigh.

"Wait, how did you not know you're married? That seems like something you'd know about. Were you drugged or something?" Luke chuckled.

"No. Hell, I was 19. She thought she was knocked up and I did the honorable thing."

"But I'm not understanding why you're still married." Luke's confused expression mirrored Cole's.

"I don't either. I signed the damn divorce papers over 12 years ago."

"Maybe they made a mistake." Luke propped himself up on the edge of the large metal object.

"If there's a mistake this big, my faith in the judicial system is fucked."

"Seems like an easy fix though. File again and get rid of her."

"Yeah, I'll get it taken care of. She's gonna be in town for a few weeks. I'm sure we can get it done then."

"Sounds like a plan. Listen, I'm gonna head out. Ava's cooking fried chicken and rhubarb pie." Luke rubbed his stomach.

"You're so whipped." Cole busted out laughing.

"No, I'm in love with the most amazing woman on the planet."

Cole didn't envy the googly-eyed look Luke wore when he talked about his girlfriend. In fact, Cole had sworn off all emotional attachment to the fairer sex ever since he'd first signed those damn divorce papers.

If there was ever a woman he was head over heels in love with, it was her. Gracie Callahan. With her spitfire attitude, her glowing red hair and those emerald eyes;

every man in a 5 block radius turned to look at her when she walked by. Cole hadn't seen her since they'd split though. He wondered what she'd look like as a completely filled-out woman. Would she be the same innocent beauty she'd been years ago? Or had she changed over the years like he had? Damn this was going to suck big time. As if he didn't have enough shit on his plate, now he had to entertain Gracie while she was in town. Well fuck a duck.

"Are you sure we have to go?"

Gracie looked at her daughter who was whining. "Yes, for the umpteenth time, we have to go," Gracie declared as she continued to toss articles of clothing into her bright red suitcase.

"But I could stay with Aunt Jenna. I'm sure she wouldn't mind." Her daughter pleaded with her while digging through Gracie's jewelry box — something the almost-teenager did quite frequently.

"Cora, I need you to come with me. Please don't make

this an argument." She lowered her voice.

Cora tossed a pair of earrings back into the wooden box and turned to look at her mom. "Mom, this's my summer vacation. I don't want to spend it in Mississippi!" The dark-haired girl threw her hands in the air and stomped out of the room.

Gracie yelled at her back, "I'm your mother and what I say is the law around here! You're going and that's final!"

She heard her daughter call from the hallway, "Whatever!"

That was Cora's go-to response for something she didn't like. When things didn't please her, she just said 'whatever' and stormed off. The 12-year-old was becoming more like her hard-headed father with each passing day. The only thing was Cora had never met her father. And he had no idea he had a daughter. It wasn't as if she was a terrible human being for not telling him about their daughter. It was for self-preservation. Gracie knew he wasn't in the relationship 100 percent and she refused to keep him around just because they created

offspring. Was keeping that information from him the
right thing to do? No. But it had been the easy thing to
do.

Cole Matthews wasn't someone Gracie would
consider 'daddy material.' His wild ways and refusal to
be tied down were just a couple of the reasons she'd felt
compelled to be tight-lipped about Cora. Yeah, they'd
dated all through Junior and Senior years in high school
and, of course, thought they were destined to be
together. They'd even waited until the night of Senior
Prom to take their relationship to the next level. In room
265 at the local Super 8 Motel they'd kicked things up a
notch and had sex. Actually, "having sex" wasn't really
the word for it. Cole had blown her mind and body into
the stratosphere. She'd expected her first time to be
rough and uncomfortable but Cole made sure he took the
time to make her at ease and cared for. Boy, did she feel
cared for that night. After the initial nervousness had
worn off, he'd taken her to heights she never dared to
imagine, even a few days later she could feel the places
on and in her body he'd been. Even now her cheeks

flamed and her panties became damp at just the thought of what he'd done to her. But all good things must come to an end. And their end had been when she found out she was pregnant at 19. Fresh out of high school Gracie didn't know what she'd do. When she'd gotten up the nerve to finally tell Cole about the baby, he'd proposed and they were married less than a week later. At the time it seemed like a good idea but after being together for only a month, Gracie knew it wasn't going to work out. Cole wasn't there emotionally and there was no way in hell she'd raise a child in that type of environment. So she did the only thing she could think of; she lied. Telling Cole the pregnancy was a fluke might've been a terrible thing to do but it was better than keeping a man around who clearly didn't want to be there.

Right now, her plan was to fly to Biloxi, get Cole to sign the divorce papers and get out. It was time to move on for good. Even though Cora would be with her, she had her fib ready in case he suspected anything. She'd pass Cora off as a one-night stand after they'd broken up all those years ago. He'd believe it; he had to. If Cole caught on to her sham, she'd be knee-deep in shit and the consequences of that were life-threatening. Getting in and getting the job done quickly was crucial.

Zipping up her bags she began carrying them to the front door.

"Cora, time to go!" Gracie called through the house.

"I'm coming," her daughter popped out of her bedroom dragging her own suitcase behind her. Yeah, Cora had a bit of an attitude. But Gracie blamed it on the fact that her own Irish heritage must've bled into Cora's genes a bit too much.

Glancing at the bags by the door, she sighed. This wasn't a trip she wanted to make, but right now, the safety of her daughter and herself were hanging in the balance. She'd do anything to protect Cora and this was a step she had to take. She'd lay down her life for the sassy 12-year-old no matter what. Time to put that theory to the test.

～ *Chapter Two* ～

"HEY AVA. Could I get a quick trim?" Cole walked into Ava's one-chair salon and took a seat on the sofa in the waiting area.

"Sure thing. Just gotta finish up with Jack here." Ava smiled one of her sweet grins and went back to running the electric clippers over the old man's head.

Grabbing a magazine from the stack on a small table, he flipped through it while waiting. After scanning a few articles about '*how to please your lover with food in the bedroom*' and '*make any man want you with just a look,*' Cole tossed the useless piece of garbage to the side. He knew how to please a lover and as for making a guy want him, just *no*.

"Come on over, Cole," Ava called.

He watched the other client make his way out the door as he walked over and took a seat in the black styling chair. "Thanks for working me in," he said as Ava spread the cutting cloth over him and snapped it around his neck.

"No problem. You have a date tonight?" She looked at him in the mirror and winked.

"Don't *even* act like you don't know what's going on. I know for a fact your boy toy is a big blabber mouth." Cole groaned.

"You're right." She grabbed her water bottle and began spraying his hair down. "So, you're married?"

"Seems that way."

Ava snorted. "What's she like?"

"Hell, I don't know. Haven't seen her in years. She could weigh 600 pounds and have an eye patch for all I know."

"Big girls need love too, ya know," Ava laughed.

"Yeah well, I'm not in the loving mood for *anyone*. I just wanna get this shit signed and over with."

Ava began to snip the ends of his hair. "I understand."

Before long Ava had him all trimmed up and looking somewhat presentable. He was in serious need of a shave but he was becoming attached to the scruffy look he had going on. No use trying to impress anyone, especially Gracie. He wasn't planning on spending any time with her anyway. It was simple; sign the papers and walk away. If she wanted to rehash old times, that was too damn bad. He didn't have time for that shit.

"Just wonderful." Gracie sighed as she stood on the curb outside the airport.

"What's wrong, mom?"

"I called to confirm our hotel and they lost the reservation. Now they're booked."

"Just get another one," Cora said. "Make sure it has a pool too."

"That's the thing, there's some sort of convention going on and all the hotels are booked for the week."

"Great. Are we going to have to sleep in a cardboard box while we're here?"

"No, I'll figure something out." Gracie knew what that *something* was, too. Although she really didn't want to go with door number two. She took a steadying breath and faced down her phone like it was a lion getting ready to devour her if she made one wrong move. "I *can* do this." With the phone in her hand she turned it over and hit the name on the screen. Her foot tapped the concrete as she listened to it ring on the other end.

"Matthews." Cole's voice filtered through the phone and into her brain, immediately putting her body on high alert. "Hello?" he said, pulling her out of her lackadaisical state of judgment.

"Hi, it's me, Gracie," she stated with a shaky voice. Looking down at her free hand, she rolled her eyes to see it trembling like she had some type of disorder.

"Gracie, how are you?" He sounded out of breath.

"I'm good. Did I catch you at a bad time?" She couldn't help but hear the way he was breathing. Damn, it sounded a lot like he'd been having sex. Shit. What if he *was* having sex?

"Nope, just out for a run. What can I do for ya?"

"I hate to ask this. I know it's an inconvenience, and you don't have to say yes..."

"Spit it out, Gracie."

She hesitated. "There was a problem with the hotel reservation. I don't have a place to stay while I'm here." She looked around again.

"Where are you now?" *Crap*, he sounded irritated.

"At the airport." *Ugh* she hated asking him for help.

"Be there in 15," he said and then hung up.

Well that was quick. She didn't expect him to play *Captain America* and come to the rescue so fast.

As Cole drove to the airport, a fit of nervousness swamped him. He shook his head at the thought that *he* could become nervous. Hell, his job was beyond dangerous, he dealt with the worst kind of criminals and he'd been shot numerous times. *None* of those things made him anxious. But driving to meet Gracie? Yeah, he was about to shit himself.

Nothing on this earth could've prepared him for what he saw when he pulled to the curb in front of the airport. First of all, he'd recognize that hair anywhere. The reddish-golden hue was even more vibrant in the Mississippi sunlight than it'd been back in Chicago. Cole smiled at the memory of his hands buried in those fiery locks. Even though it seemed like ages had passed since he'd been with her, his hands would never forget the way she felt beneath them. The way her body ebbed and flowed when she was on top of him. And the way her breath came out in barely audible pants as she neared orgasm. Heck, Cole's workout shorts were becoming tented with just the thought.

Finally getting up the courage, he pulled the truck right next to her. He watched as her head shot up and she made eye contact with him for the first time in more than 12 years. Damn, he was fucking toast. So much for the thought of her being some hideous creature now. It was the exact opposite. Gracie Callahan had grown into a stunning woman with just the right amount of lush curves lining her body. Cole's fingers flexed as he sat there in the idling truck.

"Cole?" The confused redhead tapped on the passenger side window.

"Just a sec," Cole said. He had to get himself under control and fast. No way was he exiting the truck with a boner that made his shorts look like the equivalent of a Coleman tent. "Grandma, baseball, Brussel sprouts." he chanted over and over. Finally his problem down south diminished. He flung open his door and jumped down. When he rounded the front of the vehicle, Gracie's scent carried to his nose, the spicy smell stopping him dead in his tracks.

"Are you okay?" She pinned him with a worried stare.

"I'm good." He mentally slapped himself upside the head and continued toward her. "Here, I'll throw your bags in the back." He picked up one and heaved it over the side of the bed.

"Thanks." She handed him a second one, her fingers brushing his as he accepted it. His mouth watered as he reminisced about gliding his palm over the rest of her alabaster skin.

"Mom, they didn't have Diet Coke so I got you a Sprite instead." Cole stood up straight as a dark-haired girl approached Gracie. The suitcase he'd been holding clattered to the pavement.

"Thank you." Gracie took the drink from the girl and looked over at him. "Cole, this is my daughter Cora. Cora, this is Cole Matthews."

"Oh, hey," the young girl said and then proceeded to shove earbuds into her ears.

"You have a *kid*?" He braced his hands on his hips and pinned Gracie with a stare.

"Yes, Cole. I have a daughter."

"You failed to mention that."

"I'm sorry. I didn't think you'd help me with a place to stay if I told you."

"You're right." He raked a hand through his sweat-damp hair. "Jesus. If I'd known about her I would've at least run home and hid a few things." Cole panicked.

"What could you possibly have to hide? It can't be

that bad." The sound of Gracie's laughter went straight to his dick.

He stepped closer to her. "For starters, my coffee table is littered with *Playboy* magazines. But let's not forget the fucking posters on the walls."

"They can't be *that* bad." Her eyes dilated as he stepped even closer.

"Sure, they aren't *that* bad. Black and white posters of naked women are just what a young kid needs to see."

"Oh."

"Yeah, *oh*." This was bad. His house was his sanctuary, a place free of judgement. So he had nude posters and dirty magazines everywhere, big fucking deal. He'd just have to figure out a way to take them down and do some quick cleaning before Gracie and her kid came into the house. "Look, I have a friend who has a small salon in town, her name is Ava. I'm going to drop the two of you off for about an hour while I run home and clean up the place." He grabbed her bag again and tossed it in the back of the truck.

"Okay. That's fine. Could you run by somewhere and

grab something to eat first? Cora's diabetic and she needs
to eat frequently."

"Yeah, sure. Come on." He tossed the kid's bag into
the bed of the truck and motioned for them to hop in.

Wasn't this just a good old fashioned cluster fuck?

Chapter Three

GRACIE COULDN'T HELP but notice Cole was in an irritable mood as he drove them to his friend's salon. He'd taken her and Cora to a fast food place where he argued with her about paying for their lunch. She didn't want *anything* from him but a signature on the divorce papers, but as usual Cole had a stubborn streak. He whipped out cash and paid for the food before she could even dig her wallet out of her purse. And of course her daughter didn't pay a lick of attention to what was going on. Her ears were stuffed with earbuds that were connected to an iPod. Gracie would be surprised if the poor girl didn't have to have hearing aids by the time she was 20. Heck, you could hear the actual song lyrics even when standing a few feet away.

"How often does she need to eat?" Cole spoke up and pulled Gracie from her worries.

"Every few hours. She's on insulin but we make sure to keep her blood sugar balanced by eating small meals," she explained.

He glanced toward the back seat. "That hardly seems like a small meal."

She glimpsed back to see Cora take a huge bite of a double bacon cheeseburger. "Yeah, but that's what she wanted." She shrugged.

"Do you let her eat unhealthy shit like that all the time?" he inquired in a condescending tone.

"I don't see how any of this is your business. But no, we tend to eat healthier foods."

"You're right. It *isn't* my business." He sounded hurt.

"Cole, I'm sorry. I didn't mean to come off like a bitch. I'm just tired from the flight." Yeah, that was part of why she was worn out. The other part? No, she wasn't telling him about that. She'd get it figured out on her own, just like everything else in her life.

As he drove through the center of town, Gracie took in her surroundings. This was a nice town and for some reason she felt extremely comfortable being there. She'd lived in the suburb of Schaumburg, Illinois her entire life. Her job was in the city which she loved. It was nice to drive 45 minutes and be able to see the tall buildings of Chicago six days a week. But Biloxi was great too, so far. It was clearly smaller than where she lived, but the southern feel of everything was drawing her right in.

"So, how old is she?" Cole broke through her thoughts once more.

"Cora's 12." She seriously hoped he wouldn't catch on and figure out Cora was *actually* his.

"She'll be in what, 6th grade this year?" Cole asked.

"Seventh."

He seemed to be contemplating something and she hoped it wasn't a timeline for Cora's birth. If he put two and two together, she'd have some major explaining to do. That one complication she didn't want to interrupt this little trip.

"Here we are," Cole said as he pulled the truck in

front of a small strip mall.

"Are we staying here?" Cora asked, leaning forward.

"No, Cole has to go clean his house up a bit. He wasn't expecting us. We're going to hang out here while he's gone." Gracie explained.

"Cool," Cora said before stuffing the earbuds back into her ears.

As Cole got out, Gracie watched him round the front of the truck and come to her door. He opened it and motioned for her to climb down. As she did, he grabbed her hand. The warmth that shot up her arm took her by surprise. It was like she'd stepped into a time machine and was transported back to prom night all those years ago. The breath caught in her throat as the memories swamped her like an ocean wave taking her under the sparkling blue water.

"You okay?" Cole asked.

Gracie jerked her hand back as she put both feet on the pavement. "Just fine, thanks," she grumbled. "Come on, Cora." She called to her daughter who was now furiously texting on her cell phone.

"Gotta love teenagers," Cole chuckled.

"She's not a teen just yet. I have a week and a half until *that* officially happens. But I'm not looking forward to it." It was hard to believe Cora had been in her life almost 13 years now. Sure, there were times that made her want to rip her hair out of its follicles, but for the most part, Cora was a great kid. She was blessed to have her in her life.

"Come on, I'll introduce you to Ava." Cole gestured for the both of them to follow him into the small building. When they walked through the door, the smell of hairspray surrounded her. "Ava? You in here?" Cole called.

"Be right out!" Cole's female friend yelled from the back of the salon. It was about 30 seconds later when the gorgeous blonde made her way out. "Sorry about that, had to toss some towels in the dryer."

"Can they hang out here for about an hour?" Cole asked Ava.

"Yeah sure. I don't have any clients for the next hour anyway. I could use some company." Ava smiled.

Gracie became envious all of a sudden. This other woman was downright stunning. Her golden hair, blue eyes and slightly curvy figure were things Cole always went after. It was a given that he'd be attracted to Ava.

"I'm Ava. It's nice to meet you." Ava extended her hand.

"Gracie Callahan. And this is my daughter Cora. I'm an old friend of Cole's."

Cole snorted behind her. "Old friend? We're technically married. I think that makes us *more* than friends, don't you?" She ignored his rhetorical question and walked further into the salon. She eyed the sofa in the waiting area and took a seat. "Okay then. I'll be back in an hour." Cole retreated, leaving her and Cora with Ava. An uncomfortable feeling came over her.

"How long have you and Cole been an item?" The question slipped out before Gracie had a chance to censor herself.

Ava began laughing hysterically but when she finally caught her breath, she said, "Cole and I aren't an item. He's my boyfriend's partner."

With cheeks flaming from embarrassment, Gracie apologized. "Oh, my God, I'm so sorry. I just assumed…"

"It's okay. The three of us spend quite a bit of time together. I'm sure it looks strange to some people. But Cole moved here when Luke did so he doesn't really know too many people."

"That's nice of you to take him in." Gracie smiled at the beautiful blonde's generosity.

"Thank you. So, what do you do?" Ava walked over to her styling station and used a small brush to dust hair from the seat of the hydraulic chair.

"I'm a hair stylist," Gracie admitted.

Ava turned to face her with a surprised look. "Really? Wow, that's awesome!"

"Thanks. I went to school a few months after I gave birth to Cora."

"It's nice to have a kindred spirit around." Ava seemed to be contemplating something. Then spoke, "I don't want to put you on the spot but it's been ages since I had a trim. Would you want to give me one while you're here?"

She stood from her seat on the couch. "I'd love to." This was something she knew. Even though being in Biloxi was new and she felt somewhat out of her element in the situation, she was completely at ease with doing hair.

"Wonderful," Ava said as she made her way back to the shampoo bowl.

Gracie's professionalism kicked in as she followed the other woman back and began prepping her for shampooing. She couldn't help but smile as she reached for the hose and made sure the water temperature was just right. As Ava leaned back in the bowl she began talking again, "Is Cora's father still in the picture?" Okay this was pushing a little beyond her comfort zone.

"No. He left before she was born." Gracie figured *that* lie was closest to the truth. She didn't feel so bad when the falsehood slipped past her lips.

"Are you seeing anyone back home?" Ava pressed.

"No, I focus on Cora. I don't really need that sort of complication in my life. Besides, it would be hard bringing in a stranger while my daughter is a teen." That wasn't the complete truth. She'd gone on a few dates and that was part of the reason she was down here in the first place.

"Makes sense." Ava didn't continue with her game of 20 questions and for that, Gracie was thankful. Once she finished shampooing the other woman's hair, she gave it a quick towel dry and walked her now client over to the lone chair in the place. "If you and Cole need some alone time to talk, I can take Cora with me to Luke's house. It's this huge plantation home and property; she'd probably love it."

"I appreciate the offer but I think she needs to stay with me." Panic rose in Gracie's gut as she thought about the dangers of not having her daughter close.

"Okay. But if you change your mind, let me know."

Gracie nodded and began combing the wet, blonde locks that covered Ava's head. She was so deep in concentration that she didn't hear Cole come back through the door until he said, "Holy shit, what the hell is going on here?" She spun around and saw the shock on his face.

"Gracie is giving me a trim," Ava answered.

"When did you learn how to cut hair?" he asked. "I thought you were going to school for some kind of journalism degree." He sat in a chair nearby. Gracie could feel the heat of his stare as she began to slide her fingers through the hair and snip off the ends, letting them fall to the floor.

"That *was* the plan. But after I found out I was pregnant with my daughter, plans changed."

"Yeah, I guess they did," he said through a clenched jaw.

Why Cole would be pissed about her not going to school for journalism was beyond her. At the time, she did what she thought could support her and Cora. Taking four years of her life and devoting it to college wasn't in the cards. Taking care of her baby by herself was. She'd had to make a grown up decision all those years ago. And truth be told, she didn't regret it in the least. She loved her job, loved her daughter and would love it if Cole would back the fuck off while she was in

Mississippi.

So Gracie didn't go to school for what she'd said she would. That was news to Cole. The woman had had so much determination when she was younger and he'd bet money back then that she would've been working to help clean up crime in Chicago. But alas, she was a hair stylist just like Ava. Sure it was a perfectly respectable career but for some reason he couldn't picture Gracie standing behind a chair hacking off chunks of hair all day. But sitting there watching her work on Ava made him see the light. The woman looked like she was in her element. Her every move was precise and focused. He'd be lying if he said watching her didn't cause blood to rush to a certain manly part of his body. Cole had never expected to be attracted to her again, but seeing her after all this time he knew there would be no getting over Gracie. She was the one. But now, it was way too late to make a go of it. The unwavering redhead was here to divorce him. And if he knew one thing, it was you couldn't change her mind once she had it set.

"Mom, I'm bored." Gracie's daughter stepped over to where they were.

"Almost done, honey. Are you getting hungry again?" Cole watched as she looked at Cora with concern in her eyes.

"Jeez, I'm fine. Ugh." The almost-teen stomped her feet as she made her way to the waiting area and plopped down on the sofa.

"I don't envy you." Ava giggled.

"Some days I don't envy *me* either." Gracie finished up and took the cape off of Ava. "All done." Her satisfied smile transported him back to the days when that same smile was aimed at him. Damn he missed that.

He missed having someone there for him when he needed it. He longed for someone to chat with when he had a shitty day. But there wasn't just anyone who could fill that void. The sexy woman just a few feet away was the only one who could fit the bill.

"Come on Cora. Let's go get settled in at Cole's." She grabbed her purse, said goodbye to Ava and waited for him at the door of the shop.

Cole—being the somewhat southern gentleman now—rushed ahead and opened the door. She gave him a strange look but went through it anyway, followed by her head-bobbing daughter. He'd never understand teenagers. They were all like zombies with their loud music and faces plastered to a tiny screen in their hands. Cole shook his head. Yeah, kids were weird.

Chapter Four

"WOW, THIS IS…well it's…" Gracie trailed off as she took in the sparse area of Cole's living room.

Cole stood to the side and rubbed the back of his neck. Was he *self-conscious* about his living conditions? "You know, it's just me here. I wasn't really expecting company." He stammered a bit while the excuse fell from his mouth.

She stepped further into the room and surveyed what was in front of her. A beat-up putrid green sofa from circa 1970 took up an entire wall while a 3-legged coffee table sat in front of it looking like it could topple over at any given moment. Hell, the only thing that looked modern in this room was the giant flat screen television and gaming console.

"No way! You have the limited edition PS4?" Cora knelt down and ran her fingers over the dust-free device.

"It's how I unwind. You a gamer?" Cole asked her daughter.

"Mom won't let me have one, says it'll rot my brain." Cora shrugged.

"Rot your brain?" Cole looked directly at Gracie. She flashed him a *'don't argue with the mom'* look and he immediately backed down. "Point taken. Maybe she'll let you take mine for a spin while you're here?" He flashed his blues at her and she almost melted.

"Maybe," she answered.

"The bedrooms are this way," he pointed down the hallway and Gracie followed. Her eyes should've been on the floor, or even the walls. But they weren't. Both of them were targeted on the ass of the built man walking in front of her. His jeans hugged the muscles of his glutes like they were painted on and the pockets were like neon signs that screamed *'grab me!'* She wouldn't of course. She wasn't that type of woman anymore. Sure, she'd have squeezed both of those taut cheeks, dug her nails in and moaned about it years ago. Now though, she was a mom. A mom trying her best to keep her daughter safe and healthy. Not even the sexy-as-sin Cole Matthews could make her deviate from her goal. It would be one of the hardest things saying no to what he would more than likely offer her, but Gracie had will power. It was time she started using it.

"There's only two bedrooms, Cora can have the spare and you can take mine." Cole led Gracie into his bedroom and his entire body went on red alert. How many times had he laid in that bed and dreamt of the sizzling redhead since he'd moved into this house? Some nights it was the only thing that kept him from losing his mind. He'd close his eyes and transport himself back to the times when she was in his arms and everything seemed right in the world. Behind those closed lids he'd remember what it'd felt like to run his hands over the expanse of her form while she lay completely naked next to him. The small sounds that'd escape her lips as he'd push himself into her tight body, filling her up. God, she was something. Gracie was somewhat of a shy lover. She didn't express what she wanted, she'd just let him take the lead and show her how her body was supposed to react to him. Even when she came, he'd have to strain to hear any sort of sound coming from her. But that was her and he never faulted her for it. He embraced and celebrated it because every moment he'd spent with her was like a small slice of heaven had been handed to him for safe-keeping.

Gracie turned to him with a saddened look in her eyes. Had she been thinking of the past like he had? "I don't want to take your room, Cole." Well, apparently she wasn't.

"It's fine. I'll crash on the couch." He backed out of the room before he reached for her and tugged her into his arms. One thing he needed to remember was the fact that they weren't an item anymore. That ship sailed a long time ago and he was left on the shore bidding farewell as the sails flapped in the wind.

"If you're sure," Gracie replied.

"I'm sure, so stop making a big deal out of it." He left the room, feeling remorseful for being snippy with her. But there was only so much a man could take. Clearly she was now an ice queen and if he didn't want to be frozen solid, it was best to walk the fuck away.

"Fuck," Cole cussed as he reached the kitchen and found that the fridge was bare. He could really go for a beer about right now.

"Mom says you're not supposed to say that word. Says is makes a person look like a jackass," Cora's voice behind him caused Cole to whip around and see the kid with a half-smile on her face.

"But it's okay to say 'jackass'?" He raised an eyebrow.

"I don't know. Mom's kind of weird," Cora snorted.

"Don't I know it."

"Your house kinda sucks," Cora stated.

"Wow, you don't hold anything back do you?" He leaned his back against the counter and crossed his arms over his chest.

"I'm almost a teenager. I'm *supposed* to be rude." She

smiled.

"There's a difference between being rude and just plain being an asshole." Cole pushed past the dark-haired girl.

"Yeah, you're right. Sorry. I get like this when I don't feel good," Cora explained.

Cole turned back. "You sick?"

"It's a blood sugar thing. I hate that I'm like this." The young girl had a sad look on her face. He supposed it would be shitty to have to deal with an illness like diabetes at such a young age. The disease was in his family and he'd seen many relatives have to deal with it, but for some reason, *he* wasn't struck with it.

"Do you need something to eat?" He knew there wasn't much in the way of food around. He'd have to remedy that fairly quickly so Cora didn't end up in a coma.

"Yeah, I should have a snack soon." She sat slowly on the worn-out sofa and stared at him.

Cole couldn't help but stare back. This chick looked familiar for some reason. Like he'd seen her somewhere

before but couldn't place her. He shrugged—no use
trying to figure insignificant shit out right now. Getting
some food for the girl was the number one priority.

"I'll run to the store and grab some stuff. Anything
special you want?"

Cora hopped off the couch and said, "I'll go with
you." She smiled a megawatt smile—which looked a lot
like her mother's.

"Hey Cora, do you have your medicine? I need to get
it in the refrigerator." Gracie came down the hallway and
found him and the girl standing in the middle of the
living room. "What's going on?"

"I'm headed to the grocery store. Gotta get some
food." He grabbed his keys from the small rickety table
by the door.

"I'm going, too," Cora proclaimed.

"Not so fast," Gracie said in a stern mother-like tone.
"You can't go running off with strangers, Cora."

"He's not a stranger, mom, we're staying in his house,
remember?"

"She's got a point," Cole chuckled.

"Go put your medicine in the fridge. I need to have a chat with him." Gracie pinned him with a no-nonsense look and motioned to the front door. Why did he feel like he was being scolded for something he didn't do?

Once outside, Cole turned to her and planted his hands on his hips. "What the hell did I do?"

"You didn't do anything. But I need you to listen to me."

"Fine."

"That girl is the only thing in this world that I would give my life for. If you in any way cause her harm, I will make you hurt so bad you won't know what hit you. Do you understand?"

Cole threw his hands up in a surrendering gesture. "Jesus, who the hell do you think I am? Are you listening to yourself right now? For fuck sake, Gracie, I work for the FBI. What makes you think I would do anything to harm that kid?"

She backed down a bit. "I'm sorry. Yes, I'm overprotective of my daughter but I have to be."

Cole saw something a lot like fear on her face. "Is

something going on that I should know about?"

Her head shot up and she narrowed her green eyes at him. "No. Everything's fine. Just be careful." Her hand reached inside her front pocket and she pulled out a wad of cash and a plastic tube. "Here's some money for groceries. And these," she passed him the tube, "are glucose tablets. If Cora starts feeling faint or looks like she's going to pass out, give her a couple of these to chew. They'll elevate her blood sugar."

He grabbed the tablets, pocketed them but pushed her hand away that held the bills. "I don't want your money."

"Cole, we aren't here to use up your resources. Take the money." She held it out again.

He stepped forward—enough that he was now in her personal space. Grabbing the hand that held the money, he tugged her closer. "There're a few things I want from you, but money isn't one of them." He watched as Gracie's eyes fluttered closed and the pulse point at her neck visibly thumped against her skin. "Do you like that, Gracie? You like me touching you, don't you?"

"No," she whispered.

"You're a bad liar." He leaned down and blew lightly on the shell of her ear then casually said, "Keep up this ice princess act all you want. I know what it's like to have the warm and soft Gracie underneath me." He then dropped her hand and backed away. He shouldn't have done that but the magnetic pull between the two of them was *too* intense. She didn't know it yet, but Cole had plans for her. He'd work double time to show her what she meant to him. Then she'd be the one who was tugging *him* to *her*. It was only a matter of time.

Cole was now on a mission. He was calling it *"Operation Melt the Ice Queen."* Gracie had another thing coming if she thought she could shut him out after the history they'd shared. Hell, he knew her body better than she did and he was determined to show her just how well.

"So, you and my mom?" Cora sat in the passenger side of his truck while he drove the 15 minutes into town. Cole was surprised she hadn't stuck the earbuds in her ears again to ignore him.

"Yeah." He wasn't sure what to say to Gracie's kid. In fact, carrying on a conversation with a minor was a little out of his league anyway.

"Mom says you two were married. What happened?"

Cole shifted in his seat—feeling uncomfortable with the way this conversation was headed. Should he tell her about being married to her mom? Or keep his trap shut? He decided that some conversation was better than an awkward silence. "Things didn't work out," he decided on the safe route.

"That sounds like a cop out." Okay this kid was smarter than he gave her credit for, a trait he admired.

"Look, I don't think you want to hear about my past with your mom."

"Why not? Mom won't talk about it. Might as well get the info from you," she sassed.

"Damn, you're a lot like her." Cole looked over at the young lady who still looked so familiar to him.

"She tells me that too."

"Does she ever talk about your dad?" Cole wasn't sure why the hell he would ask her that. It wasn't any of his business about the kid's father.

"Not really. She said he didn't want to be in our lives. I guess I can live with that. It would be nice to meet him though."

"Have you asked her if she'll get in contact with him? Maybe let you guys meet?" Cole asked.

"Yeah, but you know my mom. She's hard-headed."

"I *do* know your mom." He chuckled as the she rolled her eyes and looked out the window beside her.

"It's probably for the best though, ya know? If some douche biscuit didn't want to stick around, I probably don't wanna meet him anyway." Cora shrugged nonchalantly but he could see a bit of sadness in her profile.

It must've been rough for Gracie—raising a child all by herself. Hell, when she'd revealed her pregnancy to him when they were together, an urgent panic took up residence in every part of him. He wasn't ready to be a dad. Dads were supposed to be strong and supportive.

He wasn't either. Cole knew back then it was for the best that the test was a false positive. He would've been the worst kind of parent to a baby.

"I've found that things work out the way they're supposed to in life," Cole said.

"No need to get philosophical over there. I'm a kid, remember?"

"Touché." He couldn't help but laugh at her. Cora was smart, sassy and ready to go toe-to-toe with the best of them.

It was another five minutes until they reached the grocery store. As he parked his truck Cora bounded out and rounded the hood to meet him. They walked side by side to the cart caddy at the front entrance and Cole grabbed a handle and jerked it from the other carts. As he pushed it through the automatic doors, Cora bumped him out of the way with her hip and grabbed the handle.

"What the hell?" Cole demanded, staring at her.

"Mom says I need to push the cart when we shop. If I feel sick I'll have something to hang onto to support me," she explained.

"Okay, but you didn't have to hip-check me out of the way."

"Sorry." She smiled causing him to smile.

"Damn, kid. I'd swear you were mine with the way you act like a bull in a china shop."

"No offense, but I wouldn't want to be your kid. You're kind of a dick." She pushed the cart toward the produce section.

"I think you need to cool it with the language."

"Fine." She reached for a bag of mini carrots and turned toward him. "Don't tell my mom, okay? She'll ground me from my phone or something." The look of panic on her face struck him.

"My lips are sealed. Just chill out with the adult words." He grabbed the carrots from her hand and tossed them into the cart. "Where did you learn to talk like that anyway? You sound like a sailor."

"Movies," she said.

"What's the world coming to?" He sat a bag of apples in the cart. Kids liked apples, right?

"According to *The Walking Dead*, the world's headed

for a zombie apocalypse," Cora said seriously.

"Maybe I should have my cable cancelled while you're staying with me. Doesn't sound like you need any more shows to corrupt you."

She was silent while they lined the cart with fresh fruits and vegetables—something that surprised him. Didn't most kids go for potato chips and Twinkies? Clearly Gracie taught her daughter the right way to eat to control her disease. Cole was struck with pride at that thought. She might've been handed the short end of the stick when the asshole left her with a kid on her own, but she'd raised her daughter right.

Cole followed her down another aisle. "What do you do for fun besides blow your eardrums out with music?"

"I like to draw, read books and I play the piano." She sounded proud.

"The piano?" Okay that was something Cole thought twice about.

"Yeah, mom put me in piano lessons when I was five. It's pretty cool. Although she couldn't really afford to buy me a professional keyboard to practice at home on. I get to use the one in the band room at school sometimes though."

"Are you any good?"

"*Puh*-lease. I've won three state championships in my age group and was invited to the national competition last year." she boasted.

"Did you go?"

"Nope. We didn't have the extra money. But it's okay, I'm sure I'll get to go one day."

Sadness swamped him as he heard she couldn't do what she wanted because of money restrictions. But it wasn't his problem. This wasn't his kid or responsibility so he needed to stop feeling sorry for her.

Gracie sat all alone at the kitchen table in Cole's house. The sliding glass doors at the back of the room gave her a prime view of his backyard which was just like the inside of the house…lacking. She shouldn't judge him; her life was far from perfect. But for some reason, she'd pictured Cole having a house full of the finest furniture money could buy. He always had a taste for the more expensive things when they were younger. He'd grown up with money since his father was a successful investment banker in Chicago and his mom's family was part owner of the Chicago White Sox baseball team. Cole didn't want for anything so why the hell was he living in what Gracie would consider almost squander? Surely he had some sort of trust fund to buy things. If he did, you couldn't tell it by looking around his house. The furniture all looked as if it'd been purchased at yard sales, the house itself was nice, but it didn't seem to fit him.

She began to drum her fingers on the beat-up wood table top and stare out the transparent doors. Her mind transported her back to prom night so many years ago.

"We don't have to do this," Cole said as he peered at her standing in the motel room in her glittering prom dress.

"I know, but I want to," Gracie replied nervously.

He looked at her with such loving eyes. It almost scared her even more than she was already. They were both 18 and had dated for two years, it was time to take the next step in their relationship.

He pulled her to him and began to kiss her—a kiss that conveyed everything he was feeling in that moment. Anxiousness, desire...it was all there in the way he moved his lips over hers and explored her mouth. As she stood there, Cole began to reach around her and gently pulled the zipper of her dress down. The cool air in the room brushed her skin and sent another shiver over her body.

"You okay?" he asked, gazing into her eyes.

Gracie nodded. He was going too slowly for her liking, but she'd never tell him that. For some reason it seemed as if he wanted to savor this moment between them, not rush it. His hands began to caress the bare skin on her back and Gracie felt moisture gather in her satin panties. She didn't wear a bra with her prom dress— there wasn't a need for one. The only thing covering anything underneath her sparkly dress was her white string bikini underwear.

Standing there with labored breathing, she watched

as he pushed the straps of her dress off her shoulders and let it fall at her feet. She instinctively stepped out of it, leaving her in nothing but the scrap of white satin and a pair of heels.

"Damn," Cole breathed. Gracie became self-conscious and covered her breasts with her hands. "No, don't."

"Cole, I'm sorry if you don't think I'm…"

"Don't think you're what? Beautiful?" He stepped closer and pulled her hands from her body. "Baby, I think you're the most beautiful thing I've ever seen." He then kissed her with an urgency she'd never felt from him before. Her arms trembled as she untied the bowtie at his collar then fumbled with the buttons on his shirt until they were all free. Pushing the stark white garment from his shoulders, she trailed her fingers down the smooth expanse of his chest. A few dark hairs peppered the area and his stomach was already developing muscles that bunched under her touch.

But what she really wanted to see was the part of him that was still concealed beneath his black tuxedo pants. Gracie's nerves got the best of her, causing her hand to brush the front of his fly then yank it back.

"This isn't gonna go very far if you don't want to touch me, Gracie," Cole snickered.

"I don't know what to do," she admitted. This was all new to her. Yes, she trusted Cole; he was someone she could count on no matter what. But this was far from her realm of expertise.

He gently placed his hands on both sides of her face and made eye contact with her. "If you aren't ready for this, I'll wait. I don't want you to think I'm pressuring you into this, Gracie," he said in a tender tone.

"I really want to do this," she replied with more enthusiasm than she was feeling.

"Come here." Cole grabbed her hand and led her to the bed in the room. Sitting on the end, Gracie looked up while he stood in front of her. He crouched down and grabbed her hands. "I love you," he said softly.

"I love you, too." She smiled, feeling more at ease.

Cole then stood but leaned down and began kissing her once more. Gracie felt her body recline until her back was flat on the mattress. Cole was still above her, his hands roaming her heated body.

"Touch me," slipped from her lips.

"Where?" he asked.

Gracie—feeling slightly brazen, pushed his hand until it was right above the juncture between her thighs. The breaths she was concentrating on stuck in her throat when his fingers swept through the wetness gathered between her legs.

"Fuck," Cole cursed.

"What? Is everything okay? Is something wrong?" Her eyes now wide, focused on his face where his eyes were heavy lidded.

He grinned as he trailed his fingers through her moist folds. "Everything is perfect."

All she could do was lay there and revel in the sensations he bestowed on her body. She was powerless to control the heat he'd stirred up inside her. Part of her wanted to cry out when he circled one finger around her entrance, and the other part? Well, it wanted to push him away because things were getting serious super-fast. But even so, all she could do was let out a barely audible mewl as he removed his hand and lifted his body over her. One of Cole's legs pressed on her knee, silently asking her to open further to him. He was still clothed from the waist down which made what they were doing even more forbidden.

"You have no idea how much I want you right now," Cole said as he brought his weight down on her—being careful not to crush her.

Gracie couldn't mistake his arousal prodding her center through the fabric of his pants. To know he was so close to her had her own arousal climbing a few notches. "I'm ready to feel you," she didn't recognize her voice as it came out.

"You sure?" He raised himself off her to look in her eyes. She nodded.

Cole stood and began to unbutton his pants, shoving them to the floor when he was finished. Propping herself up on her elbows she took in the sight of her longtime boyfriend, standing there in only his boxer briefs. As he reached down to his discarded pants, she watched him pull a square foil packet from his wallet. A sigh of relief tore through her as he palmed the condom. His hand folded around it as he tucked his fingers in the waistband of his underwear and slid the fabric down his defined legs. Gracie's eyes shot up to take in his cock that was now bobbing freely. Sure, she knew what a dick looked like but she'd never actually seen Cole's. Surprise hit her as the awkwardness seemed to dissipate and he stepped forward toward the bed.

"Will you touch me?" he asked.

Gracie bit her lip as she looked as his erect shaft. Her hand raised and fingers wrapped around him, a hiss tearing through his lips. "Like this?" She began to stroke him up and down, his rigid length twitching with each motion she made.

But soon Cole wrapped his hand around hers and halted her ministrations. "Maybe that's not such a good idea," he joked and she understood. "How about you lay back on the pillows?" Cole motioned to the head of the bed.

She stood from her spot and reached for the blankets, pulling them down to reveal the white linens beneath them. With shaking hands, she climbed on the bed and lay her head on one of the firm pillows. Cole then climbed over her and knelt between her spread thighs. His head was bent in concentration as he tore open the foil packet, tossed the wrapper to the side and began to roll the latex over his engorged cock. Gracie tried to control her breathing as he finished and settled himself over her.

"Spread your legs a little more, baby." Cole reached between them and ran his fingers through her cleft once more. "That's it," he soothed. "You okay?" he asked as he fit the head of his cock against her entrance.

"Uh huh," was all she could manage to choke out at this point.

"Ready?"

Gracie nodded and said, "Go slow, please?"

"Of course I will. I don't want to hurt you." He came down a little more and she could feel his cock brush against her wet folds. "Damn, baby, you're so wet." Gracie felt more moisture seep from her at his statement.

She closed her eyes as Cole pressed himself forward

and begin to enter her. Gracie half expected to be in excruciating pain at this point but all she felt was extreme desire for the man poised above her. "More?" he asked when he was only an inch or so inside her channel.

"Yes, more."

Cole pressed forward some more and Gracie felt the tugging inside her. She was tight and It was starting to feel uncomfortable. She squirmed trying to acclimate her body to his.

"Baby, you're squeezing me right now. Holy hell, you feel good," he said in a strangled voice. "I need to be all the way inside you."

"Okay." She wrapped her arms around his neck and pulled his face to hers. "Kiss me."

As their lips met, Cole surged forward and buried himself in her tight pussy. Her breath held as the burning sensation intensified then began to dissipate. She hung onto his neck for dear life while he pulled out a fraction and thrust back in her. The feel of his cock touching her most intimate area was causing a tingling sensation to rack her body. She didn't know what was happening as he continued to thrust in and out of her but whatever it was, it felt as if it were coming at her like a freight train.

"Shit, I'm close," Cole warned.

"Close?" She wasn't sure what he was talking about.

"I'm gonna come soon." His warning hit something deep in her and suddenly a sensation began at the tips of her toes and crawled up her body. It landed right where Cole was moving his cock inside of her. Gracie didn't know what was going on so she closed her eyes and kept quiet. But whatever it was, felt fucking amazing. "Yeah, you're coming baby!" Cole shouted as he picked up speed and thrust into her. He then roared as he ceased his movements and pressed into her as hard as he could. She lay there as he buried his face in her neck and let out heavy breaths. When his breathing seemed to be under control, he lifted and looked in to her eyes. "You alright? Did I hurt you?" He pushed the sweat-drenched hairs from her face and waited for her answer.

She lifted a hand and stroked the side of his face. "You didn't hurt me. It was perfect." She smiled.

"God, I love you so damn much." He bent down and

kissed her forehead.

"And I love you."

"I'd better get cleaned up. Be right back." Cole pulled himself from her body, Gracie wincing as he did.

She giggled a bit as his naked ass made its way to the bathroom. Wow, she'd never expected her first time to be that amazing. Sure it had some awkward moments, but it was nothing shy of fantastic. She sat up in the bed and felt wetness trail from her folds.

"Uh, baby. We have a problem."

Her head shot up and looked at a more than worried Cole in the bathroom doorway.

"What?" she asked.

"The condom broke."

Chapter Five

"HONEY! WE'RE HOME!" Gracie startled as Cole's voice called through the front door.

"You're so weird," she heard her daughter say to Cole.

"Back at ya, kid."

She stood from her seat and let the blood travel back into her legs. Crossing her arms over her chest, Gracie tried to conceal her hard nipples poking against the thin material of her blouse. She watched intently as Cole plopped bags of groceries on the counter and turned to face her. "You sick or something?" he cocked his head to the side.

"No, why?" She gawked at him.

"Your cheeks are all red."

Her shaking hands flew to her face and felt the heat residing there. Shit, it was all that reminiscing about her and Cole on prom night. Dammit she didn't want him to know she'd been daydreaming about him. That would give him one more reason to think he had a chance with her. And he certainly *did not*. "You know, I might be coming down with something after all. Excuse me." She ducked her head and made a quick retreat. There was no way in hell she'd stay in a confined space with Cole for any length of time. That was a recipe for disaster. She might've been a coward running away with her tail tucked between her legs, but it was better than staying there with him, which would eventually lead to him having his body parts tucked into hers.

Cole scratched his head and wondered what the hell was up with Gracie. The woman looked suspicious when he'd walked into the kitchen. And if there was one thing he was an ace at spotting, it was suspicion. It was his job to spot people who were on a path to deception and from what he could tell, Gracie Callahan was hiding something.

Cora popped into the kitchen. "Where's my mom?"

"She fled when I walked in." He grabbed a bag of groceries and headed to the fridge. "You need a snack?" he asked her.

"Sure." Yet again the girl hip-checked him out of the way and began digging around in the bags of produce. She yanked out the bag of mini carrots and tore it open like a famished rabbit. "What?" she said with her mouth full of orange crunchy food.

"I'm assuming your mom didn't teach you about manners?"

Cora shrugged. "Just like nobody taught you about interior decorating." She smiled with shreds of the vegetable stuck between her teeth.

Cole shook his head and laughed. "You're not cutting me any slack on my house are you?"

"Nope." She tossed another carrot in her mouth and exited the room.

As he filled the crisper drawers with the produce,

Cole smiled to himself. It was strange having two females staying with him, but honestly, he wouldn't have it any other way. Cora was a typical smartass kid, and Gracie, well, he'd take care of her eventually. Her *and* those red cheeks.

Just as he finished with the last of the groceries, Cole heard footsteps on the wood floor behind him. He turned to see Gracie standing there with a look of uncertainty on her face.

"Yeah?" he asked.

"This is your house, and I'd understand if you told me no, but..." She reached up and tucked a stray lock of hair behind her ear.

"Spit it out, Gracie."

"Do you mind if I cook dinner tonight?"

That was what she wanted? Hell, he'd thought maybe she wanted to redecorate, or put a pool in the backyard. Not cook food.

"Knock yourself out." He stepped around her.

"Thank you," she said in a small voice.

"How about a game of *Call of Duty*?" Cole entered the

living room and hit the power button on the PS4.

"Really?" Cora sat up from her reclined position on the couch, her eyebrows shooting up.

"Yes, really. Jeez, does your mom keep you in a fucking bubble?" he asked.

"Language!" He heard Gracie shout from the kitchen.

"My bad," he apologized while Cora was laughing hard behind him.

"And no, I don't keep her in a bubble!" Gracie confirmed. "But if you keep running your mouth, you'll be sleeping on the porch," she warned.

"Does she realize this is *my* house?" Cole asked Cora.

Cora shrugged and reached for one of the game controllers on the coffee table. "What's with this table anyway?" she asked. "It only has three legs."

"Saw it on the side of the road one day. Kinda felt bad for it so I took it in." He explained.

"So this place is like a shelter for all the crappy furniture in the area?" She snorted.

"Something like that."

"'*The house of misfit furniture*', it has a nice ring to it."

She giggled as he took a seat next to her on the sofa.

Once the game was started, Cole sat back and relaxed while blowing the shit out of the enemy while his trusty sidekick had his six. Cora could hold her own in the game and the two of them fell into a companionable silence. Soon he caught the unmistakable fragrance of home-cooked food filtering from the kitchen to the living room.

"Alright, that's enough rotting your brain for one night." Cole saved the game and tossed his controller on the table. Cora did the same and disappeared into the kitchen.

"I can set the table," she offered to her mom.

It wasn't a feeling he'd ever experienced before, but Cole suddenly felt out of place in his own house. The two ladies worked in the kitchen and here he was lounged out on the couch like he was waiting to be fed grapes and fanned with a palm frond. Damn, it sucked to have his personal space invaded.

"Everything's ready in here," Gracie called from the other room.

He bounded off his perch and made his way to where she was. "Whoa, that's quite a spread," he commented as he sat in the chair closest to the wall.

"Figured you might be hungry. It's the least I can do for you letting us stay here." She smiled.

Finally, a genuine smile from her. Cole would put a checkmark in the point column for himself on that one.

The girls took their seats and began to scoop portions of food onto their plates. Cole watched intently as Gracie's hands worked the utensils, piling meat and vegetables on the mismatched dinnerware. Those same hands knew just where to touch him once upon a time. They'd graze his skin and set him ablaze in a matter of seconds when they were together. The way she'd trace his nipple with her fingernail causing him to shudder was one of his favorite things she did. She'd take her time torturing him until he couldn't take it any longer. Then he'd flip her over and bury himself deep inside her when he'd had enough. He used to spend what seemed like hours exploring every smooth inch of her until the two of them fell asleep in each other's arms. On more than one occasion he'd even woken her up to the motion of him stroking his cock in and out of her. Even in sleep her body knew how to react to him. He'd toy with her pussy while she slept until she was dripping wet, then he'd slide himself between her thighs. Most of the time she'd come right after she woke up. Her back would bow off the bed, her eyes would slam shut again and her channel would grip him tight enough to make him explode, too.

"Fuck," Cole cursed as he realized he'd been having a major sexual fantasy at the dinner table. He wouldn't doubt his dick was hard enough to tenderize a steak at this point.

"Something wrong?" Gracie asked.

"N-no." He tried for a smile but it came out forced. He was saved from further stammering by a knock at the front door. "I'll get it." Cole jumped from the table so fast he banged his knee on one of the legs while trying to escape his chair.

On the way to the door he once again chanted about stupid shit to get his dick to play nice, "Colonoscopy, grandma, nut sac in a vice," he repeated in his head as he reached the door. Thank fuck things down south were under control now. Throwing the door open, Cole found Ava on the porch with a sweet smile on her face.

"Hey, Ava. What brings you by?" He motioned for her to come in.

"I wanted to talk to Gracie," she said and looked around him. "Is she here?"

"Gracie?" He tilted his head to the side.

"Yep," Ava chuckled.

"You hungry?" he asked.

"No, I ate already. But thanks for the offer."

He lost his train of thought for a second as Ava stood in the living room gawking at him. "Oh shit. Yeah, she's in the kitchen." Putting one foot in front of the other he led the petite blonde through the house. When he crossed the threshold to the kitchen the breath was nearly sucked out of him at the sight of Gracie and Cora sitting there eating their dinner. What shocked him the most though was the fact that it looked so fucking normal. Seeing that scene was like looking in on someone else's life. The way they both sat there like they really belonged in his simple home. Damn, it really hit home for the first time in his life. He could've had something like that if he'd just acted less like a dumbass and more like an adult at the age of 18.

"Hi Ava!" Cora jumped from her seat, the legs of the chair scraping on the tile floor. She rounded the table and went up to Ava giving her a hug. Wow, they'd been in town for less than a day and already the kid was friendly with Ava.

"Hey, there. You two get settled in okay?" Ava asked and then looked directly at Cole.

"What?" He narrowed his eyes at the other woman.

"Nothing. Just wanted to make sure you weren't being an ass to them." The normally sweet blonde wasn't one to trifle with. She'd rip you a new asshole and feed the old one to you with a syringe if you weren't careful.

"I'm insulted if you think I'm not a gracious host. Hell, I gave Gracie my damn bedroom," his voice rose in exasperation.

Ava laughed and glanced at Gracie. "I hope for your

sake he changed his sheets."

The room erupted in laughter, save for him and Cora who didn't get the adult humor Ava was dishing out. Good thing, too. The poor kid didn't need an education about how *that* part of the world worked right now.

"Everything is fine," Gracie assured Ava, making Cole feel more at ease.

"That's good to hear. Listen, I wanted to stop by and see if Cora could stay with me this weekend? Luke is on assignment in Gulfport until Monday and it'd be nice to have some company."

"Shit, I forgot about that." Cole rubbed his face and sighed. He and Luke were attached at the hip it seemed like. They'd been partners for quite some time and having the other man gone for a few days felt like he was missing a limb.

"I don't know if that's such a good idea," Gracie said with a look of extreme trepidation on her face. Cole hadn't really seen her like this. She almost looked scared.

"She'll be fine. Luke has all kinds of guns and shit out there in case someone tries anything stupid," Cole confirmed.

"I don't doubt that, but I really don't think…" she began, but he cut her off with his hands on her shoulders.

"Would I tell you to send your kid somewhere that wasn't safe?" he asked.

"No, I guess not. But…"

"No 'Buts.' She'll be fine and it's just for the damn weekend. She has a phone. If anything is wrong, she'll call you."

"What about her medicine?"

"Mom, I know how to take my shot. I know how to eat right. And I know the warning signs. I'll pack my glucose monitor like I do when I stay with my friend Torrance. Pleeeeease let me go?" Cora begged.

Indecision blanketed Gracie as she toyed with the idea of letting her daughter stay the weekend with a near-stranger. "Okay, I suppose it'll be alright."

Cora did a fist pump and ran out of the room to grab her things. She was back in no time and at Ava's side. "I promise to take good care of her," Ava assured.

"Alright. If you need anything, call me, okay?" Gracie

hugged Cora and let her go.

"Will do, mom."

It wasn't long and Cole could hear Ava's car pulling away from the house. He stood at the front window making sure they were gone before he turned to face Gracie.

"Guess it's just you and me now." He smiled.

∽ Chapter Six ∽

GRACIE KNEW THAT LOOK; it was one she'd recognize even with her eyes closed. It meant that Cole had an idea in his head and he wasn't taking no for an answer.

"Looks to be that way," she agreed then walked back into the kitchen to escape him. Her best bet was to keep busy and avoid the dangerous man in the other room. So she did just that by cleaning up the table from dinner and running water to wash the dishes. Once her hands were submerged in the soapy water, she worked to keep her mind from traveling to a place where it wasn't welcome to go. A place where Cole was the star of her dreams and if there was an award for *'best orgasm donor'* he'd win it hands down.

"Need any help?" She felt him behind her before he spoke. That was the thing about knowing someone so well. You could sense their presence in a room before they revealed themselves. You could feel the heat coming off their skin, smell the unique fragrance that melded with their body chemistry, creating something that was special only to them. It was like possessing a sixth sense when she was around him. Even though they'd spent so many years apart, the sensations never really faded. They only lay dormant for a period of time and now, they were back with a vengeance. *Now* she had to fight every overactive nerve in her body so this moment didn't result in something she'd regret in the morning.

"No, I'm good." Gracie heard her voice crack as she answered him. *Get yourself under control, Gracie Callahan.* But upon seeing the stricken look on Cole's face, she realized that her answer had come out more abrupt than she'd planned. She pulled her hands from the warm, soapy water and grabbed the drying towel nearby. As she wiped the moisture from her hands she decided to try again. "I'm sorry, I don't really know why everything

I say comes out bitchy." Cole didn't reply, he only stood there, staring at her with a stoic expression. She turned to glance at the clock on the wall behind the table. "It's getting late. I'll uh, see you in the morning." She forced a smile and tried to push past him. The breath was sucked out of her when he grabbed her wrist and pulled her back to his front.

"I think you should see me now, Gracie." His breath on her ear caused her head to fall back and her eyelids to flutter closed.

"Cole, please don't." Her plea was weak at best.

"We have a few things that need clearing up."

"Like what?" Okay this type of conversation she could handle…maybe.

"Like why the hell you all but decided I wasn't good enough to be in your life anymore for starters." He released her and Gracie stepped forward.

"Are you kidding me right now?"

Cole crossed his arms over his chest and glared at her. "No, I want to know."

"It wasn't even like that and you know it," she bit out.

"Then what *was* it? Hell, you come to me and tell me you're pregnant and then after we're married you say it was a fluke? Damn it, Gracie, did you even for one second think I might've wanted to stay married to you either way?"

"It wouldn't have worked and you know it."

"How do you figure?"

She had to think fast. How could she shoot him down and end this conversation quickly? "Because you weren't ready to grow up!" Gracie tossed her arms in the air and hoped that hit the nail on the head.

"We were 18 years old. Neither of us was ready to grow the fuck up."

"I was," she whispered.

The room became silent for what seemed like ages. When Cole finally spoke, she was floored by what came out of his mouth. "Do you ever sit and think about that night at prom?" Just at the mention of that event, Gracie's face flamed, her palms began to sweat and she felt like squirming. "The night when two dumb kids decided to go further than they'd ever gone before?" He stepped closer, causing her to bump into the counter behind her. "The night when you felt me inside you for the first time?" Even closer he came until he was standing toe-to-toe with her. "The night when I watched you come all over me for the first time." One of his hands lifted to brush across her cheek. "The night when you felt me stroking my cock in and out of you until I couldn't take anymore and exploded inside you?" His face came dangerously close to hers. Lips within kissing distance, breaths mingling with hers and hormones raging inside her like a beast trying to claw its way to the surface. "Tell me, did you ever think about any of that in all the years we've been apart?"

"I can't do this," Gracie choked out.

"Why? Why can't you open up to me like you used to?"

"Because I don't know you anymore." She raised her chin and looked him in the eyes.

"You don't forget someone that easily." He backed away and she missed his warmth. "I sure as hell didn't forget you." That was the last thing he said before he disappeared from the kitchen and she heard the front door slam.

Gracie stood there alone again—something she'd come to know all too well—and tried to calm herself. She was so close to giving in. So close to letting Cole ease the ache he'd created all those years ago. So fucking close to telling him everything that was going on in her life and letting him fix it. But the reality of the situation was far worse than the fantasy. Cole wasn't her hero. He was a stumbling block to fix what'd been broken in her life. Nothing more, nothing less.

Cole felt like shit after walking away from Gracie but being so close to her was driving him insane. The urge to kiss her was causing every synapsis in his body to misfire. But he'd proven one thing when he asked her all those questions, he *still* affected her. The way her eyes dilated, her breaths came out more ragged and the slight squirming told him she wasn't as over him as she led him *and* herself to believe. She wanted him, plain and simple. Sure he was patting himself on the back for that fact, but the ten-thousand-dollar question was *how do I get her to act on how she's feeling*? There was no doubt he wanted her; hell, the hard-on he sported when he walked out of the room would attest to the urgency he felt when near her. But he refused to force himself on her. If she wanted him, he'd wait it out and make her come to him. Then when she did, he'd have her coming so hard, she fly clear into the next fucking galaxy.

The furthest he got was the front porch though. He didn't feel like driving anywhere and even if he did, he'd more than likely end up at Luke's house and he wasn't home. Luke was the only personal relationship he had in Biloxi. So he sat there on the step breathing in the night air and wishing for things he had no business wishing for.

"Cole?" His head shot up at the sound of Gracie's voice behind him. "Can we just…I don't know. Start over?"

His answer was clear, "No. We can't Gracie."

"I don't want us to be like this. We have too much

history to act like a couple of pissed-off teenagers."

"What would you expect me to do? Pretend I don't give a damn about you anymore?"

Her footfalls on the wood of the old porch told him she was coming closer and soon she was sitting on the step next to him. Her perfume or soap or whatever floral smelling shit she was wearing decided to invade his nose and drive him mad once more.

"I'm here to get the papers signed and that's it. I can't rehash old times."

"I didn't ask you to."

"Then what do you want?"

Cole had had enough. If she wanted to know what he wanted, well, he'd fucking show her. His body swiveled around on the step and faced her. Without thinking about it too much he extended his hand and grabbed the back of her neck, pulling her closer. Her eyes went wide, she sucked in a breath and the last thing he heard before his lips crashed down on hers was the beginning of a protest. She didn't get far with it though, he made sure of that.

With his lips on hers, Cole did his best to show her what he wanted. He caressed her mouth with his, his tongue tracing the seam of her perfectly plump lips. The hand at the back of her neck found its way into the silky strands of her hair and began to tug lightly as she opened for him to sweep his hot tongue further into her depths. Small sounds rang through his ears as he realized she was actually kissing him back instead of pushing him away. Her body pressed closer as if it were searching for something. But the one thing he *didn't* expect from his once shy lover was when her hand swept down and began to caress his erection through the fabric of his jeans.

Startled, Cole broke the kiss and looked into an equally startled set of green eyes.

Gracie's mouth rounded in a 'O' shape like she was surprised at what she'd done as well. "Oh, God. I'm *so* sorry." She reached up and ran a finger over her now swollen lips.

"No, you're not."

"This isn't a good idea." She began slipping back into

responsible adult mode again and Cole hated it. "I'm sorry I uh, touched you."

He watched as she glanced down at the front of his pants. Thinking that he'd go balls to the wall, Cole grabbed her hand and placed it back on his crotch. When she didn't attempt to move it, he leaned forward again and brushed his lips on hers. "Do it again," he ordered. She nodded and began to rub him. "Fuck," he bit out as her hand stroked over and over again, the rough denim heightening the sensations. When he heard her moan he about lost it. "Inside. Gotta take this inside." He quickly stood and grabbed her hand.

"Wait!" She stopped him as soon as he closed the front door and they stood in the living room once more.

"I don't think I can." Cole pointed to the insistent erection behind his zipper.

"One time. This can't go beyond tonight and my daughter can't ever know about this," she bargained.

"Jesus. Fine. One night," he agreed and trapped her against the far wall in the living room. "But for *this* one night, you're *mine*."

This was it; Cole knew if he could show her just this one time how good they were together, she'd be hooked.

∽ Chapter Seven ∽

GRACIE WAS IN A STATE of panic as she stood there staring at the man who'd haunted every bit of her life for the past 13 years. He was the same in so many ways, but completely different, too. It was strange seeing him again and knowing she had a part of him with her every day in the form of her daughter. Standing there, she felt somewhat guilty for keeping Cole from knowing Cora was his. But now wasn't the time to feel remorseful. No, it was a time to get Cole out of her system for good. *One time.* That's all it would take. She'd roll in the sheets with him for a while, more than likely get a good orgasm or two and be able to walk away. That was the plan and Gracie was one who could stick with a plan no matter what. This situation wouldn't be any different than the schedule she kept at work.

"Hey," Cole approached her with a caring look on his face. She tilted her head back to be able to gaze into his blue eyes. "I don't know what's going on up here," he tapped the side of her temple lightly, "but I need you here with me. Not in your head."

Gracie's better judgment slipped in and the panic that was just a dull lull, became a roar that she couldn't ignore. "I don't think we should do this."

"You're right. This isn't a good idea." His words shocked her. Cole wasn't a responsible person. Most of his life was spent throwing caution to the wind and not giving a fuck what the consequences were. So *this* Cole? This man scared the ever-loving shit out of her.

"Really?" She couldn't help but feel a spark of disappointment at his statement. Yes, this was a terrible idea, but somewhere deep down inside, she wanted to know what it was like to be with Cole after all these years. To see if the spark they'd had before was still there beneath the surface just waiting to be unleashed.

"This's your call. I won't stand here and pressure you into jumping into bed with me, Gracie."

"I appreciate that." She gave a small smile.

"Can I tell you something though?" He asked and she nodded. "I'm not trying to give you a line when I say this, but Gracie Callahan, you're even more beautiful than I remember." His words weren't only sweet, they were sincere. Something she'd never expected from the likes of Cole Matthews. Shell-shocked would've been an understatement to how she felt about his endearment.

"Thank you," Gracie whispered.

Cole began to come closer and the attraction she'd tried to bury just a few minutes earlier came bubbling to the surface like a hot spring in the forest. "I want this," she heard herself say.

"Tell me again," he said. She could tell he wanted reassurance before he laid another hand on her. In a way, she was grateful for that.

"I want this," she repeated.

That was the green light for Cole. Her breath left her body in a *whoosh* as he took one long step and backed her against the plaster wall. His hands were in her hair, tugging her head back to give him better access to her lips. When his mouth crashed down on hers, she felt it clear down to a cellular level. This was it. She'd have her wish of one last time with Cole. She only hoped that one time would be enough to work him out of her system.

When the kiss was finally broken, Cole backed away slightly and grabbed her by the hand. She expected him to lead her to the bedroom but was surprised when they ended up in the kitchen. "Please tell me you don't have some sort of utensil fetish," she said on a laugh.

He didn't answer her, he only began to unbutton and unzip her jeans as she stood there trying not to lose her mind from the sexual heat being conducted between them. Was it hot in here or was it just her? When her pants were undone, Cole hooked his fingers in the waist and pulled them down her legs. "Step out of these." He tapped her ankle with his finger. Everywhere the man touched—even if it was a light pat—sent shock waves through her body. But she did as he said and soon she stood there in nothing but a skimpy lace thong. Brushing a finger over the white fabric, he shot her a look of disapproval. "The Gracie I knew wouldn't wear something like this," he murmured.

"Maybe I'm not that girl anymore."

"I'm not sure I like the thought of you wearing something that barely covers this." He cupped her between her legs and Gracie's eyes rolled back in their sockets.

"Oh, God," she moaned.

Cole cocked an eyebrow and asked, "How attached are you to these?" He began to ball the side of the lace garment in his hand.

"Not very."

"Good." He yanked on the flimsy fabric, the sounds of them shredding echoed through the hollow space of the kitchen. The cool air wisped over her bare skin and she shivered. He then grabbed her around the waist and lifted her until her ass was on the countertop. "I want you right here." He began to slide his hands across her upper thighs, gooseflesh peppering every inch that he touched.

When his hands wrapped around her knees and pulled them apart, the inner sex crazed maniac in her almost snapped. But she held herself back, waiting to see what he'd do. It didn't take long either. Cole began to softly run his fingers on the outside edge of her folds. His voice was low as he leaned forward and spoke, "I can't wait to spread you open and see how wet you are already." Her leg muscles began to shake. "Are you soaked?" he asked.

"Yes." She didn't hold back on her answer at all. She wanted him to know what he was doing to her. What he'd *always* done to her. This was so stupid but she couldn't bring herself to stop it. The magnetism was too powerful to yank it apart.

Cole had always taken his time with her when they'd been intimate. He didn't rush anything or fumble through it. For some reason, he was quite the master at what he'd done, even though they been each other's firsts.

"If you want me to touch you, I have to hear the words. Or else I walk away."

"Cole, I need you to touch me."

"How bad?"

Oh, God, he was just torturing her now.

"*So* bad," she mewled.

Without warning Cole reached down and buried two fingers in her soaking wet pussy. She cried out at the invasion. "Fuck, baby, you're tight." He began to pull his fingers out and slide them back in, her hips thrusting to match his movements. "When was the last time you came?" he asked as his fingers worked magic inside her body.

"I don't know," she lied.

"Bullshit," Cole hooked his fingers and hit a spot that caused a whimper to force its way out of her mouth. "Was I the last man to give you an orgasm, Gracie?"

She didn't want to admit it, but yes, he was the only man who could get her off. She didn't have much to compare it to though. Besides Cole, there was only one other man she'd let inside her body. Truth be told, she wished that'd never happened. That was the reason she found herself in the mess she was in.

"Damn it. I want you to admit to me I was the last one who made you come." He continued to stoke the fire building slowly inside her. "Baby, I know you. And I know your body."

"Yes, Cole! You were the last person to make me come!" Her hips bucked off the counter as his fingers dove further inside her channel. Damn it, she wanted the release she was chasing. It was so close she could feel the stirrings creeping up like a silent stalker. But for some reason, Cole kept changing his rhythm, ultimately denying what she was reaching for. "I want it," she admitted.

"Do you realize how hot you look right now? Sitting on the counter, my fingers deep inside your pussy, your nipples pressing against your shirt like that."

"Give it to me, Cole," she demanded through gritted teeth.

"Then take it," he said with a look of determination on his face.

Gracie had never *taken* anything when it came to sex. She'd let the man take the lead, always. But due to circumstances in her past, she wanted the control now. She wanted to be the one demanding and taking. So she did what she felt the need to.

Watching Cole intently, Gracie began to snake her hand down her body until it rested right above the bundle of nerves that would send her over the edge. She'd never touched herself in front of Cole and from the look on his face, he was shocked that she might do so now. But he didn't know the *new* Gracie. The one who wasn't ashamed to show her sexual desires and act them out.

"Touch yourself," he urged.

She used two fingers to spread her folds further apart and expose her swollen clit. She began to tease herself with the tip of her finger and soon added more pressure and a circular motion.

"*Mmmmm*," her own moan spurred her on further.

"That's it. Rub that clit while I finger fuck this pussy."

"Yeah," she agreed.

"You gonna come for me, baby?"

"Yes. I'm gonna come for you."

"Good girl. Come for me, show me how sexy you are when you come."

"Oh, god. I want to come so hard for you." Gracie worked her clit until the unmistakable tingling sensation began to spread over her skin.

"I bet you're thinking of every single time my cock was deep in this pussy aren't you? The times when I fucked you until you were sore." His dirty talk heightened the feelings.

"Keep talking." She needed him to dirty talk with her, it was leading her toward the path of an epic orgasm.

"God damn it. You'd better fucking come. I need to have my cock in you soon," he bit out.

Working relentlessly, Gracie finally felt the beginnings of her release. The awareness that spread throughout her pulled a scream from her throat as the orgasm tore through her. The feelings were foreign and familiar at the same time as she bucked her hips and rode Cole's fingers through her entire release. It'd been years since she felt something like that. Something that left her feeling satisfied and confused all in the same breath. But now wasn't the time to be analyzing the situation. This was the time to feel and act out what she needed right now. Cole was here and willing to take care of the need burning brightly within her and she needed him to keep that alive, even if it was only for one night.

"Jesus. I missed this." Cole slowly pulled his fingers from her core and brought them to his lips. Gracie watched with hooded eyes as he opened his mouth and licked her wetness from his digits, his eyes on hers the entire time. When he was done enjoying her flavor, he reached his arms forward and scooped her up. Her legs twined around his ripped torso as his hands dug into the globes of her ass. She couldn't help but press herself closer as he backed up and began to walk them down the hallway.

"Where are we going?" she asked on a whisper. Her voice was already failing her with the remnants of the potent orgasm still hanging on to her body.

"My bed," he grunted.

Gracie could feel his urgency as he continued down the hall. The solid evidence of it was pressing firmly against her front. With each step he took he pressed further into her causing a gasp to escape her lips.

When they reached the bedroom, he loosened his hold and let her slide down his body. Once her feet hit the floor, nervousness swamped her.

"Hey, look at me," Cole said as he tilted her chin up to meet his gaze. "I know what you're thinking." A small smile spread across his handsome face. "You're thinking this is a bad idea. And you're probably right."

"Then what do we do?" Confusion began to set in further.

"I'll leave that up to you." He shrugged.

It wasn't hard to tell he was in pain, he'd watched her come on his kitchen counter and hadn't gotten off himself. But was this a good idea just because he needed to get his rocks off? No, it wasn't. But it'd been years since she'd had a sexual experience to write home about. She'd been alone for the longest time and the one thing she missed was having someone worship her body. This wasn't about feelings, no, it was about needs. And right now she *needed* to feel Cole moving himself inside her body more than she needed her next breath.

"Take your clothes off and lie down on the bed," she instructed.

Cole cocked an eyebrow but didn't question her. He began to remove his clothing piece by piece. When everything was in a pile at their feet, he leaned forward and gave her a light kiss on the lips. She watched him walk toward the bed and lie on his back like she'd said. It was such a painful sight, seeing Cole stretched out, waiting for what she'd do next. Gracie was ready to show him just what she had planned.

ᳬ Chapter Eight ᳬ

COLE'S BREATHING accelerated as he laid on his bed completely naked. He didn't have a clue what Gracie was up to but something about her was different. So different in fact that Cole wanted to put a stop to this whole thing and see what the hell was up with her. The once docile kitten had morphed into a jungle cat that was now stalking her prey. He watched as she strode around the bed and took in his nakedness from head to toe. The way her eyes raked over his body made him feel self-conscience for the first time in his life. He wasn't a small man in the guy parts department, but the way she was staring at him made him feel lacking. Afraid to say anything for the fear she might leave, he lay there quietly as she surveyed him.

"Do you have any ties?" she asked.

Cole's eyebrows shot up as he realized what she'd said. "Ties? Like neckties?" he asked.

"Yes."

"Yeah. In the top drawer of the dresser. There should be a few in there."

Gracie went to the weathered dresser and pulled on the handles of the top drawer. She rifled around a bit until she found what she was looking for. When she turned to him, he sure as fuck didn't expect her to be holding his service weapon. "Why do you keep this in here?" She held the gun in her hands and looked at him.

"Seemed like a good a place as any. Just stick it back in there." He became nervous that she'd pop him for all the grief he'd cause her in the past. But she didn't aim at him or threaten him with it, she only slid it back in the drawer and pulled out two neckties. One was the blue and grey one he'd worn to his commendation ceremony and the other was the purple one he'd worn to his grandfather's 90th birthday party two years ago. A satisfied smile crossed her face as she came back to the bed with the strips of fabric.

"Put your hands above your head and grab the rails on the headboard," she all but ordered.

"Gracie, I don't think…"

"If you want me to do this tonight, this is how it has to be."

He scrubbed a hand over his face in frustration. "I'm not letting you tie me up. That's insane," he complained.

"Fine," Gracie dropped the ties on the bed and began to exit the room.

No way was she leaving him in the condition he was in. With his dick at full mast, he jumped from the bed and followed her down the hall. Before she reached the end, Cole grabbed her arm and spun her around. "What the fuck is going on with you?" he bit out.

Gracie jerked her arm out of his grasp and stared him down. "Nothing is *going on* with me."

"I beg to differ. You want to tie me up like that crazy ass sex book all the women are reading. Cleary *something* is going on."

"It's nothing."

"Look, I'll admit, I've been a dick in the past. But even so, you always talked to me."

"Maybe I wanted to do something exciting," she admitted.

"But this isn't *you*."

"What if it is?"

Silence covered the space but soon Cole realized tears were streaking down her face. He stepped closed and wiped a few away. "Please talk to me. You know I hate seeing you cry."

"I'm really sorry." She cried as she came closer and buried her face in his bare chest. The warm salty tears began to pour across his skin.

"Hey, there's nothing to be sorry for. Look at me." He lifted her head and looked into her perfect green eyes. "Maybe I'm the one who should be sorry. If you thought you had to be like this to please me, then I obviously put off the wrong vibes." He chuckled.

"It has nothing to do with you."

"Then *what* does it have to do with?" he questioned.

"It's not important." Gracie shook her head.

"You may not believe it, but anything you have to tell me is important. Can you please talk to me?"

"I feel so out of control with my life. Like everything that was supposed to happen for me, didn't," she sighed.

"I can't seem to see where you have a shitty life."

"I never said I have a shitty life, Cole. But it wasn't the way it was supposed to be. You know damn well the plans I had. Being here with you brought all of that back to the forefront."

"Yeah, and plans change. You think I ever saw myself working for the FBI? I didn't. Hell, I doubted I'd even make it past my 25th birthday with half the shit I pulled in my teenage years." He laughed which had her chuckling in turn. "Is there any way we can have this conversation in there?" He pointed back down the hall to his bedroom. "Me standing here with my dick hanging out isn't conducive to an ideal conversation."

"Sure," she said meekly.

Cole led Gracie back to his bedroom, pulled a throw blanket off the end of the bed and wrapped it around her.

It was fairly warm in the house but he could see goosebumps raised on her creamy skin. She sighed when he placed it on her shoulders.

"Thank you." She smiled.

Not wanting to have a talk when *he* was naked, Cole grabbed a pair of boxers from his dresser and yanked them on. When he turned back around Gracie was snuggled in his bed under the covers. He decided to crawl in next to her.

"You okay?" He brushed her hair away from her face so he could see her eyes.

"Not really. Cole, I'm so sorry for acting the way I did. I know you wanted to, you know."

"Have sex with you?" He laughed.

"Yes, that."

"I'd rather you tell me what's going on with you."

With another sigh, Gracie began to talk again, "Some days I miss my old hopes and dreams. I love my daughter, I wouldn't trade her for all the gold in the world, but I can't help mourn the things I thought I'd be doing now."

"Like what?" Keep her talking, that was his plan.

"Like going to Stanford, getting my degree in investigative journalism and traveling the world, dredging up stories."

"There's still time to do all of that."

"I know. But what makes me more scared than anything is that I love what I do now. I don't think I'd want to leave it at this point."

"Then don't. If you have a good thing going, no use trying to fix what isn't broken." He reached up and pulled the blanket over her shoulder where it'd slipped free. It was instinct to want to run his fingers over the velvety expanse of her skin, but he thought better of it. This wasn't the time to get all sexual on her; she was opening up and that's what he wanted more than having his dick buried in her.

"I know I freaked you out with wanting to tie you up but I thought maybe it would make me feel more in control for once."

"Sex isn't the place you need to feel in control, baby. You need to start seeing you for who you are. That will make you feel in control."

"Who am I?" Her voice dropped lower and took on a husky quality.

"You're someone who's managed a career, a life, and raised a daughter even when some fuck-tard left all the responsibility on your shoulders."

"I guess. But Cole I..." She trailed off but he could see she had something more to say.

"You what?"

"Never mind. It doesn't really matter." Gracie pulled her hand above the blankets and began to stroke it over the stubble on his face. He closed his eyes and took in the rasping sound of her soft palm against his rough features. As he lay there with his eyes shut, he felt her warm lips touch his. "I want this, Cole," she whispered.

Slowly opening his eyes, Cole looked into hers. "Are you sure?"

She nodded. "I want to remember what it was like when things seemed okay."

He couldn't convey in words what he was feeling, so he did it with a kiss. Their mouths connected, tongues twined and bodies pressed together as they lost themselves in each other. He didn't know if he could make her feel any better about herself—she had to do that on her own—but he could make her feel good for a little while at least.

Breaking the kiss, Cole reached over and grabbed her around the waist. She tossed her leg over his body and straddled him, his hard cock pressing against her naked center through his underwear. Only a thin piece of cotton separated him from her moist heat.

"You have control, baby," he offered.

"I just want to feel you."

"Then let's get rid of these." He lifted her up and began to shimmy his boxers down his legs. Once they were disposed of, he pulled her back on top of him. "Condoms are in the top drawer." He pointed to his nightstand.

Gracie leaned over, her breasts bobbing near his face, tempting him to take one of her hard nipples in his mouth. But he wouldn't do that right now, no; this was about her having control of this. He wouldn't force anything on her she didn't want.

It was pure torture watching her sit back on his upper thighs, tearing off the end of the foil packet. She pulled the circular object out and tossed the empty wrapper to the side. When she placed the condom on the tip of his cock, Cole had to yet again concentrate on something other than what was going on. Gracie however was getting turned on by rolling the latex down his shaft. He could feel the evidence of her arousal on his thigh. He couldn't wait to have that wrapped around him.

"Baby, do you realize what you're doing to me right now?" he groaned.

"I think I do," She smiled.

"You'd better hurry up with that or we might have to wait a bit longer," he joked.

She finished rolling the condom down his cock and stroked it a couple times. When she was satisfied it was in place, she lifted her body up and positioned the head of his erection at her entrance. Cole held his breath as she glanced at his face and sank down. The moment he felt himself completely buried in her heat, he let out a moan along with her.

"Fuck," he cursed.

"You feel…" her eyes closed as she tried to finish her thought.

"Ride me." Cole grabbed her hips and dug his fingers into the soft flesh.

When she began to move and glide over him, Cole knew what heaven must be like. The way she rocked her hips, the way her clit slid over him and the small whimpers that escaped her lips were second to none.

"I want to come so bad," she admitted.

"I can't wait to feel you come on me."

"I don't think I can like this." She continued to rock back and forth, chasing her orgasm. She'd always had trouble reaching orgasm during intercourse. It'd become his main mission to get her off each and every time. As far as missions went, it was one he was always willing to give a hundred and ten percent to.

"Tell me what you need."

"I think I need you on top of me." She halted her motions and Cole let out a groan of disapproval.

"Are you sure?" He wanted to make damn sure she wanted it.

"Yes, I'm sure."

He didn't waste any time flipping her over and burying himself back inside her.

"Oh, my God!" she shouted.

"Remember this?" He grabbed one of her legs and placed her heel on his shoulder. He raised up a bit and changed the angle. When he thrust his cock inside her, Gracie let out a half scream. "Am I hurting you?" He wanted to make sure she was okay.

"No, yes...just fuck me!" she shouted.

Cole began to fuck her hard and deep. With each forward thrust, he felt her pussy become wetter and begin to clamp down on his dick. "Damn I love that feeling. Your pussy getting ready to milk my cock."

"Yes!" He pounded into her again and again. "Make me come."

"Yeah? You want me to fuck you until you come? Is that what you want, baby?"

"Yes, please!" she cried out.

Cole wasn't used to the vocal woman beneath him but he loved it. The way she shouted and screamed with each drive he gave her spurred him on further. "Hear that? Your pussy is so fucking wet. Damn."

"I feel it. Oh fuck." She spread her free leg further to let him in deeper.

Cole didn't think he could go deeper but she proved him wrong. "I need you to come for me, Gracie."

"I will!"

"Now, baby. Go ahead and come all over my cock." He lifted up a little more, hitting something inside her that made her scream again.

"More, I need more."

Cole gave her more. He knew she'd be sore in the morning, but damn it, he wanted her to come so hard she'd almost black out. "Damn it, I'm gonna fill this condom," he groaned.

Just then he felt the walls of her pussy begin to clamp down on him. He knew she was right there but needed some help. He reached down and began to furiously rub her over-swollen clit. When he did, Gracie let out a guttural scream and he felt her pussy yank him in further. He stopped rubbing and began to thrust in to her depths once more. As she milked him, Cole came with a loud groan. His cock twitched inside her as her heat enveloped him.

Once he was spent, he collapsed, making sure not to crush her with his weight. Their breathing finally came down to a normal level and Cole lifted himself off her. When he looked down, her forehead was beaded with sweat and her cheeks were flushed. There was nothing sexier than a sated woman.

"Cole, that was…"

"Fucking phenomenal." As he said it, he felt his cock threatening an encore performance. He pulled himself from her body and jumped from the bed. After cleaning up, he returned to find Gracie fast asleep. Her gorgeous body lay on its side, her cheek rested on one of his pillows and her left hand rested just below her chin. The same left hand that once wore a simple white gold band, signifying she was his.

Should he crawl back in bed with her? Or should he

go sleep on the couch and be a good southern gentleman? The decision weighed on his mind for a few moments while he stood there watching her sleep. Finally, he'd made his decision; he'd take the couch. Yeah, they'd just had sex. Probably the best fucking sex of his life, but he wasn't about to curl up next to her not knowing if he was welcome to or not. It was better to tuck tail and get the hell out of there.

The house was quiet as he made his way to the living room. When the couch was situated with a pillow and a sheet, Cole laid there on his back and looked up at the ceiling. Damn, what a night. Him and Gracie were over as far as *she* was concerned, but him? He wasn't about to sign those papers without a fight. It should've bothered him that she had a kid now, but for some reason it didn't. Cora was a good kid, he got along with her okay. Sure, they'd only been there for a day, but his plan was to drag this thing out until Gracie admitted she still had feelings for him. If she didn't, he'd hang his head and let her go one last time. But he wasn't going down without a fight.

Chapter Nine

GRACIE OPENED HER EYES the next morning and shot straight up in bed. The blanket slipped down her body causing a cool rush of air to brush her naked breasts.

"No, no, no," she chanted. She reached down and pulled the fabric up to conceal herself. What the hell had she done? Cole, *that's* what. Her lapse in judgement the night before had her now sitting in Cole's bed completely naked. This wasn't good for so many reasons.

"Morning," Cole strode in the room with a shit-eating grin on his face. When he saw the look plastered across hers, he paused. "Whoa, you okay?"

Gracie jumped from her spot, wrapping the sheet

around her body. "No, I'm not okay." She brushed past him and into the bathroom down the hall. Cole was hot on her heels but she managed to slam the door just before he could reach out and stop her. Once inside the small room, Gracie stood there shaking. This wasn't supposed to happen. What'd started out as a simple task had now turned into a major fuck-up on her part and she'd surely pay for it now.

"Gracie, let me in." Cole knocked on the door.

"I need a few minutes please," she called. A few minutes was a gross understatement. What she needed was a bunker to hide herself and her daughter in.

"I think we need to talk," his muffled voice came from the other side of the door.

"No, I don't want to talk."

"Come on. It wasn't *that* bad, was it?" She heard the humor in his voice. Something he was known for. Cole never did take much seriously. He'd play and joke his way through any situation. It was a wonder he could be undercover with the FBI. Keeping a straight face wasn't his strong suit.

"Cole, can you just go the fuck away for a few minutes!" she all but screamed.

"Okay then." She heard his retreating footsteps and let out a puff of air.

Bracing her hands on the sides of the sink, Gracie peered at her reflection in the mirror on the wall. Her hair was a mess, tangles flying everywhere, her face was all splotchy—that wasn't Cole's fault though, her Irish heritage played a huge role in that. And her lips were swollen and well-kissed. Okay, *that* was Cole's fault. Gracie lifted her fingers to her lips and sucked in a breath. Her eyes closed and her mind transported her to what'd happened just hours earlier. Regret sunk in and tears formed at the back of her eyes. How could she fix this? How could she make this go away and still keep Cora and Dash safe? Gracie shook her head at her own stupidity. How the hell was she supposed to resist her former flame when he was looking all sexy and saying things that made her want to fall into a puddle on the floor? She'd thought her mind and body were stronger than falling for a well-muscled stomach, strong capable arms and a mouth that was solely designed for sin. Clearly those things weren't on the same page when it came to Cole Matthews. That man could unwind a fucking grapevine so fast it would shatter the bottle of wine it'd already produced. Damn him.

"It's been a few minutes, Gracie. Don't make me bust this door down. I have training in this," he called.

It wasn't possible to hide out in the bathroom forever. And she knew he'd make good on his promise. Cole wasn't just the goofball who could charm the panties off a rabid skunk, he was perfectly capable of breaking down doors and anything else that got in his way. Hell, her heart had gotten in his way at one time and the bastard broke it until she thought she'd needed to buy stock in Krazy Glue to repair it.

"I'm counting to five. You know what happens at five," he warned.

Oh, yes, she knew what happened at five. When his mouth said that dreaded number, he charged in like a rhino with PMS. It was best to keep the beast at bay so she grabbed the knob and flung the door open. Cole stood on the other side with his arms braced on the frame above him and the planes of his stomach in perfect view, not obstructed by clothing.

"Ah, so you remember what happens at five," he flashed a sinister grin her way.

Gracie pushed past him once more and made a b-line for the bedroom. "Yes, I know what happens at five," she grumbled as she darted out of his way.

"Either you're upset at something or you'd like to play cat and mouse today. I could go for a little chase," he teased.

"I'm fine, Cole." Grabbing her suitcase, she yanked out a pair of shorts, tank and underwear. The sheet was still firmly wrapped around her body when she gawked at him standing just inside the doorway. "Can you please turn around?"

"What the hell for?"

"I'd like to get dressed if that's okay with you."

Cole let out a '*pffft*' sound, "Honey, I've seen every damn part of you."

"Don't remind me," she blurted out. Before she had a

chance to take a breath, Cole was across the room and in front of her.

"Really? We're playing *that* game?" He reached out, grabbed her and tossed her on the bed. The sheet fell away, Gracie trying desperately to pull it back across her naked body. When Cole placed his body over hers though, she wasn't sure if she wanted to be nude or not. "I think I *do* need to remind you," his hand began to slide up her body, landing below one of her breasts, then cupping it. "I haven't only *seen* every part of you," he used a thumb to graze her traitor of a nipple that was already responding to his touch, "I've touched every part of you," his head lowered, the breaths coming from his lips warming her chilled flesh, "I've tasted every part of you," her back bowed as if she wanted him to suck her nipple into his mouth further when he snaked his tongue out to lightly lick her. "Wanna know what else I've done?" Gracie began to panic when his hand left her upper body and trailed further south. This wasn't going in the direction she'd hoped. And why in the hell were her legs falling open, waiting for him to touch her? Oh, and he did. He wisped his fingers over the outside of her sex then used them to spread her open. "I've fucked every single part of you, Gracie." Gliding his fingers through the gathering wetness, Cole then penetrated her, Gracie moaning at the invasion. "I've fucked your pussy," one finger reached lower to feather over her ass, "I've fucked your ass," he then began to plunge his fingers further into her channel, "And I've made you come for me. Every. Single. Time."

"Cole," she moaned.

"What, baby? Do you need something?" She didn't answer. "Tell me to fuck you."

"No."

"I know you. You'd rather come all over my cock than my fingers."

"I can't," she whispered.

"Fine," Cole said as he removed his fingers from her wet heat, leaving her bereft.

"No, wait!" She panicked as he stood from the bed.

"Yes?" he looked down at her.

Gracie found herself blinded by the need of a good

orgasm yet again. Was it *that* bad for her to be with him again? Surely it wouldn't catch up with her later, right? Could she take that chance?

"Did you need something?" he asked as she tried to make her inner turmoil go the fuck away.

Thoughts of right and wrong flew out the window as she also stood from the bed and turned around, her back to him. She then leaned down and placed her hands on the edge of the mattress. Her ass perfectly in line with the front of his shorts. "Fuck me like this," she all but ordered.

"Damn," he said as a whoosh of air hit her. She looked around to find him grabbing a condom from his nightstand.

Gracie's patience wore thin even as he sheathed himself and placed the head of his cock at her dripping entrance. She wiggled her ass hoping he'd get the point and hurry the hell up. It wasn't until Cole slammed into her that she realized she didn't have patience. A scream ripped through her throat as he bottomed out.

"Are you remembering how deep this position feels

now?" he asked.

"Oh, God, yes," she groaned while grinding her ass against him.

"I want to fuck you so God-damned hard right now," he admitted.

"Then do it. I need you to fuck me, Cole. Don't hold back."

"Yeah?"

"Yes!" she demanded.

Suddenly Cole dug his fingers into her hips and pulled his cock almost completely free of her. It wasn't long though until he slammed back into her. Over and over he'd remove himself and thrust relentlessly into her channel until Gracie felt her release begin to creep up on her.

"I think I'm going to come," she said.

"Damn right you are. Touch your clit," he said as he plunged himself inside her once more.

She positioned her arm and reached underneath to massage her clit. Damn she was so fucking close. Her vision blurred and everything seemed to disappear as she reached for that amazing peak. Just a little more and she would be able to fly over the edge.

"Come on Gracie, work those fingers and make yourself come," Cole instructed. The pace quickened with the way he fucked her as he kept talking, "Baby, my cock feels so fucking good inside you. You're making me wanna come."

"Cole, I can't," she whined. It was hard trying to come. It wasn't something that came easy to her and right now, the crest she thought she'd reached was fading.

Cole didn't hesitate to help her though. He pushed down on her shoulders, putting her in a different position than before. Gracie groaned as she felt his erection press even further into her. "Don't stop touching yourself," he demanded. So she kept up with flicking her fingers over her more than swollen clit.

It wasn't long and the sensations returned. This was it, she was going to come this time. When the first pulses of her orgasm began, Gracie screamed into the mattress below her. It muffled the sounds that didn't even seem human. Cole shortened his strokes which prolonged her release. By the time her orgasm finally faded, she felt like she'd just experienced heaven and hell all in the course of a minute. But she noticed he hadn't come yet. She waited for the familiar guttural sound to escape his mouth but it didn't. He only slowed his pace inside her sensitive core. Feeling somewhat unabashed, Gracie shifted forward and let his cock ease out of her.

"What are you doing?" he asked.

Rolling her body over she sat up on the edge of the mattress. She reached up and rolled the condom from his cock and tossed it to the floor. Cole stood in front of her bewildered as she began to stroke him. The low moans that filtered from his mouth spurred her on. Leaning forward she then began to tease the slit of his cock with her tongue.

"Holy fuck." His hips jutted forward as if he wanted more. She'd show him *more* alright.

"What do you want, Cole?" She decided to turn the tables on him this time.

"I want you to suck me. Fuck me with your mouth."

A breath *whooshed* out of him as she did just that. Her mouth encased him like a tomb of ecstasy as she slid her lips up and down his shaft. She wouldn't admit it out loud, but doing this to him was making *her* wet too. Her sex began to flutter with awareness as she kept on licking and sucking him.

"Fuck yeah, that's it," he urged.

Gracie pulled her mouth away and began stroking with her hand again. Her eyes were focused on his as she felt him harden even more in her palm.

"Keep that up and I'm gonna come." He smiled.

"Then come."

"Where do you want it? On those pretty tits?"

"No, I want you to come in my mouth," just as she said it, Cole's cock twitched in her hand. It excited her that he was finding enjoyment in what she was doing.

"Really? You want me to come in that mouth? You gonna swallow for me?" he asked, his voice coming out pained.

"Yes," Gracie hissed.

"Put me in your mouth, baby. I'm so fucking close."

Leaning forward once more she began to stroke him with her mouth like she'd done with her hand just moments before. Again his cock hardened more and she applied more suction.

"*Mmmmm,* yeah. Keep doing that."

Her mouth felt like it was performing an erotic ballet as she brought him closer to completion.

"Gonna come," he groaned.

Soon Gracie felt the warm tangy jets hit her tongue. She sucked hard as he released into her mouth. Working her throat muscles, she swallowed every last drop her gave her. When he was finished, he pulled himself from her mouth, his chest heaving like he'd just run a marathon. He looked down at her flushed face and smiled.

"I don't really know what to say about that."

"Bad?"

"Fuck no, it wasn't bad. Damn Gracie, that was the single most amazing blowjob of my life," he said, making her proud.

Even though she was filled with pride, worry began

to creep in as before. She couldn't keep this up. There was nothing but warranted trouble at the end of this road and she'd be in deep shit if someone found out.

Jumping from her seat, she began to grab her clothes, ignoring a still naked Cole in the room. "I need to shower and call Cora. I'd like to make sure she's okay."

"I'm sure she's fine," Cole said, making her anger rise. What the hell did he know about raising a kid? Nothing, that's what.

"Unless you're some kind of fortune teller, I don't think you have the right to tell me if my child is fine or not," she bit out.

"Jesus, what the hell, Gracie?" He began to shrug on his underwear and then a pair of faded jeans. She'd always loved him in faded jeans.

"I need to check on her. That's that, Cole. She has a disease and I worry about her."

"Yeah but less than five minutes ago you had my dick down your throat."

"Yeah? So *fucking* what?" she sassed.

"Really?" He ran a hand through his hair making his

normally perfect mane messy. "You're giving me whiplash here. One minute you're all into what we're doing and as soon as we're done, you're back to being a bitch again. What gives?" He looked genuinely hurt at the way she was acting. Rightly so. But she had to distance herself before she hopped into the bed again and played the equivalent of naked twister.

"I'm sorry. I'm just stressed out, okay? I have a responsibility to take care of Cora and make sure she's okay," she tried to explain. Too bad she couldn't explain *all* of what was troubling her.

"I get it, I really do. But you have to take time for yourself, too. Hell, that kid can hold her own, trust me." He laughed.

"That's because she's just like her father," Gracie said it and regretted it instantly.

"I thought you didn't really know her dad." His eyebrows shot up in curiosity.

"I didn't." She shrugged and slipped her feet into her flip flops.

"Then how do you know she's like him if you didn't

know him?"

"I was assuming. She's not like me in that aspect so I'm assuming it's a trait passed down from him." It sounded like a legitimate excuse, one she was happy with.

"Fine. I've gotta get some shit done at the office today. Feel free to hang out here or whatever," he offered.

"Okay, thanks."

No, she wasn't planning on hanging out at his house for the day. It was time to try and figure some things out. But first, she did need to give Cora a call to make sure she was doing okay. She worried about her daughter. It was kind of in the job description of *being* a mom. Ever since the day she laid eyes on that tiny bald human being, nothing had ever been the same again.

~ Chapter Ten ~

"MAN YOU LOOK like someone took the wrong end of a hammer to you," Luke joked as he made his way over to Cole's desk.

"You can just shut the fuck up."

"Clearly you didn't get laid this weekend," Luke snorted.

"Clearly you're a dipshit." Cole tossed back. This was how it went with them. They'd insult the hell out of each other until they were bored with it. But Cole wasn't in the mood to play these fucking games today. "Not in the mood, man."

"You need to go do some target practice to get your head clear?" Luke asked. Damn him, he knew what would perk Cole right up.

"Damn right I do." Jumping from his chair, he switched off his computer and darted toward the door. "You're driving!" he yelled over his shoulder.

"Why the hell do I always have to drive?" Luke whined.

"Because you're an asshole and I like you paying for gas."

"Fucker," Luke accused.

There was nothing that made Cole feel better than feeling the slight jerk of his rifle when he squeezed the trigger at a target. Sex was a close second at this point in his life, but somehow reconnecting with Gracie, being with her was vying for the top spot now.

"Dude, you look like someone kicked your puppy," Luke commented as he drove them to the shooting range.

"Not really in the mood to talk about it right now."

"That's it, clam up and let that shit fester. That's a great way to handle your shit."

"Man, fuck you. You didn't wanna talk about you and Ava when shit happened with that whole deal."

"There was a reason for it, we were undercover for

fuck sake."

"Doesn't matter. I'm your partner, the one who shoots the bad guy before he puts a bullet in you."

"Didn't do too good of a job of that did you?" Luke laughed.

"Oh, shut the hell up. You didn't die did you?"

"No, but my spine still feels like it's gonna shoot out my ass when the weather's shitty."

"Pansy ass," Cole teased. It was nice joking around with his best friend and partner right now. If he wasn't doing this, he'd probably be putting his fist through a wall somewhere. "She's got me so fucked up already and she's not been here but a day. How the hell is that possible?"

"Love tends to grab you by the balls and twists them into a pretzel."

"Yeah, I guess it does. But she's different now. Something isn't right with her and I can't put my finger on it."

"Maybe nothing's different and you're just looking for an excuse to tell yourself you don't have feelings for her anymore. You're an investigative person by nature, could it be there isn't anything wrong here?"

"Could be. But I don't believe that for one second. She acts like she's scared of something. I'd like to know what that *something* is."

"Have you talked to the kid about it? Kids tend to know more than they let on about with their parents," Luke suggested.

"I'm not gonna sit and grill the kid about this shit. That's some sort of unwritten rule. I'm sure Gracie would turn into a terrifying mama bear if I did some dumb shit like that."

"You're probably right. I'd hate to see Ava with our kids someday if someone fucked with them."

"Wait. You're planning the whole family thing already?"

"We've been talking about it." Luke looked over and grinned like a total lovesick dipshit.

"Is she knocked up already?"

"No. I'd like to get married first. I'm old fashioned like that I guess." Luke leaned over and popped the glovebox of his truck open. After pushing aside his holstered service weapon, he then grabbed ahold of a small black velvet box. He slammed the door shut and dropped the box in Cole's lap. "Check that out."

Cole snatched up the box and flipped open the hinged lid. The brilliance of the diamond centered between two emeralds was nothing shy of stunning. "Wow, that's impressive."

"Think she'll like it?" Luke sounded nervous.

"I think you could give that woman a damn kidney stone and she'd be happy with it. When are you planning on popping the question?" Cole shut the lid.

"Not sure yet. I've had that damn thing since I came back from D.C."

"Having second thoughts?" Cole raised his eyebrows.

"Not at all. This is probably the easiest decision I've ever made. I just haven't figured out a good time to ask her. She's always busy with work and so am I. It's not like I wanna ask her while we're in bed at night."

"Not very romantic."

"Exactly. But I do need a favor," Luke said.

"Yeah?"

"I need you to hang onto that for me. Ava's gonna eventually find it and I don't want to ruin the surprise. She deserves a big gesture and I'd like to give that to her."

"It's good to see you like this."

"Like what?"

"Happy. You deserve it, man. And Ava is one hell of a woman to put up with your cranky ass."

"I'm not cranky," Luke defended.

"The fuck you aren't. You're even more so with that damn beard. Are you auditioning for a role on *Duck Dynasty*?"

"She likes my beard!"

"Aright then," Cole jammed the small box in his pocket just as they pulled into the gravel parking lot of the range.

Each and every time the opportunity arose to get some target practice in, Cole was there. He knew what he was doing—his marksman training was well-used. But it was always a good idea to have more practice.

"Let's shoot some targets and maybe you'll feel better." Luke grabbed his bag and jumped down out of the truck.

"Hell yeah."

Gracie didn't have a vehicle to drive so she took off on foot from Cole's house. She wasn't sure where she was going since nothing was familiar but she had to get out of his house. His scent lingered so much that it was driving her to the brink of insanity. Everything reminded her of what they'd done last night and even just a few hours ago. A blush crept up her neck as the thoughts intensified. As she tamped her arousal down, her phone began to ring in her pocket. The number on the display screen reminded her what was at stake if she didn't get those papers signed soon and get the hell back to Illinois.

"Hello?"

"Hey," the semi-depressed voice came over the phone.

"How's everything going?" she asked.

"As good as can be expected. How're things with you?" the male voice inquired.

"Everything is going fine. I miss you so much." Gracie tried to keep the emotion from her voice but was failing.

"I miss you, too. But we'll get to see each other soon." He sounded optimistic.

"I know we will." She smiled.

After chatting for a few minutes, he said, "Shit, I've gotta get off here. I'll call you again when I can. Love you."

"I love you, too," she replied just before the line when dead.

Damn it. She wanted more time to talk to him. The short phone calls weren't enough for her liking. But if that was all she'd get with Dash, she'd take it. And he was right, they'd get to be together again soon. She had to hold out hope that it would really happen. Gracie loved him with all her heart and would make sure they'd see each other soon.

"Mom!" Her head shot up when she heard the

unmistakable screech of Cora's voice.

Coming down the sidewalk toward her was her daughter and Ava. Cora wore a huge smile as she bounded to her mom.

"Hey, what're you two doing?" Gracie shoved her phone into her back pocket.

"Ava took me to this super cool vintage store. They have some rad clothes in there!" Cora looked so happy and carefree. Exactly as a soon-to-be teen should be.

Shit. Gracie almost forgot her daughter's birthday was in a week and a half. Hopefully she'd get Cole to sign the papers and get the hell back home. She didn't want Cora to have to celebrate such a milestone birthday while in a place that wasn't home.

"Hi, Gracie. Hope you don't mind I took her shopping." Ava stood back with a look of trepidation on her face.

"No, not at all. She loves to shop." Gracie grinned even though she *was* a bit uncomfortable knowing she wasn't asked beforehand.

"Mom, Ava wants us all over for dinner tonight. Will

you go? Her house is awesome!"

Gracie smiled again at her daughter's excitement. This was a side of Cora she hadn't really seen much lately. It was mostly iPods and headphones.

"Uh, sure." Gracie shrugged.

"You don't have to bring anything. We're grilling some steaks and Cora promised to help me with the sides for the meal."

Ava was one of the good ones, Gracie could tell. The woman had clearly been through some rough shit but showed kindness to those around her.

"How about I bring a cake? I don't want to show up empty-handed."

"That works, too."

"Can I go with her and you just pick me up tonight?" Cora asked.

"That's fine. Are you feeling okay? Taking your medicine like you should?"

"Yes, mom." Cora rolled her eyes at the question.

"Then it's fine by me."

Her daughter joined Ava once more and the two of

them took off down the sidewalk. Great, she had to spend even more time with Cole this evening. This was starting to feel like a normal life, but if there was one thing she knew, the illusion of normalcy was just that.

Not knowing where to get the ingredients to make a cake, Gracie pulled out her phone and hit the search engine for a local market. There were three in a mile radius, but the closest one was only two blocks away. She took off walking in that direction. Thoughts of everything that was going on traveled along with her and yet again she worried herself with how it would all turn out in the end. It was all going to be fine. Dash would be safe and sound, Cora wouldn't know what was going on and Cole would just sign the papers and be out of her life for good. Why the hell did that last one make her pause though? Cole wasn't good for her on so many levels. Hell, his job was the first one at this point. It was dangerous. Who knew if he'd come home in one piece each night. Ugh, she had no business thinking about shit like that. Cole wasn't going to be in her life *at all*. The thing that'd happened with them was only a hiccup, a minor bump in the road to be reunited with Dash. He was the one who mattered, not Cole.

"Feeling any better?" Luke asked Cole as they drove back to the office.

"Marginally." Cole scrubbed a hand over his face and blew out a frustrated breath.

"Why don't you just bite the bullet and tell her you don't want to sign the papers? Tell her you'd like to try and make this work."

"Because I know Gracie. She'd only try because I wanted her to. If her heart isn't in it a hundred percent, I don't want it."

"Wow, that's pretty harsh."

"How so?"

"Wouldn't you rather have part of her than nothing at all?"

"*No.* If someone doesn't want to turn over the entire set of keys to me, then I don't have any business trying to pick the remaining locks. It's not fair to either of us. Do I love her? Of course I do, always have. But I'm not gonna force her to love me back."

"I guess it makes sense." Luke shrugged.

"You can't sit there and tell me if Ava wasn't completely in love with you, you'd want to stay with her?"

"But she *is* in love with me."

"That's not the point, jackass. All I'm saying is you wouldn't want her walking around with doubt. Doubting that you were who she's supposed to be with."

"Ava doesn't have doubts."

"Why do I even bother talking to you about this shit? I could have a heart-to-heart with my dick and get a better response."

"A hard-on isn't a response." Laughter bubbled from Luke's chest.

"Man, fuck you. Just drive the damn truck." Cole motioned to the road.

"You really need to work on your anger issues."

"And you need to work on your comprehension skills."

Cole wasn't one who liked his faults tossed in his face and Luke was doing just that. If Luke hadn't saved him from several bullets, he'd be tempted to reach over and plant his fist in the side of the other man's nose right now. But he wouldn't do that because it would only prove one thing, that Luke was right about him being an angry fucker. He wasn't an angry guy, things and circumstances made him angry and aggravated. In fact, Cole was a pretty calm guy considering the shit he went through in his daily life. Hell, he'd been shot more times than he could count at this point, earning him the nickname *"Bullet"* back in the D.C. field office. He'd taken it in stride just like everything else in his life. There was one thing he wasn't sure he could take in stride though, this shit with Gracie.

As he sat in the truck contemplating his next move, Luke's phone began playing the tell-tale ringtone that said Ava was calling. Luke never seemed embarrassed when Taylor Swift began crooning while in the office. But hey, to each his own.

"Well hey there, sweetheart," Luke answered. Gag a

maggot. The sugary way he spoke to the petite blonde was causing Cole major acid reflux. "Really?" Luke looked over at Cole. "Will do. Love you." Then he hung up.

"Something tells me I'm either hiding a body tonight or there's something else up."

"Dinner at my place. Gracie and Cora will be there too."

"Great."

"Stop acting like someone put your Johnson in a guillotine. It's just dinner. Besides, I thought you wanted to spend more time with her, wasn't that the point of all this?"

"It would be if I knew what the final outcome of this thing would be."

"Good luck with that. You'd have better luck trying to wipe a cat's ass with sandpaper."

"How many…never mind." Cole shook his head and clamped his mouth shut. It was better to shut the hell up before he found out more info than he wanted to.

Gracie stood in Cole's kitchen watching the timer on the oven like a hawk. It would be a catastrophe if the chocolate cake burned because of carelessness but she wasn't about to let that happen. It would turn out perfect as usual and everyone would love it. Hopefully This was Cole's favorite cake. "Damn it. Why do I even care?" she said aloud.

"Why do you care about what?" Cole's deep timbre of a voice sounded behind her causing her to startle. The oven mitt in her hand went flying and landed on the kitchen table beside her. "Sorry." He swaggered into the room with her and suddenly it felt significantly smaller. "Just came in to get some water." He stepped around her like she was a caged animal.

"It's your house." Gracie smiled as he yanked on the door of the fridge. Her eye went wide as the handle of the 1970s model appliance gave out and Cole stood there with the handle in his hand.

"Shit." He gawked at the fake wood.

"Might be time for an upgrade?" She snorted.

"Did you do something to it?" He sat the handle on the counter and stalked toward her.

"No. I don't even know how to loosen one of those!" she dodged him just as he tried to pounce. "Cole, stop it. I have a cake in the oven," she warned.

His head snapped up and gaze went to the door of the matching pea-green oven. "What kind?" He leaned over trying to sneak a peek through the grease-laden window.

"Chocolate."

"You're making chocolate cake? For *me*?"

"I'm making chocolate cake for everyone at Luke and Ava's house."

"So, me. Right?" His boyish grin brought on one of hers.

"Fine, if it makes you feel good about yourself, I made it just for you," she replied sarcastically.

"Awww." He stepped closer and pulled her into a crushing hug. "Thank you." Before he stepped away she felt him kiss the top of her head.

Luckily the timer went off and she was saved from further intimate shit. As she took the cake from the oven and placed it on the counter, she could feel Cole's eyes on her. To be honest, it felt nice to have someone looking at her. Would she admit that to him? Hell *no*. He didn't need to know any of the thoughts he currently inspired. Some of them included the chocolate frosting that was sitting in the now handle-less fridge.

"I need to get dressed while that cools." Gracie wiped her hands on a towel and stepped around Cole.

"Wait." Grabbing her hand he halted her steps. Goosebumps rose on her skin from the contact of his touch.

"Cole, don't," she again warned.

"Look, I know you don't want me anymore, you've made that abundantly clear. I just want to make sure you're alright."

"Of course I am." No, she wasn't okay at all but she'd be damned if she dragged him into her problems.

"Okay." He shrugged and let her hand go.

Once she made it safely down the hallway and into

the bedroom, she shut herself in and rested her back against the door. Blowing out a breath she realized just how close she'd been to asking him to kiss her when he stopped her in the hallway. Comfort was what she needed right now and she'd always found that in Cole, even if he *did* only have the emotional maturity of sea kelp. She needed to cool her jets when it came to him or she'd be in even more of a pickle than she was in now. Dash was waiting on her back home and he was the important one, not Cole.

Slipping off her clothing, Gracie grabbed the dress from the bed she'd found at the vintage clothing store Cora had been raving about earlier. Surprisingly the prices weren't terrible and they had tons of stuff to fit her curvy figure. The 1950s sundress she picked out was somewhat sweet but fit her conservative personality to a T. The squared neckline would keep everything concealed, but the full skirt was slightly flirty to balance it out. Pink wasn't a color she'd normally choose but the small red polka dots made it work.

"You about ready? Luke keeps texting me." Cole

knocked on the door making her jump.

"Just slipping my shoes on," she called out. Once her feet were covered in the white flats, Gracie took one last look in the mirror. It would have to do; it wasn't as if she was going there to impress anyone.

Cole tapped his foot as he waited for Gracie to come out of his bedroom. He'd taken the liberty of frosting the cake while she was changing and had more than one fantasy about the multiple places on her body he could lick the creamy stuff off of. He smiled knowing he saved some of it and stuffed the bowl behind some other stuff in the fridge to hide it. Maybe she'd be willing to let loose again later.

"Sorry, it took me a while with the zipper." Cole's head shot up when she walked down the hallway.

"Fuck me," he groaned.

"What?" Her eyes went wide.

Cole had a thing for vintage-looking women. It was kind of a weakness of his. And right now with Gracie standing there in that damn dress and those full lips painted red, he might need to spend a few minutes in the bathroom to get *'bullet junior'* to play nice for the evening. "Nothing. You look nice." His smile came across pained so he swiftly turned to the kitchen to grab the cake.

"Crap, I need to put the frosting on the cake."

"Got it taken care of. Hope this looks okay?" Cole held up the cake hoping it would meet her approval. He'd felt like a prissy chef as he swirled the icing around with a small spatula.

"Wow, that actually looks great!" Her smile gave him hope that she didn't actually hate his guts.

"Thanks. Let's get on the road." He grabbed the cake and ushered her out the door. It was a bitch trying to keep his eyes from going to her ass swaying perfectly in that damn red and pink fabric. But he took one for the team so he didn't get a cake smashed in his face.

When he had her situated in his truck, he started it up and backed out of the driveway. Just as he did, a thought hit him.

"Hey, since I've been working quite a bit and haven't

had time to go buy stuff for the house, I thought maybe you and Cora could do it for me."

"I don't think so."

"Why not? You both expressed how lame my shit is. I'll give you the money and you can get it fixed up."

"Cole, that's your personal domain. I'm not about to go in and make it all girly."

"You don't have to make it look like a sorority house. Just order some new appliances, a couch and maybe some rugs and shit."

"Okay. I guess we could." She looked like she was on the verge of asking him something but he watched her clamp her mouth shut.

"Whatever's on your mind seems like it wants out." He chuckled.

"It's none of my business." She smiled sweetly and looked out the front window again.

"For fuck sake, just ask me."

She shifted in her seat, "Why don't you have nicer things in your house? With your parents…" she snapped her mouth closed once more.

"With my parents being loaded?"

"Yeah, that." Her cute little nose scrunched up.

It took him a few moments to answer her, but he was nothing if not transparent. "Dad was pissed when I decided to take the job for the FBI. It wasn't like he cut me out of the money train but I felt like he was disappointed in me. I don't know, I've always been that guy who doesn't want shit handed to him."

"Your trust fund?" she asked.

"Got it when I was 25 and donated the entire thing to the American Cancer Society."

"Wow, that's amazing."

Cole shrugged as if it weren't a big deal. "I still talk to mom and dad but there's still that feeling that they hate what I do for a living."

"Maybe they're scared they'll get a phone call saying you're gone."

"Could be. But honestly, I don't think about it that often. It's part of the job. Just like you cutting your finger with your shears is part of your job."

"There's a huge difference in me nicking a knuckle

and you getting a bullet lodged in your heart or head."

"Yeah, but I've had a pretty good life. I've lived and loved, not much more you could want, ya know?"

"Yeah." She sighed.

"But I really would like you to do something with my house. You guys are right; it looks like a homeless person's been squatting there. It needs to feel more like a home."

"I'll think about it."

He was taking a huge risk letting her do this for him. Truth was, he didn't give a shit what his house looked like. More than on one occasion he'd spent the night on the floor at the office. His house was just a place to take a shower and eat a meal every now and then. For the most part if he wasn't at the office, he was gracing Luke and Ava with his signature charm and wit. But maybe this would make her feel like he wanted her in his life more. It sure couldn't hurt, right?

When he turned down the driveway toward Luke's plantation home, Gracie's eyes widened. He pretty much expected it. Most people went nuts over this place. It was pretty damn spectacular if he was honest. But after staying with Luke for a few weeks after he moved to Biloxi, he realized he wouldn't want a house that big. It was hell when you were a little drunk and trying to find your way to one of the bathrooms. More than once he'd given up and taken a piss on Ava's rose bushes by the front steps. Heck, one of them *still* wasn't growing right. Not that he'd want Gracie to know about his loathing times when he'd first moved here. It was some kind of hell watching your best friend fall in love and get all gross about it. Then there were the noises he'd heard coming from the upstairs bedroom, yeah, no. Cole was surprised he hadn't smothered himself with a pillow one of the many times he tried to cover his ears. Those two sounded like a couple of cats in heat when they went at it.

"You okay?" Gracie asked from the passenger side of the truck.

"Right as rain. C'mon."

"I couldn't imagine living in a place like this. It's like a fairy tale." The gorgeous redhead spun around wistfully. Hell, that was the most carefree he'd seen her since picking her up at the airport.

"What is it with chicks and houses?" he grumbled.

"I don't know. Maybe we associate a home with settling down and raising a family." She took off walking ahead of him.

"Men do that shit, too. But we do it with power tools and 72 inch flat screens with NFL Sunday Ticket packages."

"Can I get you a club with that, Mr. Caveman?" she joked.

"Only if I can yank on that fiery mane you've got there." The words left his mouth before he thought better of it. The crazy thing was, the look that crossed her face told him she might be more than interested in being dragged back to his cave. But as soon as it revealed itself, it was gone and replaced by '*hard ass Gracie*' again.

"Let's get one thing straight," she stepped closer and poked his chest with the tip of her finger, "Cora isn't to know about us. So for the love of God, please keep your fucking mouth shut." She punctuated the last word with another sharp poke to his sternum.

Cole stood there rubbing the spot and then said, "What will you give me if I keep it shut?"

She whirled around with venom in her eyes. "Are you seriously bribing me?"

"Maybe." Cole stepped so close his shoes were touching hers. "But we both know I don't need to bribe you, now don't we? Because the fact of the matter is, I touch you, and you beg for more."

She stepped back like she'd been singed. Her alabaster skin reddened and she placed her palms on her cheeks. "I don't beg." She thrust her chin up in defiance.

"Really? I think I remember the words *'fuck me Cole'* being yelled recently. Sounded like begging to me." He shrugged his broad shoulders.

"It won't happen again."

"Fine. I'll remember that. But I'm not making you come until you do beg me."

"That'll never happen."

"Oh, it will. You've gotta sleep sometime." He flashed a cocky grin and brushed past her. Yeah, he had her. She was now remembering the lazy weekends they'd spent in bed their senior year of high school. The times when he woke her up with his hand between her legs. The moments when he'd push his cock into her while she slept on her side. She'd flutter her eyes open and beg him to either go deeper, harder or faster. She'd be in that same position again and he'd wait until he had her begging so hard she was fucking breathless this time. Gracie Callahan thought she could one-up him? Not a chance in hell.

~ Chapter Eleven ~

"MOM!" CORA SCREAMED so loud it caused Gracie to cringe. "This place is sooooo cool!" This wasn't a side of her daughter she was used to seeing. The sullen soon-to-be-teen? Of course. This chipper smiling kid? Not so much. But it caused Gracie's mood to perk up. Seeing her child happy was one of the greatest joys in life.

"It does look cool." Pulling Cora in for a hug she grabbed her daughter tightly. As she released her, she noticed Cole standing back watching the interaction between them.

"We should move down here." Cora grabbed her mom's hand and started dragging her toward the back of the house. "Maybe when things get ironed out with Dash?" Cora asked.

"Wait, how did you know about that?" Gracie grabbed her shoulders and lightly shook her.

"Mom, I hear you talk on the phone all the time. I'm not an idiot." Cora rolled her eyes in that perfect teen way.

Glancing around to make sure they were alone, Gracie lowered her voice. "Listen, I don't want you talking to anyone about Dash, okay? That's private stuff and I'd like to keep it that way."

"Okay." Cora looked frightened for a split second.

"How about we find Ava?"

Cora nodded. Gracie hoped her daughter wouldn't ask any more questions and just let the entire thing go. This wasn't the time or place to bring up things happening back home.

Gracie had to admit this was a really beautiful place. The history on the property was utterly astounding but it wasn't as if she wanted huge place like this. It was too much to take care of—too much maintenance. Her apartment back home was more than enough space for her and Cora.

"You gonna join everyone or you thinking about hanging out over here all by your lonesome?" Cole's voice pulled her out of her observations of the place.

"Sorry. Was just taking all of this in." She smiled sweetly at Cole.

"If you don't want to be here let me know. I'm more than happy to take you back to my house." He waggled his eyebrows in a suggestive manner.

"Uh, no. I'm good." Brushing past him she put an extra pep in her step hoping it would taunt him.

"This's your first warning, darlin'," Cole groaned.

She decided to play along just a bit more to torture him. "What *evah* do you mean?" she feigned innocence in a southern Scarlett O' Hara voice.

"Shake that ass at me one more time and we'll be finding a dark corner somewhere around here."

"You wouldn't."

"I think you know damn well I would."

"Leave me alone, Cole." She backed up as the more

than sexy man stalked toward her. "Don't!" She shrieked as he leapt forward and grabbed her around the waist. Her hands began to beat the corded muscles of his back as he effortlessly swung her over his shoulders and smacked her ass. She shouldn't have been excited about any of it but her damn body was a traitor. "This isn't cool. Put me down!" The laughter that bubbled out of her chest surprised her. Damn it, she was actually having a good time. That wasn't supposed to be happening.

"Nope. I've got you right where I want you." He chuckled.

"You're such an ass," a grumbling Gracie said.

"What are you two doing?" Cora began giggling as they rounded the house and found the rest of the gang in the backyard by the barbecue grill.

"Cole decided to be an ass today," Gracie mentioned as she was still slung over his shoulder with her ass shining in the air. Panic set in as she wondered if her actual ass was sticking out for all to see. The panic soon became squashed though. If it really was sticking out, Cora would've said something for sure.

"Time to put you down." Cole slid her body down his, Gracie sucking in a sharp breath as she found out how much what he was doing to her affected *him*. Not wanting to have him embarrassed, she stood in front of him so he could compose himself. He leaned down and whispered, "Thanks."

"Gracie, would you mind coming in and helping me?" Ava asked in a sweet voice.

"I'd love to." It would give her an excuse to get away from the reason her underwear were becoming damp. Following Ava, Gracie ended up in the kitchen. The smells inundating the room were comforting as she took in the history in the space. It all had such a homie atmosphere to it. It wasn't as if everything was in a certain place; no, it was a bit of organized chaos. The counters had things strewn on them like someone actually *lived* in this house. It reminded her of her own apartment. She wasn't one to have everything in its place especially with a kid in the house. Cora wasn't the most organized either. Must've learned that from her mom. Gracie laughed internally at the thought.

"How're things going? I mean staying with Cole and all?" Ava asked.

Gracie shrugged, trying to act nonchalant. Truth was, she became restless when thinking of the man who'd all but haunted her dreams for so many years. "Things are fine." Busying herself by grabbing a nearby cookbook, Gracie worked at not making eye contact with the other woman. That was the thing, women knew when you were telling a tall-tale. It was something engrained in a woman's DNA that gave them the almost Marvel superhero ability to sniff out bullshitters.

"Why do I not believe that?" Bingo. Gracie was dead-on.

"I don't know what to say. He's giving us a place to crash while we get this situation sorted out." She shrugged once more.

"Cora seems to like him," Ava pointed out the window.

Sure enough, Cole was horsing around with her daughter who was laughing so hard her pale cheeks were pink. Damn it. She didn't want Cora getting attached to the man who would undoubtedly lead her to heartbreak like he did every other female who graced his doorstep. Her motherly instinct was to run out there and tell Cole to back the hell off. She didn't notice she was making good on that thought until she felt a hand on her arm.

"They're fine," Ava soothed.

"I just don't want her to get hurt," she replied lamely.

She knew Cora could hold her own. Hell, the kid had been booted off the cheer squad for punching a preppy snob in the nose for saying Cora's ass looked like two giant bowls of cottage cheese in the flimsy uniform skirt. No, it was the fact that Cole had no regard for anyone but himself. He'd easily walked away from her all those years ago. She'd given him an out and he took it, no questions asked. Maybe she'd expected him to argue, to tell her he loved her so much it didn't matter if there was a baby or not. That he wanted to stay and build a life with her. Maybe she was deluding herself, though. Cole wasn't built for long term and if he found out that Cora was his daughter, well, that wouldn't be good for anyone.

"Look, I know there's something between you and Cole. Anyone with two eyes can see it. Why don't you guys try to work things out?"

"Because with Cole, there isn't any working things out. He made up his mind a long time ago." A sigh of sadness escaped her lips as she spoke. "Once upon a time I wished he'd stick around but after I lied and said the…" Gracie snapped her mouth shut. Oh no. She didn't mean to say that much. Why in the hell was she even talking to Ava about her past relationship with Cole?

"Lied?" Ava prodded.

"Oh, it's nothing," She waved her hands in the air and forced a huge smile. Hopefully the other woman would buy it.

"You know what? It's none of my business. I apologize for sticking my nose where it doesn't belong. Luke always tells me they teach you how to be nosy in cosmetology training. He says I'd make a great interrogator for the FBI," Ava snorted.

"We are quite the nosy bunch, aren't we?" Gracie

began laughing. Damn it felt good to let loose for a few moments and laugh.

"Care to let me in on the joke?" Cole stepped into the kitchen with one of his perfect eyebrows raised. Gracie had a hard time keeping her breathing under control with just the sight of him.

"A lady never tells." Ava winked and grabbed a large bowl from the fridge. "I'm gonna run and see if Luke needs help outside." Then she was gone.

"Were you talking about me?" Cole asked as he came closer, invading her space.

"Trust me, I have better things to do with my time than chat about you."

"Oh? What kinds of things?" He kept advancing until her back was against the edge of the countertop.

"None of your business." Gracie stuck out her chin hoping it would dissuade him from further advances.

Instead of warding him off, he reached up and ran a finger right under one of the small straps that held her dress up. "I always wondered how you got your skin so smooth." The rough pad of his finger now shooting tingles of awareness coursing through her entire body.

"Please stop," she whispered.

"Why?" Cole leaned down, his lips just a hair from hers.

"You *know* why."

"Because you might start begging?" he teased.

"I'm not doing this here, Cole." A grumble left her chest.

"Fine."

Faster than she could screech, Cole snatched up her hand and was pulling her through the Civil War-era home.

"Where are you taking me?" She struggled to keep up as she tried to at least get a bearing for what type of room they were in. But Cole didn't speak he only pulled her further into the house until they reached a small room on the opposite side.

"In here," he rasped.

Once she'd entered the room, he closed the door and clicked a skeleton key in place to lock it. He then pocketed the key, trapping her and an extremely turned-on man in the room. Oh, this wasn't going to end well at all.

"Beg me," Cole demanded as he stalked forward.

"I'm not begging you for anything." She was determined to hold her ground and not give into him.

"Remember the time after graduation when we took my truck to the lake?" He began telling a story that would surely be her undoing. "We spread that blanket out in the back and laid there, looking up at the stars."

Oh how she wished he would shut up now. She didn't need this.

"But the stargazing didn't last long, did it? You rolled on top of me and started grinding."

"Cole, *don't*," the words coming out barely a whisper.

"I can still remember how damn hot you were, even through those skin-tight jeans." He stepped closer, running the back of his fingers across her bare shoulder. "How each time you rocked your hips back and forth it felt like you were trying to kill me." His hand left her arm and reached down to tip her chin so she could look into his eyes. "Do you remember what you said right before I flipped you over and pulled those pants off?"

"No," she lied. Gracie remembered exactly what she'd said but she wasn't willing to admit it to him right now.

"Bullshit. Tell me what you said," he urged as he brought his lips closer to hers but not yet touching.

"I told you, I don't remember." Looking away, she worked to take her mind somewhere else. Somewhere where—what used to be—the love of her life wasn't turning her on in ways only he could do.

"You looked down at me, the moon shining on your face and said, 'I can't imagine how anything in this world could be any more perfect than this moment right here'."

She considered him as he waited for her reply. "That moment *was* perfect but it was just a moment. A fleeting fraction of time that came and went."

Tears began to build in her eyes as she thought back to that night. How the frogs croaked across the expanse of the pond, how the stars glittered above them like each one had been strategically placed just to balance out the enormity of the moon. How she felt so small in the big picture of everything around her. Sure, who *wouldn't* feel sentimental when reminiscing about a time when everything in your life was flawless? Her future was bright, the man in her life was there for her in every possible way and their lives seemed to be going down a path of pure bliss.

"Gracie, stop overthinking it." Cole brushed his lips across hers in the gentlest of motions as she fluttered her eyes closed. "I just want you to remember what we had. That there was something here at one point in time."

As her eyes flew open, reality came crashing down once more. No, this wasn't how this was supposed to go. Cole was not allowed back in her life. He'd made the choice to walk away long ago and Gracie Callahan didn't believe in second chances. "You can't honestly expect me to just go back to the way things were, can you?"

"Not exactly the way they were," his voice took on an irritated tone.

"No, Cole. This," she pointed between the two of them, "Can't happen. I have a daughter to protect and take care of."

"She's a good kid." Cole shoved his hands in his pockets.

"Listen, you had a chance at a life with me. You threw it away. You tossed me away like I didn't even matter to you."

"I was confused, Gracie. Hell, we were 18! There's not an 18-year-old on this planet who doesn't get confused by their life and where it's headed."

"But you acted like you wanted to spend the rest of your life with me. You were the one who had to calm *me* down when we got to the courthouse to get married. I honestly thought I could count on you."

"You *can* count on me!" He tossed his hands in the air and raised his voice.

"No. I. Can't!" Gracie shoved at his shoulder and made her way to the door. She grabbed ahold of the knob and remembered he'd locked them both in. "Give me the key." She held out her palm.

"Not until you calm down and talk to me."

"There's nothing to talk about." Crossing her arms over her chest, she hoped he would just drop it and let her out of the room that was beginning to suffocate her.

"Then I guess we'll be in here until we find something to talk about, now won't we?" He chuckled.

"Why are you such an ass all the time?"

"Probably the same reason you're such a little shit all the time."

"Ugh. I'm not going to stand here and trade insults with you like a couple of pissed-off teenagers, Cole."

"I want to make you a deal." He crossed his arms over his broad chest and stared her down.

"What?"

"Stay here in Biloxi for two weeks. If after that two weeks you still want me to sign the divorce papers, I'll sign them."

"I want you to sign them now."

"I'm not going to sign them now. Two weeks."

"And what am I supposed to do in those two weeks?" She watched as Cole moved to the door and stuck the antiquated key in the lock.

He popped it to the right and twisted the knob. "Fall in love with me again." He swung the door open and stepped through leaving Gracie standing there with her mouth agape.

Seriously? Fall in love with Cole again? Not happening. But if she didn't get those papers signed, things would be more than bad for Dash and she couldn't let that happen. Two Weeks. Yeah, she'd have to stay here and make sure the papers were signed. Dash was counting on her to make it happen and she wouldn't let him down. She loved him way too much to let him go. So she'd hang out in Biloxi for a while longer and prove to Cole she didn't have any sort of feelings for him. Once the 14th day hit, she'd hand him a pen and watch as he scribbled his name by the X. It wouldn't be hard at all. Gracie was a pro at hiding things. Hell, she'd hid the fact Cole shared a daughter with her all these years, what was two more weeks?

Chapter Twelve

COLE KNEW BEYOND a shadow of a doubt Gracie would fall in love with him again. He could tell by the way she looked at him and the way her body reacted to him that she'd be saying those three little words again. And he'd do just about anything to make that happen. No, he wouldn't force her to stay with him, he wasn't that type of man. But he would pull out his bag of romance tricks and show her that what they'd had could in fact last longer than it did before.

As he walked down the hallway to make his way outside, Cole almost expected Gracie to trail behind him and argue this whole two weeks deal. She wasn't one to back down so it surprised him that she wasn't there.

Maybe she wanted to see what he had in store for her. Maybe deep down, Gracie knew they were meant to be together. Or maybe he'd just surprised the hell out of her and she was left with nothing to say. Either way, he was going to start right now with his devious little plan. Part of it was connecting with Gracie's daughter. If he wanted to win over the mom, he had to win over the kid. It wouldn't be too hard either. Cora was a good kid who was looking for fun. He was a fun guy and he'd show the teen just that.

"Where's Gracie?" Ava met him in the kitchen as he walked through.

Cole looked behind him and she still wasn't there. "I don't know. She's probably looking around at the house."

"Cole, don't mess with her, okay?"

"I'm not messing with her." Yeah, that was a huge lie.

"She's a single mom. You can't just butt in and try to disrupt their lives."

"How the hell am I disrupting anything?" He was a little hurt that his best friend's girlfriend would think of him as someone who did nothing but cause drama. Okay, the thing with Ava's best friend Brandi and him was a small nugget of drama, but that was in the past. "I'm just trying to get her to see what we used to have, that's all."

"Yeah but maybe the stuff in the past needs to stay in the past. Have you even asked her if she's seeing someone?"

"No. But I don't think she is."

"How would you know if you haven't asked?" Ava pinned him with an incredulous stare.

He lowered his voice so as to not let anyone else catch wind of what he was about to divulge. "Because we've had sex, Ava. Gracie isn't the type to cheat."

"Ugh, she hasn't even been here for a week and you've taken a go at her. Have you no shame?" the small blonde scolded.

"It takes two to tango." He shrugged.

"Yeah, and you have two heads; start thinking with the bigger one for a change." Ava grabbed a couple bags of potato chips and headed out the back door.

How dare Ava judge him like that? What he did in the privacy of his home was *his* business. Well, his and Gracie's business. It wasn't like he held her down and forced her to fuck him. She was with him one hundred and ten percent in the whole thing.

"Where's my mom?" Cora asked as she came through the door.

"I think she's through there." Cole pointed down the hallway.

"Okay," She headed in the direction of her mom and Cole stood there watching her.

For some reason that kid looked familiar but he couldn't put his finger on why. Yeah, she looked like her mom a bit but not as much as he'd thought she might. Oh, well. Maybe he was overanalyzing shit again.

"Hope everyone is hungry," Ava said as they all finally sat down at the patio table to eat.

"Thank you for cooking this, it looks incredible." Gracie eyed the food and couldn't wait to dig in. She waited for everyone else to fill their plates before doing the same to hers though; she was a guest and didn't want to forgo her manners.

Once everyone—including herself—had their plates piled high with grilled steaks, potato salad, chips and mac & cheese, Gracie began cutting her meat.

"Hold on, before we eat I'd like to say a few things." Cole stood causing everyone to put down their forks. He jammed his hands in his pockets like he was nervous. "I just want to say thank you to Luke and Ava for having us over this afternoon. It's good to have close friends to hang with while getting used to living in a new place. I couldn't be more grateful for you guys kind of taking me under your wings and letting me be a part of your lives for a little while." Cole jerked his hands out of his pockets. The sunlight hit a shiny metal object as it flew out and landed right on top of the creamy chucks of potato in the potato salad. Upon further investigation, Gracie could see it was a ring. *An engagement ring.*

Panic rose in her gut as the prospect of what he was fixing to do hit her. *No.* He was not going to propose here and embarrass her in front of these people and her daughter. They were technically already married for heaven's sake. Why would he propose anyway? She had to do something. Reaching forward she plucked the ring from the salad and handed it back to Cole. "Don't do this right now, please?"

He looked at the ring as panic spread over his handsome features. "Fuck!" he bit out.

"What the hell, man?" Luke stood and snatched the ring from Cole's fingers.

"I'm so sorry, I forgot it was even in there. It must've fallen out of the box," Cole tried to explain.

"What is going on?" Gracie stood too and pinned both men with a stare full of questions.

"Is that a ring?" Ava got up and went to the side of the table with the two men. "Were you gonna ask Gracie to marry you again?" Ava sounded flabbergasted.

"That isn't mine, damn it." Cole pointed to the ring in Luke's hand.

"I'm so sorry. This wasn't how this was supposed to go." Luke looked down at Ava who had a bewildered look on her face. "This is for you, sweetheart." Sadness crossed his bearded face and Gracie suddenly felt bad for the guy. Yet again, *Hurricane Cole* blew through and screwed everything up.

"Oh, my God," Ava whispered.

Luke grabbed her small hand in his larger one and pulled her away from the table a bit. Gracie watched as he dropped to one knee on the grass below. "This was supposed to be more romantic than this because you deserve it. Hell, you deserve the best of everything, Ava. Before you, I didn't really know what love was. You showed me that there was someone out there for me and I finally found her. We've been through so much together but our broken roads intersected and we found each other. I want to spend the rest of my life making you smile and hearing you laugh. I want to wake every single morning with your hair in my face and your hand on my chest. I want to live in this house with you and watch our kids run around the yard while they drive us insane. I want it all and I want it with you. Ava, will you make me the happiest man alive and agree to be my wife?" Luke finished and Gracie felt hot tears streak down her own face.

"On one condition," Ava said while everyone held their breath.

"Anything." Luke nodded.

She dropped to her knees and grabbed both sides of his face. "Never, *ever* get rid of this beard." She laughed.

"You got it, sweetheart." Luke wrapped his arms around Ava and pulled her in for one of the most passionate kisses Gracie had ever seen. Hell, she felt it to her toes and she wasn't even the one being kissed.

When she looked over at Cole, she could see something on his face she didn't recognize. Was that *jealousy* she saw? Was Cole Matthews *envious* of what Luke and Ava had? He could've had that at one point in time. He *did* have it and was too stupid to keep it.

∽ Chapter Thirteen ∽

DAMN. **COLE FELT** like a real douche bag for screwing up Luke's proposal to Ava. He should've known better than to keep the ring in his pocket like that; who even did something like that? He could only guess that when he took the box out of his pocket earlier, the ring slipped out. What was worse though, seeing the tears streak down Gracie's porcelain face as she watched Luke give the most romantic proposal Cole had ever seen. Yeah, he was secretly a sucker for rom-com movies that ended with a happily ever after, but he'd never tell anyone that. He had a reputation as a badass FBI agent to uphold. There was no way in hell he was letting his secret obsession leak out. But something hit him as he watched Luke ask Ava to marry him. It felt akin to jealousy but Cole didn't *get* jealous. Hell, no. But this whole situation had him uneasy due to the fact that Gracie was next to him and he'd fucked things up with her a long time ago. But he wanted it all back. He was ready to give up his bachelorhood for one more chance at a life with her. The sassy Irish redhead had him by the balls and she didn't even know it.

Once dinner was through Cole stood to the side watching the women clean the table and take the leftover food inside. Cora goofed around on her phone giggling at something that flashed across the screen—he had to smile at that. When the hell did the thought of kids make him smile? When Gracie revealed she was pregnant when they were dating, he'd about keeled over from a stroke at the sight of those two pink lines on the stick test. But now? Hell, he wouldn't mind a kid.

"How about we celebrate?" Luke bumped him in the arm to get his attention. When Cole looked over, Luke was offering him a cigar. Damn, he loved a good cigar.

"Cohiba? Damn, you sprung for the good ones this

time." He chuckled and took the tobacco wrapped treat from his friend.

"I wasn't gonna smoke those damn Swisher Sweets you brought on the last stakeout. Those aren't even cigars."

"They were the best I could do at the time." Cole clipped the end off his cigar with the cutter Luke handed him. They both went about lighting them then taking puffs together. "Congrats, man. Sorry for the major fuck-up," he apologized.

"It all worked out. If she'd said no, then I would've had to kick you in the scrotum."

"It would've been well deserved, that's for sure."

"So, when you cutting Gracie loose?" Luke threw the question Cole knew was coming.

"I'm not. She's agreed to stay for two weeks." He shrugged.

"What kind of hair-brained scheme are you cooking up?"

"Not cooking up anything. I just want to see if there's still something there."

"Aw hell. You do realize she has a kid, right? If you hurt her, you hurt Cora. How're you gonna feel when they both fly out of here crying?"

"Look, I'm not gonna hurt anyone. Yeah, I was a fucking idiot when I was younger. I made a shit ton of mistakes and now I'm paying the price for them. The biggest one was letting her go. I didn't know a good thing when it was lying next to me every night. But I'm trying to change that," he admitted.

"I suppose I should wish you luck. You're gonna need it with her. She seems like a tough nut to crack." Luke took a drag off his cigar and blew the smoke into the air around them.

"Please, mom?" He could see Gracie coming out the back door with Cora hot on her heels. The girl looked like she was upset about something.

"I said no. This isn't a good night for that."

"But Ava said it was fine, mom." Cora rolled her eyes.

Gracie planted her hands on her hips and stared the almost-teenager down. "No," she bit out.

Oh, shit. This looked like it was getting ready to turn

into a major blow-up—whatever *this* was. Cole decided to intervene. After all, he *was* trained in hostage negotiations. "Hey, what seems to be the problem?" He stepped up beside Gracie, her feminine fragrance enveloping him immediately. He loved the scent of her, there was just nothing comparable to it. Those special times when the breeze carried her fragrance right under his nose were some of the best memories he had of her.

"Ava said I could stay another night, but mom said no. Ugh." Cora stomped her foot.

"First of all, you need to not stomp your foot like a toddler. Second, you need to respect your mom," he said. Gracie looked up at him like he'd lost his damn mind.

"Cole, I don't need your help with this," Gracie scolded.

"Yeah, because *clearly* you have it under control," he snickered.

"Okay then, the floor is yours. You be a parent and see how it goes." She tossed her hands up and walked back into the house, leaving him with the sullen preteen.

This was unnerving to say the least. Gracie wanted

him to be the parent but he didn't have slightest clue what to do with that type of authority. He could take down major crime syndicates, chase down a high-as-hell dope fiend and take out a target at 100 yards away in a snow storm, but this? This scared the shit out of him. Cole ran a hand across his jaw and thought for a moment. How the hell did you diffuse a situation with a hard-headed kid?

"Alright. Your mom said no, that should mean something to you."

"It does, but…" Cora wouldn't make eye contact with him and her voice took on a mousy quality.

"But it really doesn't. Did you even ask her nicely? Or did you just tell her you were staying?"

"I told her, but…"

He held up his hand to stop her. "You and I both know you're getting ready to give me an excuse of some sort. The thing is, I've heard them all. Wanna know how I've heard them all?"

"How?"

"Because I've used every excuse in the book. So spare

me the drama, okay?" Cole wasn't mean when he spoke and Cora seemed to be handling his little conversation quite well.

"Okay. I really want to stay though."

"Then maybe you need to find her and ask her in a kind manner?"

"I try to do that all the time but she's always upset about Dash," Cora said.

"What's Dash?" He raised an eyebrow in curiosity.

"Dash is a man. But I'm not supposed to talk about him." A look of panic spread across her face.

Cole wouldn't press her on the issue, but he needed to ask Gracie why she was always upset over this Dash person.

"Okay, go ask her nicely if you can stay here again." He gave her a quick pat on the shoulder and she nodded.

Of course he had ulterior motives for hoping Gracie would say yes; he wanted more time alone with her. Tomorrow he had to work and wouldn't get to spend much time with her. Each moment he got was another opportunity to show her he was in this for the long haul this time.

Cora came bounding back over with a smile on her face, "She said yes."

"Good." Cole was relieved. "Now, keep our little chat in mind next time you want something, okay?"

"Okay. Thank you!" She spun around and ran inside the house. Presumably to find Ava. He was happy the girl was bonding with his friends. If he got his way, they'd be in each other's lives from here on out.

"Thanks for talking to her. She doesn't seem to understand that I'm her mom and not her *BFF* some days. I guess I underestimated you." Gracie placed her hand on his arm and damn it if he didn't feel it all the way to his cock. How the hell could such a light, innocent touch cause his man parts to go from the park position to fifth gear all of a sudden?

"You're welcome." He turned to her to see a small smile playing on her lips.

"What? No smartass remarks about how you'd make an awesome parent? Or how I don't know how to handle my own child?"

"No. Gracie, clearly you're doing a great job with her. I'm not gonna stand here and tell you that you're not."

"Okay, come on. Hit me with an insult," she said.

Cole place his hands on her bare shoulders and looked down into her green eyes. "There are so many things I'd like to do to you, but insulting you isn't one of them."

A small shiver fell over her body, Gracie trying—and failing—to hide it from him. "You want me to beg, don't you?" she asked with challenge in her eyes.

"No, I don't want you to beg anymore. I'm sick of playing this damn cat and mouse shit. If you want to go back to my place and let me fuck you until you come all over my cock, fine. But if not, that's fine too. I'd rather take the former, but I won't pressure you into something you don't want to do."

"How do you expect me to think when you say things like that?"

"I don't expect you to think. I expect you to *feel*."

"I don't know if I can do this," she said softly.

Cole stepped closer, leaned down and whispered

close to her ear, "Right now, I want to be inside you so bad it hurts. I want to lay you out on my bed, cover your body with mine and move so slow in and out of you until you scream for me to fuck you harder. I want to bend you over the sofa, the table, hell anything, and slam into you so hard we move the damn furniture halfway across the room. But most of all, I just want to get you alone so I can kiss you. I don't give a shit if you don't let me inside this body ever again but I think if you don't let me kiss you in the next five minutes, I'll probably lose my fucking mind."

His own words shouldn't have turned him on as much as they did, but hell, just being this close to her had every nerve ending about to shatter into tiny particles. Why did he ever think it was a good idea to walk away from her? If he'd stayed, they might be watching their own kids bounce around the yard and be total smartasses. But no, he'd decided to be a coward and get the hell out when she gave him the green light. Now though, he wasn't letting her leave until she saw how he'd changed. How he was ready for her to stay in his life and take everything that came along with it.

"Let me say goodbye to Ava," she said as she turned to head back into the house.

Cole was internally jumping up and down like he was strapped to a pogo stick, but on the outside, he looked cool as a cucumber. The thoughts of what he'd do to her when he got her home played through his head and damn it if he didn't want to act out every single scenario in his mottled brain. Time to say goodbye to Luke and get the fuck out of there before his hard-on busted through the front of his pants.

"Hey, man, thanks for dinner. We're heading out." He shook hands with his partner like he always did.

"Alright. Be careful. See ya in the morning." Luke shook back.

As he turned around, Gracie was walking toward him, the slight breeze flipping the hem of her dress. Yeah, he'd be running his hands underneath that dress soon.

"I'm ready." She flashed a sweet smile that held all sorts of promises. Oh, he'd be cashing in on whatever she had in mind, that's for sure.

Once they were in his truck and on the road, Gracie sat quietly across from him. Was she upset? What the hell was she thinking? Why couldn't women just come out and say what was on their mind instead of bottling it all up and eventually exploding like a powder keg with a short fuse? Time to get her talking. He sure didn't want her changing her mind and pushing him away again.

"Talk to me, Gracie."

"About what?" She turned slightly in her seat, one of the straps of her dress sliding down her creamy shoulder.

"I don't know." He took one hand off the steering wheel, reached over and pulled the strap back up.

"Why'd you do that?" She looked at her shoulder and back to him. "Maybe I wanted it down like that."

"Really?" He cocked an eyebrow.

"Yeah," she said as she grabbed the offending strap and slid it back down. Cole was having a hell of a time trying to keep his eyes on the road instead of the bare flesh of the stunning woman beside him.

"Come here." He lifted the console and pushed it into

place revealing the small seat beside him. Patting the space, he motioned her closer to him.

Gracie didn't question him, just slid her body next to him; her thigh flush with his. Feeling her warmth against his leg had an idea cross his mind. But would she go for it? She wasn't any sort of an exhibitionist but if done right, no one would even know what they were doing. "Trust me?" he asked.

"Somewhat." Gracie laughed, the sound streaming straight to his cock.

"Keep your skirt down and spread your legs," he ordered. She immediately obeyed. "Lift a leg up and lay it on my lap." He grabbed underneath her knee and pulled it on top of his thigh. Gracie spread her other leg further, giving him total access to what he wanted. "Relax," he soothed. It wasn't hard to tell she was tensing up. She wasn't used to doing anything like this in public and although they were driving down a two-lane highway, there was always the possibility of getting busted. Good thing he had his FBI credentials on him at all times.

Cole began running his hand across her knee situated on his leg, but soon it disappeared beneath the hem of her dress. The fabric bunched up as he searched out what he was looking for. Once his fingers found her silky panties, he knew he'd struck gold. Damn she was so fucking wet already. Who knew something like this would turn her on so much? He'd have to keep that little slice of information in the memory bank for future use. Using the pads of his fingers, he ran them across the soaked fabric. Back and forth he went, watching her head fall back and rest on the top of the seat. "Feel good?" he asked.

"*Mmmm*, yes," she confirmed.

"Does this turn you on? Knowing I'm going to finger fuck you while driving down the road?" Gracie nodded. "Do me a favor, baby. Reach down and pull your panties to the side. I want full access down here." He punctuated his words with more pressure on the outside of her underwear. She did as he asked and held the satiny material to the side. "Hold them there, okay? I don't want them slipping back in my way."

"Okay," she agreed breathlessly.

They both let out a gasp as he made skin to skin contact. His fingers began to seamlessly glide through the moisture gathered between her legs and he watched her hips begin to move as if searching for more. He'd give her more, but first he wanted her to tell him what she wanted. "Tell me what to do. I wanna hear you say it."

"Cole, please."

He almost felt sorry for her with the whimper that escaped her lips. "Please, what? Come on, say it."

"I want your fingers inside me. Make me come."

Gripping the steering wheel tighter with his other hand he suddenly buried two fingers inside her. They skated easily in due to the fact that she was more than turned on. It was a bit of an awkward position but there was no way he was stopping. He didn't give a damn if after this he was diagnosed with carpal tunnel, he was going to fuck her with his fingers and make her come all over his hand even if it killed him.

"That feels so good," she breathed while her hips

reached further for him.

He removed his fingers for just a split second and plunged back in, earning a loud moan from her. With each thrust, Cole felt more wetness seep from her entrance and onto his hand. Damn if that didn't make him want to blow his load in his pants right now. Not to mention his dick was begging to replace his fingers. The white knuckle grip on the steering wheel was beginning to sting, but there was no way he was going to leave her hanging. If he had to drive around some more, he'd do just that. Either way, Gracie would give him an orgasm in his truck.

"We'll be home soon, baby. You ready to come for me?" He picked up the pace on his thrusting.

"So fucking close."

"I know you are. Your pussy is gripping my fingers. Can't wait until you come all over them. Know what I'm gonna do after you do it?"

"Wh…what?" she stammered.

"I'm gonna pull them out of you, lift them to my mouth, and lick every single bit of you off my fingers."

"Yes," the word came out as a hiss.

"I think you like knowing I'm getting ready to taste you, don't you? That I'm going to taste you and swallow your sweet flavor?"

"Oh God! Harder, *please!*" she shouted in the cab of the truck.

Cole did what she demanded. Holy hell her entire body was quaking and damn if it wasn't the hottest thing he'd ever seen. But what cranked it up a few notches was when she grabbed his wrist and began using his hand as her own personal sex toy. He may not survive this little escapade. If he didn't, it would be a fan-fucking-tastic way to go.

"I'm there, I'm ready," she confirmed.

"Me, too, baby. Come on."

A few more thrusts and Gracie was screaming his name over and over. Her hips bucked up and down while her head thrashed from side to side on the back of the seat. He felt her nails biting into his wrist but he didn't care, as long as she was having a good time, he could deal with the gouges later. And boy was she having a good time. It took a little while for her orgasm to subside, but when it did, he made good on his promise. He slid his fingers from inside her depths and brought them to his mouth. Her eyes were focused on him as he lapped and sucked her essence off his hand. He could've sworn he heard a slight moan come from her. She tasted heavenly. There was no dessert in the world comparable to the flavor of Gracie. She was honey-sweet with a hint of spice, all wrapped up in a package he couldn't quite get enough of. If he was ever sent to death row, he'd request Gracie Callahan as his last meal. She was *that* damn scrumptious. Later he would take full advantage of her though. He planned on having his mouth directly on her while she came over and over again on his tongue. That sounded like the perfect way to spend the rest of the evening and night.

Chapter Fourteen

HOLY HELL. Gracie sat in the truck as Cole pulled into his driveway. Her body had just come down from one of the hottest sexual experiences of her entire life and she damn near couldn't breathe. Watching Cole lick and suck his fingers after they were inside her about made her come again just from the sight of it. She didn't dare look at him right now.

"Here's the deal," Cole said as he looked straight ahead to the house. "When we get inside, I'm going to fuck you, Gracie. I need to be inside you as soon as possible." His urgency spurred her into action.

"Why wait until we get inside?" She lifted her skirt and climbed onto his lap. Her hips gyrating as she ground her pussy all over the front of his pants.

"*Fuck*. You're gonna make me come like that." His head lulled back.

She stopped her actions and reached between them. Quickly she flipped the button of his jeans and had the zipper down in no time. Digging around she worked until his hard cock was in her hand. "We wouldn't want you coming in your pants, now would we?"

"No, we wouldn't."

It'd been so damn long since she'd felt the skin on skin contact between her and Cole. After she'd found out she was pregnant, they didn't bother to use protection. The feeling of him inside her completely bare was a beautiful experience. She wanted to feel that again. Lifting up she began to rub the head of his cock across her slit.

"Baby, that feels so fucking good," Cole groaned.

Without warning, Gracie sank down and buried him inside her. She watched as his head shot forward and his eyes flew open.

"Gracie, don't." His voice held warning.

"Why?" She asked as she began moving her hips again.

"Because if you keep doing that, I'm going to come inside you."

"Maybe I want that," she stated.

"Do you? Do you want me to fill you up?" His voice went low as he asked.

"Yes."

"Are you on anything?" She nodded. "Damn." He grabbed her hips and began moving her more rapidly. "You're so wet. Is that all for me?"

"Yes, all for you." Her head tilted back. "Cole, I feel like coming for you again."

"Then do it. Come all over me."

She let out a scream as her pussy clamped down around him. Her body kept moving to prolong her orgasm but he dug his fingers in her flesh and held her still. Once her release passed, she looked at his face which was only lit by the moonlight.

"In the house, *now*," he ordered.

Lifting herself off him she quickly scurried to the

passenger side of the truck. She grabbed her shoes and slid them on as Cole jumped out of the vehicle. Just as she reached for the door handle, he jerked the door open and put his arms around her waist. She let out a screech as he tossed her over his shoulder and carried her toward the house.

"I can walk."

"After I'm done with you tonight, you'll be lucky to be able to walk again," he chuckled.

Holy shit. What had she gotten herself into? He was on a mission to destroy her and she was letting him do it. It was like lighting the match that would burn down your own house. But what could it hurt? Having sex with a gorgeous man for a little while wasn't a crime. As long as she made sure no one knew about it, things back home would be fine. *Dash* would be fine.

After unlocking the door, he pushed it open with the toe of his shoes and put her down right inside. "Dress. Off. Now."

"Take it off me."

"Damn it, Gracie. Take the fucking dress off."

The seriously feral look in Cole's eyes gave Gracie an idea. What would he do if she played hard to get? Yeah, she hadn't made it much of a challenge thus far but something inside her wanted to make him work for it. Make him so hot he'd be on his hands and knees begging for it.

"What if I don't want to?" She smirked.

"This isn't the time to play around. Take it off or I come over there and ruin the damn thing."

"I don't think you will." Cocking her head to the side she studied his stance and expressions.

"The hell I won't." Just then he snapped into action and had her pinned against the wall just behind them. A sharp gasp shot from her lips just as her back hit. "See? Don't mess with me. You of all people should know, when I say I'm gonna do something, I fucking do it." He then buried his face in her neck and began to run his tongue right along the pulse point there. An involuntary shudder racked her as he made his way up to her ear and clamped down lightly with his teeth. "One more chance. Take this off," he fingered the strap as he'd done back at

Ava and Luke's house, "or I rip it off."

Heart racing like the hoof beats of the prize-winning steeds at the Kentucky Derby— Gracie pushed off the wall just a bit so she could reach around and pull the zipper of her dress down. Cole stood in front of her, chest heaving, while she took her time with it. She grabbed the straps one by one and let them fall off her shoulders, exposing her naked breasts to his more than hungry gaze.

"Is this what you want?" she teased.

"More," he grunted. In a way, she loved seeing him like this. He was out of control and it was killing him. She smiled to herself as she watched him hold onto his control like a child holding a kite string in a hurricane.

Slowly she slid the dress down all the way and let it drop at her feet. It was like being on display as the man in front of her surveyed every curve and dip of her body like he was mapping out a plan of attack. Normally she would've covered her bare breasts with her hands or turned away to keep him from seeing so much of her. But tonight? No, she'd stand there proudly because the way he looked at her made her feel like the most powerful woman in the solar system.

"Are your panties still wet from earlier?" He stepped forward and she nodded. Cole shocked her again by grabbing her and turning her so she faced the wall. His foot kicked at the inside of hers signaling her to spread her legs wider. Damn, she felt like some type of criminal getting ready to be cuffed and thrown in the back of a police car. It should've been somewhat humiliating, but it was enthralling to let him have this power over her. Wasn't it amazing how in a fraction of a second, the power play between them shifted dramatically? That's how it was with them though. They played off each other like two opponents vying for the same trophy.

"I can't wait to fuck this." Cole reached between her legs and cupped her already soaked sex. "Do you want me to fuck you? Or taste you?" Wow, he was giving her the option? Was there a box to check 'all of the above' on this little quiz? "I need an answer."

Saying the first thing that came to mind, she shouted, "Fuck me!"

Her breath was stolen from her as she felt her panties being ripped off. The thud of her heart rate jumped in her ears and she barely heard the crinkle of a wrapper behind her. Cole's arm wrapped around her waist and pulled her bottom away from the wall just enough to give him access to her. She planted her hands on the wall and braced for the impact she knew was coming. It didn't take long. Cole lined himself up to her entrance and slammed home causing Gracie to cry out.

"Damn, I love it when you scream for me." He moved slowly inside her—Gracie biting her lip so hard she tasted the metallic tang of blood. "Baby, you're so fucking wet."

"*Mmmhmmmm,*" was the only response she could think of as he continued to languidly pull out of her depths and push back in.

"I wanted to make this last but I need to fuck you hard. Can you handle it?" He groaned.

"Yes. Do it. Fuck me hard."

"Good girl." He began to pound into her making her feel it everywhere. Grabbing her shoulders for extra leverage, it felt like he was going deeper than he'd ever been before. "Who does this pussy belong to?" he demanded. Gracie refused to answer. Was this a game he was playing? Did it turn him on more to know her pussy was his? Hell, at this point she'd tell him anything to catch up with the orgasm she was chasing. What would it hurt? "Tell me, Gracie. Whose pussy is this?" His voice became grittier.

"You! It belongs to you!" she wailed.

His assault quickened and she knew she'd better help her release along a bit. She reached between her legs and began rapidly massaging her clit.

"That's it, rub that clit. Make yourself come all over this cock." Tingles spread across her body and worked their way down her spine. "Come on, baby," he urged.

She'd never understood why Cole was the one who could spring her body to life like he did, but right now, she didn't give a damn. All of her focus was on the beginning waves of her release as they poured over her. The sounds in the room were those of their bodies joining and the labored breathing of the man moving himself in and out of her. She wasn't even sure it was her voice that wailed into the interior of the house when she came but when the sound was joined by that of Cole's, she knew for certain what was happening.

When it was over, he managed to pull out of her and wrap his arm around her waist once more to steady her shaking form. She tried to wiggle free but he held fast. "No way. You're coming to bed with me and you're not leaving until I've given you *at least* six more of what you just had."

"Pretty sure of yourself aren't you?" She let him lift her into his arms.

"About a thousand and ten percent." He kissed the top of her head.

"What's the extra ten percent for?"

"Just a buffer in case things don't go as planned," he winked with that air of confidence that only Cole could muster.

"Well then, let's hope everything is right on track and you don't have to look bad by using your buffer." She laughed and winked back.

∾ Chapter Fifteen ∾

DAMN SHE'S GORGEOUS, Cole thought as he watched Gracie snore lightly beside him. All night they'd driven each other insane with the special little touches and secret caresses, but nothing could compare to seeing her like this. Her hair lay sprawled across one of the white pillow cases making it seem as if it were ready to catch ablaze at any moment, the shallow dusting of freckles across her nose and cheeks made her seem younger somehow and her long eyelashes fanned across her faintly pink cheeks told him she was snoozing comfortably. He'd love nothing more than to lay there with her and never leave his bed, but in some places that was considered kidnapping. Especially if he tied her to it like he really wanted to. Since he wanted to keep his job, it was time to get up and get ready for work.

After a shower and quick shave—only nicking his chin once with the super sharp razor—he moved to the kitchen to start breakfast. He wanted to make sure Gracie had something to eat when she woke up. After the sex marathon they both received gold medals in the night before, she'd surely be famished.

"Hey," he heard a slightly shy voice behind him as he flipped a pancake to ensure it got golden brown on both sides.

He turned around to see Gracie standing in the doorway to the kitchen. She was completely dressed, looking at him expectantly. "Morning," he said gruffly, then turned back to the stove. He wasn't mad or upset with her, on the contrary actually. It was the fact that she stood there looking adorable in a short blue jean skirt and flowing blouse. His mouth dried up as soon as he'd turned around and set his eyes on her. Damn her for taking his breath away like nobody's business.

"I know you have to work today so I thought I'd get

out and see some stuff." She sidled up beside him, crossing her arms over her chest causing her already magnificent breasts to thrust upward.

Cole cocked an eyebrow, wondering why she was so damn formal this morning. "Everything okay?" he asked as he flipped the pancake onto a waiting stack.

"Of course. Why wouldn't it be?" She tilted her head to the side.

"You just seem a little…weird this morning."

"Weird?"

"Like you either don't *remember* what we did last night or you could give two shits less."

"Cole, last night was great. But we both know this isn't something long term."

"At least you *remember* it," he let out a frustrated laugh. Upon looking at her again, he noticed her cheeks were stained with a darker shade of pink now. So it *did* affect her. He mentally patted himself on the back for that one. There was no way in hell he was letting her forget any time they spent together. It didn't matter if he had to hold her down and read from a list of shit. He'd emboss every single iota of time into her memory. "These are done, make yourself a plate." He motioned to the stack of perfectly cooked flapjacks beside the stove.

Gracie shook her head, her pony tail thrashing her shoulders. "Thanks, but I'm not hungry." She then walked away.

Lovely. He'd forgone his usual morning run to stay in and make her breakfast. What a waste. Angrily he flipped the burner to the '*off*' setting and grabbed up the plate of food. Heading to the trashcan, he jammed his foot on the lever and popped it open.

"What are you doing?" she asked from behind him.

"Throwing this in the garbage since you're not gonna eat it."

"Don't waste it, Cole." She reached around him and snatched the plate from his fingers.

"What else do you expect me to do with it?"

"Put it in the fridge for later." His gaze was focused on her behind as she opened the door of the fridge and sat the plate on one of the shelves.

"No one is going to eat that later. They'll taste like a

mix of cardboard and ass." Just on principle alone he went right behind her and pulled the plate from the shelf.

"Why do you have to be so hard-headed?" She jerked the plate from his hand once more.

"You're one to talk."

"Are we really fighting over a plate of pancakes?" She sat the filled plate on the counter and crossed her arms over her chest.

"I guess we are." Cole stepped closer hoping the little spat would turn into an epic bout of make-up sex.

"Uh, back off. Don't you have to work today?" She shoved lightly at his chest. The action should've aggravated him but it did just the opposite. His pants were now fitting more snuggly than before. He watched her face as she grappled with the fact he was so close but was soon interrupted by the blare of her phone in her pocket. She yanked it out and glanced at the screen. "I have to take this."

"Luke is picking me up. If you need the truck, the keys are on the table by the door," he whispered and then turned his back.

"Thank you."

"Don't mention it." Just then Cole heard the honking of Luke's truck horn. Time to get the hell out of there before he tossed the sassy woman over his shoulder and called in sick to work.

On the way outside he replayed what he'd *'accidentally'* heard from her conversation as she made her way down the hall. It wasn't hard to hear what was on the other end of the line when someone had the volume turned all the way up on their phone. Not to mention, he was a pro at listening, it was all part of his job. Now he just needed to figure out why the hell someone was contacting Gracie from the *Illinois Department of Corrections*.

"I know that look," Luke's tone told Cole he'd already figured out something was on his mind.

"What look is that?"

"The one that says you have something you need to check out." Luke chuckled.

"Damn. We've been partners for way too long." He laughed and shook his head.

"You're not getting rid of me. Time to come clean."

Cole thought for a minute—wondering what all he should tell his partner and best friend. Should he come clean about everything he'd heard? Or just bits and pieces? It was better to just get it all out in the open and see if Luke could lend some direction on what he should do next. "I overheard Gracie on the phone as I left. She took a call from the Illinois Department of Corrections."

"Really? Probably a wrong number. Some inmate more than likely got some phone time and started dialing random numbers."

"Nah. She knew who it was. As she walked down the hall toward the bedroom I heard her say hi to some person named *Dash*." Cole blew out a frustrated breath.

"Dash? That's an odd name," Luke commented.

"For the life of me I can't remember anyone from our past with that name *or* nickname." He looked out the passenger side of the truck and became silent.

"The hamster in your head is running so fast I can

smell something burning."

"I need to look into this. What if she's in some kind of trouble?"

"Look, I know you care for her, I get it. But you can't protect her from all the shit in her life. Maybe you should leave her alone and let her handle it on her own," Luke suggested.

"Or maybe I dig into it a bit and make sure her and Cora are safe." Cole tried to reason with himself.

"I could sit here all day and tell you to leave well enough alone but I know you and I know when you have an idea in your head, you're gonna go for it no matter what."

Luke was right. Cole went balls to the wall when he got something in his head. Normally his hunches paid off and he figured out the solution to whatever problem he had. He'd find out who this Dash person was and figure out what kind of ties they had to Gracie. As long as she wasn't in danger, he'd back off. But if she was, he'd go to any lengths to make sure she was out of harm's way.

"Hey, is everything okay?" Gracie's voice was tinged with worry. Dash didn't usually call this frequent and her nerves were on edge.

"Not really," he answered with a weak voice.

"Dash, what's wrong?"

"There was a fight. I got knocked around a bit."

"Knocked around?" Her hand flew to her mouth as her bottom lip trembled.

"They said something about keeping me away from the other inmates. Guy tried to stab me with a homemade knife."

"I have to get you out of there, Dash." Tears began streaking down her face as she thought of leaving him in there to take that sort of punishment. Yeah, he'd committed a crime but the type of pain being inflicted on him wasn't what needed to happen in *that* type of setting. He *should* be safe for now.

"I don't need you fighting my battles for me. I just thought you should know in case you heard about this somewhere else."

"I'm *supposed* to help fight your battles, I love you."

"And I love you. But let me do my time and be done, Gracie. Don't stick your nose into this shit any further," Dash scolded.

He could try and boss her around all he wanted but she had a mind of her own. She wasn't going to take this lying down. "Okay. Just please try and be safe."

"Will do. Gotta run, talk to ya in a few days," Dash said and then hung up.

She sat there on the edge of Cole's bed with the phone in her hand. She was numb. Dash was the only person in her life who'd never let her down, he'd been there for her when no one else was. No way in hell she'd let him sit behind bars and get hurt or worse, killed.

∞ Chapter Sixteen ∞

"HAVE I MENTIONED how much I hate computers?" Cole groused as he pecked away on his keyboard, feeling frustrated with the progress he was making.

"Every damn day, man," Luke replied.

"The only person I can find by the name 'Dash' is some guy named Damon Hunter. But Dash is his nickname."

"What's it say about him?" Luke rolled his chair around his own desk and behind Cole's.

"Looks like he's in for manslaughter."

"Any details on the case?"

"I'll have to call in a favor, records are sealed." Cole

sat back and blew out a frustrated breath.

"That's odd. Normally records aren't sealed like that unless it's a juvenile. Looks like this guy's been in for three years and he went in when he was 29."

"Beats me. You know how fucked up things are with the State of Illinois."

"True."

"I'm gonna head out and grab some coffee that doesn't taste like peppered ass." Cole pointed to the office coffee pot. "I'll make my call while I'm out." He rose from his desk and shoved his phone in his back pocket. There was no way he'd make this type of call from the office phone. If there was one thing the FBI was tops at, it was monitoring phone calls. He needed to keep this on the down low since it wasn't official business.

"Be careful," Luke said as he rolled back to his desk.

"Always am," he replied.

As he made his way to his truck, Cole shook his head. This was one fucked-up situation. He was head over heels for a woman who was keeping so many secrets from him. He should just cut his losses and walk away but Gracie was his picket fence. He'd do anything for her including risk his job to find out what the hell was going on.

Once he was in his truck and headed down the road, Cole hit speed dial on a number in his index. It rang twice on the other end then a familiar voice came on.

"Cole Matthews, you don't call, you don't write. I'm beginning to thing you don't love me anymore," the female voice said.

"Been busy. How're things, Kat?"

"Same shit, different day. It's an interesting life being a hacker." She laughed.

"I guess so. I need a favor."

"I knew you didn't just call to hear my ultra-sexy voice. What can I do for you?"

Kat was Cole's go-to gal for anything hacker related. She was a sassy 25-year-old who could find her way in the back door of any firewall she crossed paths with. He'd originally caught her hacking the FBI database a few years back and struck a deal with her. If she'd be on call for him, he'd let her go. Luckily he was the only one who'd known about her little playtime in the FBI's system; Luke didn't even know.

"I need you to find your way into some sealed files. A man named Damon Hunter in Chicago," he explained.

"Already there," she snorted.

"How in the hell?"

"I hacked your PC, numb nuts. This isn't my first rodeo."

"Jesus," Cole huffed.

"Damon Hunter. Looks like he went away for a manslaughter a few years back."

"This is shit I already know, Kat."

"Cool your jets, Matthews. I'm getting to the good part." Cole heard Kat typing and then she whistled. "Damn, looks like he beat the shit out of some guy in a bar fight and the guy keeled over a few days later in the hospital."

"Why would something like that be sealed?" Cole pondered as he pulled in front of the local bakery and coffee shop.

"Not sure. Normally only juvie cases are sealed."

"Can you find out if there's any connection between this Damon guy and a woman named Gracie Callahan?"

"Oooh, the plot thickens."

"Don't make me arrest you, Kat."

"You wouldn't do that, I'm the best chance you have at finding out what you need."

Cole chuckled. "You're right. Find out what you can and send it to my secure email."

"Will do," Kat said and then hung up.

Well, that didn't answer his questions at all. Hopefully she'd find a connection between Damon and Gracie. If she didn't, Cole wasn't sure how the hell he was going to find out the truth.

"Can I get a large white chocolate mocha and a chocolate glazed donut please?" Gracie placed her order at the bakery and waited for it to be filled. She glanced around the small shop loving the quaint feel of everything. The chairs were all mismatched, the tables held small fresh flower arrangements and the smells of yummy baked goods and coffee permeated the air. The shops where she lived weren't like this at all. Most of them were so busy you could barely squeeze your way to the counter to place an order. Most of the time she ended up using the drive thru to avoid the hustle and bustle. But this, she could get used to this small town feel. At least the people who worked here were actually smiling and enjoying their jobs.

"Here you go." The young barista behind the counter handed her the order.

"Thank you." Gracie picked up the warm drink and spun around.

"Gracie." Cole stood right behind her looking all sexy in his dress pants and crisp white button down shirt.

"Cole. Hi." She became tongue-tied as she took in his manly stature.

"Hi, Cole. The usual?" The girl behind the counter asked him.

"Yeah, and add a black coffee to that too please." He smiled at the girl which caused a streak of envy to pass over Gracie.

With her food and drink in hand, she pushed past him and found a table near the window. She sat her stuff down and took a seat.

"Mind if I join you?" Cole pulled out the chair across from her.

"Guess not." She shrugged and continued to peer out the window.

"Something wrong?" he asked.

"Nope. Just having some coffee." She refused to look at him. He hadn't changed, he was still the same flirty player who winked and smiled at anything with a vagina.

"You seem a little, what's the word? *Bitchy*." He chuckled.

"Bitchy?"

"Yeah, like you have a stick up your ass."

Gracie leaned over the table and whispered, "Fuck you, Cole."

He leaned toward her, their lips so close together, "anytime darlin'"

"You wish," she spat.

"No, I don't wish. I've been there and done that, or did you forget?"

"How can I forget? It was the worst 30 seconds of my life."

Cole began laughing uncontrollably. "I remember it a little differently," he said as he caught his breath.

"Oh yeah?"

"Yeah. I think I remember hearing, "Oh Cole, fuck me harder. Right there, Cole."

Gracie ducked her head in embarrassment. "Would you keep it down?" She glanced around making sure none of the other customers heard him.

"Admit that I rocked your world or I start reenacting the scene from last night." His tone was teasing but his face held a stoic expression that told her he meant business.

"Fine. You rocked my world, Cole." She rolled her eyes.

"Not convincing enough," he opened his mouth to inflict mortification.

"Wait!"

"Yes?" his perfectly groomed eyebrows lifted.

Gracie once again leaned across the table and whispered, "Last night, was the best fucking I've ever had. In fact, if we were alone right now, I'd let you bend me over this table and beg you to make me come." She sat back and watched heat move into his eyes.

"Fuck." He scrubbed a hand over his face.

"Better?" She smiled sweetly.

"Damn, woman. I should know better than to go toe-to-toe with you."

Gracie was damn proud of herself for rattling Cole's cage a bit. She'd be in serious denial if she said she wasn't happy when he became flustered around her. It was a heady feeling to know the man sitting across from her was more than likely trying to get rid of a hard-on underneath the small table.

"I should go." Gracie stood from her seat and tried to walk past Cole who was still seated. He grabbed her wrist and began rubbing lazy circles across the inside of her arm.

"I'm sorry," he said as she looked down into his

soulful eyes.

"For what?" She should've pulled her arm free but the way his thumb seemed to be making love to her skin compelled her to let him continue for just a few moments longer.

"For making you say all that stuff." He glanced to where their skin was connected and hurriedly looked back up.

"Don't apologize." She then decided to jerk herself free. Even though her arm belonged to her once more, it fell as if he'd burned some sort of claim on her.

"How about dinner out tonight?" he asked.

"Cora will be back."

"Then we all go out to dinner." He stood.

"Fine. See you later." She smiled and turned to leave the bakery. If she'd stayed even a millisecond longer, she'd have been on all fours wagging her tongue and displaying her hind-end like a bitch in heat.

Damn it. Cole couldn't believe Gracie turned things

around on him like she did. But why *wouldn't* she? She'd always been the type of woman who could hold her own with anyone. He was no different. Unfortunately, even though she'd walked out of the bakery, he still sported half-wood under the table. Damn her. He smiled at the thought of her admitting that he'd rocked her world the night before. He knew he had, but hearing her say it made him want to stand up and beat his chest like an overgrown gorilla. And what he wouldn't have given to bend her fine ass over the table and make her come like she asked for.

"Need a refill?" Stacy—the barista—came over to the table and asked.

"Nah. I'm good," he responded.

"Oh, okay." She smiled and walked away from the table. Thank fuck for that. He couldn't imagine her being there witnessing his arousal. She'd more than likely think it was because of her. Yeah, they'd traded looks in the past, but that was the extent of it. There'd only been one woman he'd been with since being in Biloxi and he hadn't seen her for a while now.

Rapidly chugging down the rest of his lukewarm coffee he then snatched up the one he'd gotten for Luke. Just as he stepped out the door of the shop, his phone rang.

"Matthews," he answered.

"Where the hell are you?" Luke's pissed off voice came over the other end.

"Headed back now." He juggled his keys and the cup in his hands.

"The director is seeing red. Someone hacked the database."

Oh shit. "Really? Doesn't inspire confidence in our government when someone can hack into an impenetrable system." Cole laughed knowing it was Kat who'd done the deed.

"Whoever it was targeted your desktop," Luke mentioned.

"Really? That's odd." He played dumb.

He heard what sounded like Luke moving around and then his voice lowered. "I hope to fuck this doesn't have anything to do with you looking into this shit with

Gracie," Luke warned.

"I told you I'd be careful and I will."

"Whatever, just get your ass back here," he said and then hung up.

Normally Kat was careful so Cole hoped they didn't find out it was her who'd hacked in. If so, she'd more than likely turn on him for some sort of plea deal. He wasn't stupid enough to think she held any sort of loyalty toward him. She was a criminal, plain and simple. Either way, he needed to get back and check his secret email. The FBI had access to every piece of online life their agents had. But this email was reserved for things like he was having Kat look into. He'd learned the hard way with that one. Getting caught trying to subscribe to an online porn site had cost him a heap of humiliation in the field office in D.C.

"It's about time," Luke said in a snarky tone as Cole sat down at his desk.

"Here's your coffee." He pushed the paper cup across the desk toward his partner.

Luke picked it up and took a drink. "Hell, man. This

shit is ice cold."

"I got distracted."

"Does this distraction happen to have red hair and green eyes?"

"Fuck off." Grumbling, he then logged into his email.

He wasn't in the mood to take any sort of ribbing from his friend at the moment. He needed to get to the bottom of this crap with Gracie and then he could relax a bit...hopefully.

As he logged into his account he waited for the inbox to pop up. Sure enough there was an email from Kat. He clicked on the message line and let it load. Damn slow ass FBI internet. Cole tapped his fingers on the desk as he waited for it to load. Ten seconds seemed like 10 freaking hours. When the screen finally revealed the mail, he scanned over the words quickly. "Holy fucking shit," he breathed.

"Problems?" Luke asked, looking up from his paperwork.

"You could say that." Cole ran a hand through his hair and yanked on the ends.

"Do I *want* to know?"

"Probably better you don't." Reading the message again he let out a sigh. How in the hell did he not know Gracie had a stepbrother? He knew everything about her, didn't he? Fuck, this was insane.

"You look like someone just pissed in your Cheerios." Luke laughed.

"Feels that way." Cole then whispered, "She has a brother."

"Who?"

"Gracie. I didn't have any idea she had a brother."

"Wow. So this Dash character is her brother?"

"Yeah, come look at this." Cole motioned for Luke to take a look at the email.

Luke came around the desk and did just that. "Damon '*Dash*' Hunter. Still doesn't explain why she'd have been secretive about him."

"I intend on finding out that part of the story," Cole said with determination in his tone.

"Looks like he gets released pretty soon." Luke pointed to the date on the screen.

"Six months," Cole confirmed. "Still doesn't add up."

"Women...they're so damn complicated," Luke snickered.

"How the hell is yours complicated? You two are like watching a fucking Disney movie. I wouldn't be surprised if you guys started talking to animals and singing soon."

"We didn't start out that way." Luke took a seat back behind his own desk.

"Yeah, like I could forget."

"What in the hell are you doing on your computer, Matthews? That's evidence!" The director boomed as he came through the office.

Cole quickly signed out of his account and backed away with his hands in the air. "Sorry, I was on lunch and didn't know." He stood and walked around his desk.

"If you need to use one, use Daughtry's. For now this one is evidence. I don't want to see your damn fingers on it again, got it?"

"Absolutely, sir." At least he'd been able to check out the email before it was taken away from him. He'd just have to dig through some shit on his laptop at home when he got the opportunity.

Chapter Seventeen

ONCE GRACIE WAS FINISHED picking up Cora from Ava's salon, the two walked back to Cole's house. He'd be home in an hour or so and she wanted to be ready. So he wanted to take them out to dinner? She'd show him that it wasn't possible to wine and dine her. That sort of thing didn't attract her and it sure as hell wouldn't make her fall ass over face in love with the guy again either.

"Do I have to go?" Cora whined as Gracie tried to dig out something to wear.

"Yes."

"Ugh. I don't see why I have to tag along. You guys are just gonna sit there and make goo-goo eyes at each other all night."

She turned around to give her daughter a dirty look. "Am not. And mind your own business."

"Whatever." Cora stomped out of the room.

Damn, it was hard being a single parent. Just once she'd love to tell Cora to "*go ask your dad*" but that wasn't possible. She'd just have to play the role of both parents and hope for the best.

"Hey kid, where's your mom?" She heard Cole's voice echo down the hall.

"In the bedroom," Cora answered.

Gracie quickly tossed the sundress in her hands over her head. As she tried to yank it down her body, she became tangled up in the straps. Struggling to free herself she felt the unmistakable brush of Cole's hands on her arms.

"Lift your arms," he instructed.

She did as he said and soon he was pulling the dress into place on her body. When she brushed her hair out of her eyes she said, "Well that's a change of pace. Usually you're trying to get me *out* of my clothes, not *in* them." A nervous laugh escaped her lips.

"Give it time." She stood there as he brushed a thumb across her bottom lip causing her to shudder. "Can I ask you something?"

She shrugged. "Sure."

"What does it feel like when you stand in the same room as me?"

"I don't know. It guess it just feels like I'm standing in a room with another human being." She knew it was a lie even before she finished the damn sentence. But she wasn't about to tell him what it *really* felt like to be in his presence.

"Huh. Interesting." He managed to step even closer. So close in fact she could see the tiny blood vessels in eyes. "When I'm in a room with you," he reached out and pulled a lock of her hair into his fingers, "my entire body comes alive." He ran them down the silky strand. "It's like I have a monumental reaction to you no matter what."

"You're a man, I'm a woman. It's just hormones." She batted his hand away.

"I don't think it is, Gracie." He lifted her chin with a finger. "I think no matter how much you push me away, no matter how many times you pretend to hate me, you know as well as I do, we're meant to be together."

"That's just stupid." She brushed past him, trying like hell to get him off this sentimental nonsense. "Fate doesn't exist, Cole."

"Maybe not. But no matter what, your body will never forget what I can do to it. It will forever remember each slide of my cock, each thrust of my hips and every damn time I made you scream my name." With those statements, he left the room, ultimately leaving Gracie in a state of extreme arousal once more. If he kept this up, she'd be kissing the ground he walked on before long.

It was so much fun getting her all worked up. Cole patted himself on the back for another job well done. If Cole Matthews was good at one thing, it was persevering when the situation called for it. This was one of those times. He hadn't expected to walk in on her all tangled up in a dress and damn it if he didn't want to jerk it back over her head and run his hands all over her smooth body. He gave himself credit for being *somewhat* of a gentleman. Hell, maybe the south had changed him. He sure as heck enjoyed sweet tea since moving to Mississippi; maybe he'd adapted to being a southern gentleman now as well. Shaking his head, he laughed as he yanked open the fridge and grabbed a beer. Once the cap was twisted off he took a pull from the yeasty brew and swallowed. There was nothing like coming home after a fucked-up day at work and having a nice long neck waiting on you. At least he could count on that to quell his loneliness for the time being.

"I'm hungry," he heard Cora say from behind him.

He lowered the bottle and turned to see her leaning against the doorframe. Her face was pale and it looked like she was trembling. "When's the last time you had something to eat?" He approached her and looked her over.

"A few hours ago."

"Shit. Okay, have a seat." Cole led her to the table and

pulled out one of the mismatched chairs. Cora slumped in it and watched him work a frenzy around the room. "What sounds good?" Hell, he didn't know what she needed. This was new territory for him.

"I think I need a glucose tablet." She laid her head on the table and closed her eyes.

Cole began to panic as her body became laxer and started to slip from the chair. He caught her right before her head hit the tile floor. "Gracie!" he yelled.

Gracie came running down the hall and as soon as she saw him holding Cora on his lap, she leapt into action. He watched her as she opened the fridge and grabbed the carton of orange juice and quickly knelt. "Lift her into a sitting position," she said with an eerily calm tone. "I have to get some of this down her throat." She grabbed Cora's jaw and pried it open with her fingers. "If she starts choking just make sure her airway is straight." Cole observed as Gracie trickled the juice down her daughter's throat. "Cora, honey. Come on," she soothed.

"It's not working." Cole could hear the panic in his

voice and it freak him the hell out. He wasn't one to become a basket case in any type of situation but this one wasn't one he wanted to handle.

"It takes a few minutes. Calm down, Cole," she scorned. A couple minutes ticked by and soon the young girl was trying to sit up while coughing. Gracie sat back on the floor while he continued to hold Cora in his arms.

"I'm sorry, mom." Cora began crying.

"Sweetie, it's okay."

"No, no it's not." Tears streamed down her face and Cole felt terrible.

"We all make mistakes. At least this one was fixable. How ya feelin?" He tried to sound positive but on the inside he was still in a panic.

"I...I'm okay." She wiped her eyes. Looking up at him she smiled. "Thanks for catching me. I usually crash and bang my head on something."

As Cole sat there with this kid on his lap, he realized something and that something was, he would make a shitty parent. Hell, if he'd been alone with her he'd wouldn't have known what to do. She would've ended up in a coma or worse.

"Are you okay?" Gracie touched his arm.

"Me? Sure," he replied.

"I'm gonna lay down on the couch." Cora stood shakily on both feet. She made her way to the sofa while he sat there on the floor.

"It's fine. She's okay," Gracie tried to console him.

"What if…" he began.

"Stop it. Look, she's okay, we're okay. It happens." She shrugged her bare shoulders.

"I need some space." He stood and headed to the back door. Once there, he slid open the doors and stepped outside. The humidity did nothing to calm him nor did the solitude. What the hell was he coming out here for anyway?

"What's going on with you?" Gracie stepped out to join him.

"Jesus, Gracie. She could've fucking died." He locked his fingers behind his head.

"But she didn't."

"I just…"

"You just what, Cole? You just need to make this about you like every other thing in life? You can't let it be what it is?"

"I do *not* make everything about myself," he returned.

"Yes. You. Do. Every time there's a situation, Cole Matthews has to step in and make it about himself. He wants to be top dog and get all the attention."

"Name one time *besides* today, Gracie."

"Fine. The day I told you I was pregnant. You couldn't just accept it, you had to sit there and make it about you. How you wouldn't be able to do what you really wanted. How you would do the right thing and marry me."

"What the hell was I supposed to do?"

"You were supposed to hold me and tell me everything would be okay. I was scared shitless. There I was pregnant and barely an adult. I didn't know what I was doing." She walked over to a tree and looked up into the branches. "Cole, I needed you to be there for me. Even if things were scary, at least we could've been terrified together." She looked back at him.

"Fuck. You're right, I do make it all about me. I'm sorry."

"That's the first genuine thing I've heard come out of your mouth since we've been here."

Maybe she was right. Maybe he was a self-absorbed dickhead who really didn't deserve to have her in his life. Was he only trying to get her back because he had something to prove to himself? Was this, in a way, a dumb game he'd been playing? What would happen when she finally gave in? Would he be as serious then as he tried to be now?

"You're thinking too much." She laughed.

"Yep. Guess I'd better get some dinner made." He turned around to grab the door handle.

"We aren't going out to dinner?" she asked.

"Thought you'd want to stay in after what'd happened."

"Cora's fine. *More* than fine, actually. I'd like to go to dinner."

"Okay, let's go."

Cole wasn't missing a chance to spend time with her.

He'd fought hard to get her to open up now it was his turn to open up and ask a few questions of his own.

∞ Chapter Eighteen ∞

GRACIE FELT more comfortable about her decision to keep her daughter's father a secret after watching Cole fall into a panic. She'd experienced that type of situation many times over the course of Cora's life. It wasn't new to her at all. But seeing his reaction to what was happening? Yeah, that man didn't need kids. He needed a blanket and a pacifier.

Even though he was worried, she almost spilled the beans when she'd walked in and saw him in the floor holding Cora. It was insane how much the young girl resembled her father. The dark hair, the way her lip sat when her face was relaxed and that tiny freckle that sat just below her right temple. They were all Cole. She half-wondered if he'd ever picked up on those things. Surely if he had, he'd have said something, right? Or maybe he was so absorbed in himself that he didn't notice things like that. That was more than likely the case.

"You okay?" Cole asked as he drove the three of them to a restaurant.

"Me? I'm fine." She really wasn't though.

"Cora, how're you feeling now?" It surprised her when he asked her daughter.

"All good back here." Gracie was glad to hear pep in her voice. She knew Cora would be okay, but sometimes she worried just like any other neurotic parent.

"You have a birthday coming up, right?" Cole directed another question toward the backseat.

"Yep. In five days." Cora sighed.

"Doesn't sound like you're too happy about it." Cole chuckled.

"It's just that I won't be with my friends and get to have a party or anything since we're here."

Gracie glanced over at Cole who gave her a sad look.

"When we get back to Illinois we'll have a party." She tried to perk her daughter up.

"It's not the same, mom."

Gracie was the one who sighed now. Yeah, it wasn't the same. If this trip wasn't life or death, she'd have been home planning an epic party for Cora. But she was stuck here trying to convince Cole to sign those damn papers. If he'd hurry and do it, she could be on a flight back home and Dash would be safe.

"Here we are." Cole pulled into the parking lot of a fairly nice steakhouse. "I wasn't sure what you two are hungry for and this place has just about everything," he offered.

"I'm sure we'll find something we like." Gracie replied.

"Stay put," he ordered, then got out of the truck and rounded the front. She waited, thinking he was going to open her door but shocked her by doing Cora's first. That gesture put a little grin on her face. He didn't have to do that, but maybe he was showing her he wasn't a tool bag anymore. When Cora was out of the vehicle, Cole then opened her door. "Your turn." He extended his hand for her to grab ahold of.

"Thanks." She smiled which got her a smile from him in return. A Cole Matthews smile was dangerous. She'd have sworn that same smile could disarm a hostile nation and drop panties at the same time. She'd just have to make sure hers stayed put from now on.

"How many?" The hostess at the podium asked him.

"Three."

"Right this way." She smiled sweetly. Cole knew better than to flash any sort of grin at another woman. He'd seen how Gracie reacted to another woman giving him attention. Right now his plan was to be a good boy. No flirting and no damn smiling. If he did smile, those grins needed to be directed at her and *only* her.

"Here you go," The middle-aged woman motioned to a table.

"This place is nice," Gracie commented as they took their seats.

Why the hell did she have to look so fucking beautiful tonight? Why couldn't she be ragged and gross? What the hell was he thinking? Gracie always looked stunning. Even on her worst day she was a knockout.

"Where's the restroom?" Cora asked.

"Down that small hallway. First door on the right," he said while pointing. She got up and followed his directions until she was out of sight. Time to say a few things to Gracie now. "You look amazing tonight," he started.

"Thanks." She cocked her eyebrow waiting for him to continue.

"That color looks great on you." Fuck. He was losing his suave approach. What a stupid thing to say.

She put her elbows on the wooden table and leaned a tiny bit toward him. "Why don't you stop beating around the bush and tell me what you really want to."

"What if *that* was it?" he joked.

"It wasn't."

"How do you know?"

"Because I know you better than you know yourself."

"You're right." He leaned forward. "What I *really* wanted to say was I should've taken that dress and made sure it was nice and wrinkled on my bedroom floor."

"Keep going,"

"I also should've made sure your hair was wild. You know, that freshly fucked look."

"Is that it?"

"Of course not. I think I should've fucked you with first my fingers, then my tongue and finally my cock."

"What if I only wanted one of those things?"

"Which one would you have chosen?"

"I'm not sure."

"Let's see, your body trembles when my mouth is on you. Your back arches when my fingers are flicking your clit. And your pussy? I think you know what it does when my cock is deep inside you." He smiled with male satisfaction at the fact Gracie's cheeks now resembled the color of an overripe Fuji apple.

"*Cole*?" a female voice sounded from beside him. As he looked up he cringed.

"Brandi. When did you get back into town?" Now it

was his turn to have a red face. This wasn't good.

"Last night actually." Brandi smiled.

"Good trip?" Hell, why was he carrying on a conversation with her. Brandi was nothing but a spur of the moment bad decision he'd made months ago. There wasn't any sort of feelings involved, it was a quickie fuck to relieve the tension they'd both had that day. Now he wanted to forget that it'd ever happened.

"Yeah, it was great. Well, as great as an extended vacation can be when you're stuck with your parents," Brandi hooted.

"That's good." He hoped she was getting the coolness of his voice and she'd go away any second now.

"I'm sorry. I'm being rude." She then extended her hand to Gracie who was now on full alert across the table. "I'm Brandi. Cole and I...well, never mind." She looked back at him and realized the mistake she'd made. "I'd better go wait for my date. He should be here any minute now," she glanced down at her pricy designer watch. "Gotta run. Good seeing you again." And then she was gone.

Cole didn't want to see the expression on Gracie's face—he knew damn well she wasn't happy. But he might as well bite the bullet and get it over with. Yup, the fiery woman across from him was beyond livid. "I can explain," he began.

Her hands went up to stop him. Not a good sign. "No need to." She flashed an acidic smile.

"It was a one-time thing."

"Cole, shut up. I don't need to know what happened."

"Fuck," he bit out. "I know you're upset."

"I'm not upset. Just drop it." She looked away.

"Gracie, would you please talk to me? Shit. If I'm the self-absorbed one, you're the one who clams up when she's pissed."

When she faced him again there was venom in her eyes. "I fucking told you to drop it. What you do on your own time is your business. I don't give a damn if you fuck every pothole in the county. I don't own you and you sure as hell don't own me." She stood up quickly and tossed her napkin on the table. "I'm done with this."

He watched her walk toward the bathroom where Cora had yet to come out.

No, he was *not* letting her walk away again. He'd set out to show her he wanted her in his life and was about to do just that. As he scooted his chair back, he felt a hand on his shoulder. A female hand.

"I'm really sorry about that." Brandi said. "I had no idea you were in a relationship."

"I'm not. I mean, I am but…" Cole stammered.

"Is that her daughter in the bathroom?"

"Yeah." Cole sighed.

"Huh."

"What's that supposed to mean?" He pinned her with a questioning stare.

"Nothing. It's just, that girl has the same freckle in the same spot that you do."

"What's your point?"

"Well, her eyes and hair are the exact color of yours, too."

"Why don't you just spit out what you're trying to say, Brandi. I don't have time for this shit." He was getting angry at this point.

"Cole, she could pass for yours." As the words left her mouth a sinking feeling hit his gut.

There was no way that kid was his. Gracie told him it was a false positive on the test. Cora was a result of some one night stand she'd had after they separated.

"Not possible," he told her.

"Maybe you're right. Sorry I said anything. Have a good night." Brandi retreated once more.

Cole stared at the entrance to the small hallway waiting for his dinner companions to come back. What the hell did Brandi know anyway? That kid wasn't his. She was seeing things that weren't there.

He stared so hard he didn't even see when one of them came back to the table. "Mom said she wasn't feeling good," Cora said. Cole began to look at the young girl with a different set of eyes now. Holy shit. She did have the same freckle. "You okay?" She tilted her head to the side. Damn, her eyes were the same color as his. They even had tiny brown flecks sprinkled throughout the blue like his. It was just a coincidence. Lots of people had that eye color. "Ooookay. You're acting like a space cadet," she said and then laughed. That hair.

"No *fucking* way," he blurted.

"What is wrong with you?"

"Come on Cora, we'll call a cab." Gracie walked up and motioned for her daughter to come with her.

Cole quickly stood and stared her down, "We need to talk."

"I'm done talking, Cole."

"No, you're *not*. We have a few things to discuss."

"Like what?" She planted her hands on her hips and tossed her attitude at him like it was the strike out pitch in a World Series Game. Well fuck a bunch of that shit.

"I'm not having this conversation here or in front of her. Get your purse, we're leaving." He yanked his keys from his pocket and stomped to the front of the restaurant. He knew he was acting like an ass, but it didn't much matter. There would be answers tonight even if he had to hold her down to get them.

"What's gotten into you?" Gracie caught up with him when he was halfway across the parking lot.

He spun around to face her. "I guess I'm fucking sick and tired of being lied to, Gracie."

"What have I lied to you about?"

Cole didn't want to get into this in a public parking lot but there was no time like the present. He lowered his voice enough so Cora wouldn't hear him. "Who's her father?" he pointed at the young girl as she lollygagged around halfway between the building and them.

"I told you already. It was a one-night stand."

"Bullshit. I want the truth," he spat.

"I'm telling you the truth!" she yelled.

"I guess you are. If you lie to everyone and yourself long enough you start believing your own lies."

"What do you want me to say, Cole?" Tears began to streak down her porcelain face but he wasn't buying the weeping woman act.

"Mom, what's wrong?" Cora finally caught up with them.

"I'm fine, honey. Why don't you wait in the truck?" She motioned to his vehicle which was about 10 feet away. Cora did as she asked.

"Damn it, Gracie." He was beyond frustrated. "Is she mine?" he asked but was offered no response. "Fine, if you won't tell me the truth, I'll find out my own way." He began walking toward the truck, his legs eating up the pavement with long purposeful strides.

"What are you doing?" Gracie jogged up to him.

He spun around. "I don't know."

Even with the crickets chirping, the cars rushing by on the highway and the sound of his heartbeat roaring in his ears, everything became silent when Gracie began to speak again. "I've given her a good life," she sobbed. "I did what I thought was best for her."

Cole brought his thumb and forefinger to his face and pinched the bridge of his nose. "How could you do something like this?" he whispered.

"I didn't do it to hurt you."

"Really? Because I'm pretty fucking hurt right now. I had a kid running around somewhere and didn't know it. If you just found that out, wouldn't you be even the least bit hurt?" he yelled.

"Cole, don't do this here, please?" she begged while

tugging on the sleeve of his shirt.

He jerked his arm away and tossed his hands in the air. "Where then? Where the fuck would you like me to ask about my kid's life? Where would be a good place for me to have you tell me how you fucked me out of seeing her take her first steps or say her first word? Where is a good God-damned place?" he roared.

"I didn't think you'd want any of this," she admitted.

"You didn't give me a choice! You took that option away the day you lied to me. How the hell am I supposed to forgive that?"

"I don't expect you to forgive me, Cole. But you can't just barge into her life now."

"The hell I can't! You had 12 years, Gracie. Twelve years to send a letter, an email, hell, you could've sent a damn carrier pigeon for all I care. But you didn't. You made a selfish decision. How can you feel *good* about that?"

"Do you honestly think I'm okay with what I did? Every fucking day of her life I had to carry around guilt. Do you know how that feels?" Gracie nearly screamed while poking him in the chest.

"No. You don't get to make this about you now." Cole backed away and scrubbed both hands over his face. Turning back to her he said, "This isn't about either of us right now. It's about that girl in the truck." He let out a resonating sigh. "I can't do anything about the last 12 years, but I can do something about each and every day from this point on."

"What are you going to do?"

"I'm going to make damn sure I'm a part of Cora's life, Gracie. I'm owed that much."

"You're right. I shouldn't have done what I did to you. I'm so sorry, Cole." She stepped toward him but Cole put his hands up to stop her.

"I can't right now. Just give me some time." He then pushed past her and went to the truck. Before he rounded the hood he looked back at her, "You *will*, however, tell her about me." Then he got in and started the engine.

He wasn't joking when he said this wasn't about him or Gracie, this was about Cora. The kid spent 12 years of her life without a father figure. But that would change soon. He'd do anything and everything he could to provide for her and make sure she knew she was loved. Hell, how did you love someone you just met? It didn't matter. He'd learn to make room for her in his life. She was his main focus now. Time to step up and be a dad. Shit, how the fuck did he do that?

~∽ *Chapter Nineteen* ∽~

 **"WOW, YOU'VE BEEN** handed a few bombshells lately." Luke whistled across the office after Cole revealed that he had a kid.

"Seems that way."

"So, what now?"

"Good question. I've missed so much shit. Not even sure how to deal with this." He leaned back in his office chair and grabbed the squishy stress ball from the top drawer of his desk.

"Does Cora know yet?"

"Nope. It's been three days and Gracie has yet to tell her."

"Damn."

"Yeah. What the hell should I do? I don't want to just

walk in and say *'hey kid, you're mine, let's play catch in the back yard'*."

Luke let out a broken laugh. "Probably not the best idea. Have you urged Gracie to tell her?"

"Not really. I guess I've been distant, I don't know what to say to her. In a way I'm happy, but on the other hand I'm so pissed I could punch a hole through a titanium brick." Cole began tossing the stress ball into the air and catching it. "Doesn't change how I feel about her though. I don't think anything she did could make me lose the love I have for her. Isn't that some shit?"

"I get it. It's how I feel about Ava. Hell, she held me at gunpoint. If that isn't love, I really don't know what is." Luke got up and grabbed a cup from the top of the watercooler nearby. "How about we take Cora tonight and the two of you can have some time to discuss all of this?" Luke filled a small cup and took a gulp.

"Are you sure? I feel like I've been relying on you for a bunch of shit lately." Cole caught the ball and tossed it back into the drawer, slamming it shut.

"That's what partners are for. Plus, you're gonna pay

off your favor debt to me next year anyway," Luke said and walked back to his desk.

"I'm not killing anyone for you, if that's the payoff."

"Nope. It's worse than murder," Luke snickered.

"Aww fuck. Maybe I don't want to know."

"Oh trust me, you're fucked." Luke began laughing uncontrollably.

"Might as well tell me."

"You my friend get to be my best man, tux and all." Luke pointed at him.

"You're a sick bastard," Cole grumbled.

"Yes, yes I am. I'm thinking a powder-blue number with a ruffled ascot," Luke teased.

"You do that and I'll show up naked."

"No one wants to see *'little Cole'*."

"Little? Please, if your dick saw my dick, it'd run and hide in fear." Cole began hysterically laughing.

"Enough about your dicks, fellas. I have a case for the two of you." The director came through the office and slammed a file on Cole's desk. "And if I hear that you boys are measuring and comparing dicks on this job, I'll have you out doing recruitment faster than you can pull your tape measure out of your pocket," he warned and then walked back down the hall toward his office.

"Why does he suck all the fun out of this job?" Cole complained.

"Some are born to be fun sponges and he came out of a vagina screaming and sucking fun from life," Luke answered. "What've we got this time?"

Sliding the folder in front of him, Cole flipped it open. He scanned the first page and sat back in his seat again. "Federal judge. Looks like some sort of racketeering and possible homicide."

"Why do these federal fuckers think they can get away with everything, including murder?"

"Guess they think they can't be touched." Cole lifted the first page and read over the possible infractions. "Fuck," he cursed.

"What?"

He slid the papers across the desk, "That name ring a bell?" He pointed toward the middle of the second page.

"Damn." Luke pushed the file back his way. "If they

know you have ties to this, they'll pull you off the case."

"That's why they *won't* find out." Cole shut the file and got up. "Can I trust you on this?" He pinned Luke with a stare that meant business.

"Get your shit figured out, Matthews."

Yeah, he had some shit to figure out, all right. This was deeper than he'd originally thought. Why the fuck did *Damon 'Dash' Hunter's* name have to be in that God-damned file?

"I know it's this weekend, Cora. There's nothing I can do about it," Gracie yelled from the kitchen to the living room.

"Mom, this sucks!"

"I know. But I told you, once we get back home, *then* we can have a birthday party."

"I don't want it then, I want it *now*!"

"What the hell did I walk in on?" She heard Cole's voice from the front door.

"Mom says we can't celebrate my birthday until we

go back home."

"Really? Why can't we do it here?" Cole asked while tossing his jacket over the arm of the sofa.

Gracie came out of the kitchen and pinned him with a stare. "Can I talk to you, please?" She raised her eyebrows and used her head to motion to the kitchen.

"Sure."

Once she had him close she whispered, "Look, I know you want to jump into this with both feet and all, but can you please lay off a bit?"

"Why the hell can't she have a party here?" He opened the fridge and grabbed a beer.

"Just because." Gracie grabbed the beer from his hands and twisted the lid off. She took a long pull and handed it back to him.

"Did you forget I'm an FBI agent? I *need* a reason."

"Okay, here's your reason. I don't exactly have the funds to throw her a party, Cole." Gracie sighed and began washing the last plate in the sink.

"That's all you had to say." He pulled his wallet from his back pocket and took a seat at the table. Gracie stood at the sink staring.

"How much do you need?" She watched as he slid a thick stack of bills from the weathered leather.

"I don't want your money." She turned back to the sink and yanked the plug from the drain.

"Damn stubborn woman." She felt him behind her.

"I'm trying not to be, Cole." She let out a sigh and turned to face him.

"Clearly you're not trying very hard." He put both hands on her face and lifted her gaze to his. "Is there anything you need to tell me?" he asked.

"No." She dropped her head a bit.

"Look at me." He lifted her head once more. "Stop fighting me. Let me do this," he said softly.

"I've been doing it for 12 years, I can't just let go." She felt her eyes burning with unshed tears.

"I'm not asking you to let anything go. Just let me in and let me be a part of this."

"I'll try." She smiled.

"Good. Luke and Ava are picking Cora up in about an hour. We need to sit down and discuss some things."

"Cole…"

"Not taking 'no' for an answer!" he shouted from down the hallway.

"And he calls *me* stubborn," Gracie grumbled as she wiped down the damp counter.

Cole smiled to himself as he let the hot water slide over his body in the shower. The steaming spray quenched his aching muscles as the scent of his soap filled the air in the bathroom. It was time to stop letting Gracie have her way in every situation and time for him to step up and be a man. He'd never been one to take 'no' for an answer but with her, it was easy to back down and let her run the show. Not anymore. Tonight he would show her how he really was. She'd either love it, or run from it. Either way, Cole wasn't likely to let her control things.

As he turned the knobs to shut the water off, Cole heard a light knock on the bathroom door. "Yeah?"

"Luke and Ava are here," Gracie's muffled voice came through the door.

"Be out in a minute." He grabbed the towel from the nearby rack and wrapped it around his waist. As he looked down he could still see the faint scars of the bullets that'd struck him during his time in the FBI. Most of them were mere flesh wounds but there was one in particular that'd almost caused his end. He hated looking at that one. It was a reminder that he wasn't as perfect as he'd like to think. But in a way it was also a reminder of the fact that before the piece of metal hit him, he really wasn't *living* his life. He was simply floating through. As he looked at it in the mirror the door began to push open.

"Hey, did you hear me?" Gracie stuck her head in.

"Yes, I heard you."

"Cole, what happened?" She came all the way through and shut the door behind her. She was looking directly at the scar on his chest.

"Bullet," he answered vaguely.

"It looks like it went through your heart." She reached out and ran her smooth finger over the puckered skin. Cole grabbed her hand and held it there, letting her fingers spread across his damp chest. "How did I not see this before?"

"Almost did. 2 millimeters to the right and I wouldn't be talking to you at this moment. The one day I choose not to wear my vest..." he trailed off not wanting to rehash old wounds. "And I'm pretty sure we were thinking about *other* things when my shirt was off."

"I'm sorry." She tried to pull her hand away but he wouldn't let her.

"No need to be sorry. It happens." Shrugging, he finally let her hand go.

"I'll let them know you'll be a few." She dropped her head and reached for the door handle.

"Gracie?"

"Yeah?"

Cole stared at her wanting to say so damn much but when he opened his mouth, nothing came out but, "never mind."

Gracie didn't want to spend the evening and night with Cole; he was so damn dangerous. And the way he looked with only a towel wrapped around his waist? Holy shit. She had to hold herself back from bending down and licking the tiny water droplets that were cascading down his chest. She internally shook, biting the inside of her cheek while standing there with him in the bathroom. The man was gorgeous, even with the scars marring his tanned skin. The fact that he was almost killed by a bullet made her sad. How the hell had he managed to survive something like that? Was he just lucky? Damn, she hated to admit knowing he could've been taken from this world by something as tiny as a bullet would've sent her into a state of mourning even though they weren't together when it'd happened.

"Bye, mom." Cora pulled her from her inner state of woe by throwing her arms around her neck and hugging her goodbye.

"Bye. I love you." She squeezed her back.

"You, too." It didn't take long and she was out the door with Ava.

Once the door shut behind them, she took a deep breath. Time to face the music with Cole. She hoped he didn't have an evening full of screaming at her planned. So she'd made some shitty decisions where he was concerned but they were done because she didn't know what else to do at the time. Being 19 and pregnant, it wasn't as if she automatically thought *"okay, this is how things will be and they are going to be perfect"*. No, she was fucking petrified. But it was in the past and she hoped he would come to terms with her choices and not beat the dead horse.

"Hey," Cole said as she turned to clean up the mess from dinner in the kitchen.

"I'm just going to clean up a bit in here." She crossed the living room.

"It can wait."

"I don't want the dishes to be all nasty in the morning." Gracie knew she was using any excuse she could to prolong spending time with him.

"Gracie, the fucking dishes can wait." He sounded, not pissed but just insistent this time.

"If you're going to yell at me some more I have to tell you I'm not really in the mood for it," she huffed.

"No, I thought we could just talk."

"Really?" Doubt peppered her voice.

"Damn it. Do you think I *hate* you?"

"Maybe a little bit. I'd hate me."

"At this point you could kill my dog, if I had one, and it still wouldn't cause me to feel any sort of hate toward you." He laughed. "I guess I'm curious about things, is all."

She took a seat at the end of the sofa and drew her legs underneath her. "What would you like to know?"

Cole sat down as well and faced her. "I don't know, maybe tell me about Cora. How big was she when she was born? What was labor like?"

Gracie smiled when she thought of going into labor with her daughter. "I was at home alone when my water broke. I don't think I panicked but who knows, I probably did." She chuckled. "Jenna picked me up since I didn't have a car. I tried those stupid breathing exercises on the way to the hospital but they didn't seem to help." Cole grabbed her hand and began rubbing the top with his thumb. "When we got there I remember crying because I wasn't ready to be a mom. I wanted it to all go away. But once I saw Cora for the first time, every fear I had just...disappeared. She was perfect and beautiful. There I was, responsible for this screaming, red-faced little nugget of a human being. It was the most amazing feeling I'd ever had." Cole watched her face as she told him how big Cora was, how many nights she'd stayed in the hospital and about the first few weeks of her little life.

"I named her after you and I."

"How?"

"I used the first 2 letters of your name and added them to the second and third letters in mine. I wanted her to have something of yours even though you weren't there."

She saw the emotion pass across his face as she told him about Cora's name. It surprised her he'd feel anything about it.

"Thank you," he said when he looked into her eyes.

"Cole, I know I was wrong. I fought with my decision every day. And I want you to know that we can work this out. I'm willing to do what I have to," she offered.

"Even stay married to me?" His face was dead serious.

"I *can't*," she whispered. If she didn't get him to sign the papers, Dash was as good as dead.

"Why? I need one good reason *why*, Gracie."

"I can't give you that reason." She stood from the sofa and headed down the hallway.

"Come on. Don't sit there and tell me you'll do anything and leave me with that shit." He followed her.

"You want the person you knew years ago. I'm not *her* anymore." She tossed the excuse at him.

"Bullshit. You're grasping at straws."

How the hell was she going to get him off this subject? The man wasn't backing down. An idea popped into her head. As she stood there in his bedroom, Gracie reached for the hem of her shirt and whipped it over her head, leaving her in nothing but her bra. Cole didn't say anything. *Hmmm*, it must be working. She then grabbed the button on her shorts, popped it free, then pulled the zipper down. They were around her ankles in no time.

"Jesus." Cole's eyes heated as he raked his gaze over

her body. "This isn't going to end well for you." He stepped forward and ran a finger in between her breasts.

"I could argue that." She smiled with a hooded gaze. Success; this was distracting him.

"What do you want?"

"You."

"No, you want me to drop what we were talking about. You're using this," he slid his fingers down her stomach and landed right above her panty line. "To distract me."

"Is it working?" she asked coyly.

"I think you know it is." He reached one finger inside the top of her underwear and began to glide it back and forth over the skin of her stomach.

"Lower," Gracie whined.

"On the bed." Cole stepped back and pointed to the bed. "Now."

She hadn't meant to get herself all worked up but damn it if she wasn't ready to tear his clothes off. The only thing she could think of was his hands all over her heated skin and his cock inside of her.

Cole mentally slapped himself for letting her take control of the situation. He wanted answers and the only one she gave him was the one where his dick became hard. *Shit. Fuck. Damn.* Did it really matter he didn't get answers to his questions tonight? What would it hurt for him to lose himself in her body once more? She was offering, why not take her up on it and have some sort of bliss for even a little while.

Gracie didn't give pause when he told her to get on the bed, she did as he commanded and waited patiently for him to make a move. He'd make one alright, one that would have her wailing his name eventually. But for now, he wanted to look at the perfection that was Gracie. She was something to behold with her fiery tresses spilling over her shoulders like a cascade of crimson water. Her lips swollen slightly as she bit down on them—waiting in extreme anticipation. Her alabaster skin glowing like a siren beckoning him closer, damn, every minute detail about the woman drove him to the edge of insanity. As fucked-up as this was, he loved it. He loved her too but she didn't want to hear that, she only wanted his signature on a piece of paper that would ultimately set her free. That wasn't happening. If Gracie Callahan thought he'd bow down and do what she wanted, she was sadly mistaken. He had every intention of making her fall in love with him again. She was lying to herself and everyone else if she said she didn't have any sort of emotional attachment to him. He'd call bullshit in front of Saint Peter at the Pearly Gates for that one.

"Cole, come here." She patted the rumpled sheet beside her nude frame.

"No. I want to look at you."

"You've been looking at me for the past three minutes," she huffed.

"And if I want to look for another three, and three more after that, I will."

"But I want you," she whispered.

Cole could understand her want. But what he wanted was to hear her say she *needed* him. "What part of me do you want first?" he teased. "My fingers?" He wiggled his hands a bit. "My tongue?" He stuck it out and licked his lips in a deliberate motion to make her squirm—and she did. "Or my cock?"

"All of the above." She tried to get up but as soon as she was on all fours on the bed, Cole was on her.

"How many times are you gonna come for me tonight?" He hovered over her as she lay on her back, her hair spread across the pillow beneath her.

"I don't know."

"How about you don't worry about it and I'll keep count. Sound fair?"

"Yes."

"Let's start with this." He slid a hand down her body and ran a finger through the moisture pooling there.

This was going to be one hell of a long night.

Chapter Twenty

HE WAS GOING to break her. Not in a literal sense of course, but in one that meant she would fucking splinter into microscopic particles with each touch he inflicted on her body. He was napalm to her senses yet she was doing *nothing* to stop him. She had half a mind to get the hell out of there before he was inside her body but she knew that'd never happen. She needed him connected with her. She craved the destruction he tended to incite on every part of her. So why was it that she both wanted and didn't want this to happen again? She'd asked for distance, hell, she made it a point to throw enough space between them you could fit 19 football fields. She chalked it up to being weak. As she looked at him looming over her, Gracie assured herself it was only because in another time and place, Cole could've been a male underwear model. He oozed a masculine sex appeal that had women clawing at their own undergarments — who *wouldn't* want to fuck his brains out? Lust, of course, that's what it was

"Gracie," Cole growled as he slid his fingers inside her entrance. Her spine arched and a cry passed across her lips. "That's my girl." He chuckled as he began to fuck her with his hand.

The sensations began to build rapidly but Gracie worked hard to stave off the impending orgasm. If she didn't come, this wouldn't be so personal, right? But damn, she wanted to feel the burn of release. To watch Cole's face as he found satisfaction in taking her to the edge and pushing her right over it.

"Damn it." Shit. He realized what she was doing. Ripping his fingers from her body, Cole stared down at her while shaking his head. "I know everything about your body, Gracie. Don't think you're fooling me by holding back. I feel you." He bent down and brushed his lips across hers. "Did you forget that if I want something bad enough, I take it?"

She shook her head, her body buzzing with need. "I know you do."

"Then why aren't you giving me what I want?"

"What do you want?" she breathed.

He leaned closer to her ear and whispered, "I want you to come." Oh, how she wanted that too. "Every time you come, it gives me satisfaction. Why would you deny me that?"

"I'm not," she lied.

"Bullshit." Just then he reached between their bodies and began to massage her swollen clit. Her legs fell open wider to allow him better access. "See? I know you want to give it to me but you keep holding yourself back. Why?"

"I don't know, Cole," she said breathlessly.

Continuing his assault, Cole put even more effort into making her come. There was no way he was entering her body until she came at least once on his fingers. When he did finally push himself inside her, he wanted her so fucking soft and ready that she'd beg him for each and every inch. "Go ahead, come," he whispered in her ear.

Gracie's back bowed off the mattress as he pinched her clit between his fingers. "Oh God!" she shouted as she fought with him. Yeah, she'd go off like a missile soon—it was just a matter of time. If Cole knew one thing, it was that Gracie's body belonged to him. She'd deny it until her dying day, but he was certain no other man on the planet could make her body fall under their spell like he did.

"Give me something, darlin'. I'm dying here." He held his breath, hoping he wasn't the one who went off first.

"Ask me," she whimpered.

Oh, so they were playing *that* game? Okay. He was ready to beg her for it. "Fucking come, Gracie."

"No!" she yelled.

Cole smiled. This was the shit she loved. The power play between the two of them that would eventually lead to her screaming and thrashing on the bed. "No? I think you can do better than that." He thrust his fingers inside her as he leaned down and began to lick his way up her slit. His head lifted as he said, "How about we turn that '*no*' into a '*yes*'?" Pushing deeper he trailed his tongue through her gathering moisture. Yeah, this was going to be what would cause her to shatter.

"Fuck!" Gracie keened as he felt the first flutters of her orgasm overtake her. She'd held out as long as she possibly could but to no avail. Grinning to himself, Cole knew he had her right where he wanted her.

"You like that?" He pulled his fingers from her heat and moved up her body.

"Please don't stop," she whimpered while he looked deep into her green eyes.

"I'm not stopping, baby." Feathering his lips across hers he was surprised when she grabbed the back of his neck and pulled his face closer to hers. Cole let her have control as she deepened the kiss and thrust her tongue into his warm mouth. Here was the one thing he'd never tire of. The one thing that could turn a blue mood into a colorful one in no time at all. Her kiss. Yeah, he thought about it in some type of fairytale shit, but there was no other way to describe it. Hell, he'd bet it was so powerful it could cause a unicorn to explode into a heaping pile of glitter.

"I need you inside me," she said as she pulled back— her head digging into the pillow underneath her just a fraction more.

"How bad?" he asked, breathless from her kiss.

"*How bad?*" she looked confused.

"How bad do you want me in here?" His hand snaked down her soft stomach and cupped her between her legs. "How bad do you *need* me here?" It was instinct for him to slide his fingers through her heated moisture as he waited for her reply. "How bad do you need me to fuck you, Gracie?" Without warning he pushed his fingers forward and buried them as far as they would go. "Bad enough to come for me first?"

"Oh, God! Yes!" Her lithe body thrashed on the bed as if she were standing on the precipice of something epic. "Make me come," she demanded, locking her eyes with his.

"My pleasure." As he said it, Cole hooked two fingers to hit the perfect spot that would have her doing backflips over the edge. "That's it, I want it all." Damn he loved this. Loved making a mental tape of her in the throes of passion. Loved hearing the noises that escaped her lips when the full force of her release slammed into her. But most of all, he just plain loved being with her. It didn't have to be sex. It didn't even have to be intimate at all. It just had to be him and her in the same room. She'd always had that effect on him.

Gracie couldn't understand how one man could own her like Cole did. No, he wasn't some master who ordered her around or made her do things she didn't want to. When she was with him, she'd do anything he'd asked of her. Wasn't that just stupid? She'd spent so many years telling herself that Cole was a good for nothing piece of garbage but in reality, she was the piece of shit. She'd taken so much from him, yet he was willing to fight to the ends of the earth for her. What a slap in the face it was to know that. But what choice did she have? Dash was in trouble and if she didn't get those papers signed soon, she would be too. It was her responsibility to protect those she loved. She had to, no one else would. It made what they were getting ready to do that much harder. Cole wanted another shot at this. He wanted them to be a family but it *couldn't* happen. There was no future that included her, him and their daughter. Yeah, it was another shitty thing she'd have to do, but in the end, it would protect them all.

"I've lost you again." He loomed above her and brushed the sweat-soaked hair from her face. The look on his own face had her turning her head away. He cared. She didn't want him to care. She wanted him to hate her, to push her away and tell her what a terrible human being she was. This look on his face, though, made her want to reciprocate his feelings.

"Cole, I..." before she could finish her thought, he managed to slowly slide himself inside her body. Each inch felt as though he were trying to convey some deeper meaning than just the act of sex. Her eyes fluttered closed as he seated himself in the gentlest manner she'd ever felt from him. Sure, she adored the rough side of things with him but this? This was altogether different.

"You *what*?" He placed both hands at the sides of her face, moving them so she'd look directly at him.

With her eyes slowly opening, Gracie looked into his and said, "I love you." *Oh no!* She shouldn't have said *that*! What in the hell was she thinking? Before she could open her mouth to take it back, Cole slammed his lips on hers and began to kiss her senseless. As he did, his hips began to rock more vigorously, his cock nudging a spot that had her entire body quaking. How was she supposed to think straight with him taking her to so many familiar places? She should push him away, cover her naked form and tell him what was once a blistering passion between them was now nothing but a fizzled out spark that could never be fully ignited again. So why was she still lying there with him inside her body? Why did her brain misfire every fucking time she tried to say something…*anything*?

"You don't know how long I've waited to hear you say that again, Gracie," Cole said as he reached down and grabbed one of her wrists, extending it above her head on the soft mattress. He then reached for the other and soon she was pinned down. No, she never felt like she was in danger and Cole wasn't some dominant who exerted some sort of sexual supremacy over her. This was just him loving her like only he could do. "Every day for the past 13 years I've wanted to have you here telling me that." Gracie moaned loudly as he plunged back into her throbbing channel. "I could die right now and be a happy man. I hope you know that." Again and again he assaulted her with his lovemaking. "Tell me you'll stay here and build a life with me. Tell me it isn't too late to do this." Each word was punctuated with a thrust of his hips and a gentle grinding motion that kept her on the brink of release without tipping her over. "I've never wanted anything as bad as I've wanted you back in my life, Gracie. I would give up every fucking thing I have just to get the chance to make us work. Tell me you don't feel the same way and I'll walk away."

She opened her mouth but nothing came out. Did she care for him? Of course she did. They shared a history together and a child, how could she not have some sort of sentimentality toward the man above her right now? But even so, she wasn't willing to risk the lives that hung in the balance for a hopeless future with him. She'd spent too many years being selfish and it was time to pay the piper. There was no way in hell she'd let Dash pay for her mistakes. He deserved better than that.

"Baby, I need you to look at me," Cole spoke and pulled her out of the mess tangled inside her head like fishing twine on a weeping willow branch. This wouldn't get sorted out tonight but as long as she kept her mouth shut, she could avoid any backlash until she distanced herself from Cole. That meant she'd have to keep up this idiotic ruse until her and Cora's feet were firmly planted back in Chicago. Then she could breathe a sigh of relief.

She snapped her gaze to his. "I'm here," she whispered.

"The only place I want you to be when I'm inside you, is right here with me," Cole reminded her by snaking a hand between their bodies and pinching her clit, bringing her one step closer to the orgasm she craved. "I want to know that each time I slide my cock inside you, you're right here with me."

"*Mmmmm.*" Arching her back she groaned.

"That's it. I want to hear every fucking sound you make when I tell you how good you feel all wrapped around me."

"More," Gracie demanded.

"More? You want more of this?" He thrust forward, her body slipping up the bed just a fraction more. "How much more do you want?" She could tell he was gritting his teeth with every plunge he made.

"All of it." She thrashed her head to the side, the scent of sex permeating the air around them like a fog of hardcore sexual evidence. If this was exhibit A, she was guilty as sin in this case. The sweet smell of Cole's sweat from his exertion, the ragged breaths from each of their chests and the tingling sensations that crept from the tips of her toes to her damn hair follicles pretty well stacked the deck against them. Any jury would come back with a guilty verdict and she wouldn't blame them one fucking bit. There wasn't an air of embarrassment for the animalistic sounds coming from the room. Why should there be? What he did to her body and the heights he took her were things to be proud of. No man could ever manipulate her senses such as this. No other man could wrap her around his little finger or twist her heart in such a way that it resembled vines of ivy creeping up a stone wall. This was pure unadulterated bliss at its finest.

"Almost there," Gracie clenched her jaw as the words grated past her teeth.

"Give it to me. Come all over me," Cole urged her on with his crass bedroom lingo as he inflicted punishing strokes inside her channel. She didn't doubt her inner thighs would be bruised in the morning with the way he was determined to extract a grand orgasm from her.

The way his voice found its way into her brain cells was the ultimate aphrodisiac. All he had to do was speak and her body flew apart like a dandelion puff in a slight breeze. "I'm there!" She dug her fingernails into the flesh on his back as her sex tightened around his erection—still pounding inside her depths.

As the waves of tingling sensation began to subside, Gracie watched in awe as Cole worked his way toward his own release. It was brilliant watching him use her body in the manner he was. All she could do was move with him to make sure he came with as much fervor as she had. And of course he did. After a few more deep strokes, Cole quickly pulled himself from her opening and began stroking his length with one hand. No, that wouldn't do. If anyone was going to make him come, it would be her. Sitting up, Gracie grabbed his shaft and began caressing him from base to swollen tip. Her mouth watered for the taste of his essence as she witnessed it slowly seeping from him. She licked her lips and leant forward, gliding her tongue up the underside of him. She could taste herself mixed with his flavor as she became more brazen and engulfed all of him until he hit the back of her throat. Strangled moans sounded from above her, letting her know he was more than pleased with what was transpiring.

"Baby, I'm so close." One of his hands dove into her

hair and began pulling at the roots. "Make me come in that sexy mouth of yours." That's exactly what she wanted so she put more gusto into her actions. "Fuck yeah. I'm gonna come so hard for you." The more he spurred her on, the more she wished he was on top of her again, getting ready to come deep in her body. But she'd already had her fun, it was his turn. She could tell when it was time for him to fall apart and right now, it was time. "Ready?" he grunted. All she could do was nod as he began to furiously fuck her mouth. "Goddamn it!" he roared as she felt the first bit of salty warmth hit her tongue. Female satisfaction swamped her with each stroke she made with her mouth. Yeah, this was what she craved when it came to Cole. He didn't hold anything back. He was all male and made zero excuses for it. But soon, it was all coming to an end as he gently pulled himself from her mouth and sat in front of her on the willowy mattress. Gracie swiped the back of her hand across her mouth and tucked her hair behind her ears.

"Why do you do that?" Cole asked.

"Do what?" Her head cocked to the side in question.

"Why do you act embarrassed after sex?"

Well that wasn't exactly the question she'd expected. "I don't know. Maybe because it's really intimate."

"You don't say." He chuckled then leaned forward to kiss her—Gracie pulling away right before their lips connected. "Don't pull away."

"I didn't think you'd want to kiss me after what we just did."

Cole reached around her and placed his hand on the back of her head. "That actually makes me want to kiss you even more. Believe it or not, I like the taste of us together." Before she could even make sense of that statement, Cole had his mouth on hers sweeping his tongue around hers in a dance of genuine ecstasy.

She was right; this man was going to fucking break her.

⤳ Chapter Twenty-One ⤳

COLE SAT AT THE KITCHEN table gripping the handle of his coffee cup like the damn thing would sprout legs and walk away if he didn't hold on tight enough. His gaze stayed glued to the sliding glass doors that led into the backyard as he replayed every iota of what'd happened last night, just down the hallway in his bedroom. No, he couldn't have imagined Gracie blurting out that she loved him...could he? Was it his hormone laden grey matter that caused him to think up something as ludicrous as that? Or *had* it happened and he now sat here wondering if what she'd said had true meaning behind it. If he knew one thing, it was that human beings tended to say things just to get what they wanted. They lied and cheated so they could feel better about themselves and most of the time they didn't give two shits if they hurt anyone in the process.

"Morning," he heard her softly say as she stepped barefoot into the kitchen.

Damn she was gorgeous. "Morning." He smiled to himself while taking a sip of the lukewarm coffee in his hands. The red-haired vixen had on one of his t-shirts. Yeah, that was sexy as fuck with her bare legs peeking out from underneath the hem of the worn cotton garment and the way her breasts pressed against the FBI logo on her chest. If she didn't hurry up and sit down, Cole couldn't be sure he wouldn't tackle her to the floor and give her a morning she'd never forget.

"What?" Gracie asked as she finally slid into the chair across from him.

Cole's head snapped up. "Huh?" Jeez, this woman made his normally smart brain turn to soggy toilet paper with just one damn word.

"You were gawking at me."

He leaned back in his chair. "Just taking in the view."

A chuckle made its way from his chest.

"Not much of a view." Her sweet laugh had his dick ready to do double back flips.

"That's *your* opinion." Sitting his mug down he grabbed his phone. "I happen to think you look damn hot this morning." Without warning he snapped a quick picture of her.

"Don't you *dare* show that to anyone!" She lunged forward and tried to snatch the device from his hand but failed.

"Maybe I will and maybe I won't," he snickered. "Maybe I'll masturbate to it later."

"You've lost your damn mind." She grabbed her cup and lifted it to her lips. Lips that were still puffy from the many kisses he'd managed to give her last night.

"I'm perfectly sane. And you, Gracie Matthews are a gorgeous specimen of a woman." Reaching out he grabbed her hand and began to smooth circles with his thumb over the back.

"Why did you call me that?" He felt her trying to yank her hand away.

"What? *Gracie Matthews*? That's your name."

"No, it's not, Cole." She looked on the verge of punching him.

"We're *still* married."

"I know but I go by my maiden name."

"Jesus Christ, Gracie. Does every fucking thing have to end in an argument?"

"No, it doesn't," she said quietly.

"Good." He stood and took his empty cup to the sink. "I've gotta get to work. I'll be home later."

She didn't respond but he knew she was upset. Well, newsflash, so was he. Damn it, they were still married and she'd taken on his last name 13 years ago. Whatever, it didn't really matter. She'd get happy in the same pants—or panties—she'd gotten mad in.

"I'm sorry." As he looped his tie around his collar he heard her voice behind him in the bedroom.

"Nothing to be sorry about." He fiddled with the damn tie and couldn't get it to form a good knot.

"Let me help you with that." Gracie batted his hands away and began to fix the mess he'd made out of it.

"Thanks."

"I would've never thought in a million years you'd become what you are today, Cole."

"Neither did I."

"It suits you though. You were always so athletic and ready to take on the world. I'm proud of you," she finished and smoothed out the material.

"Can I ask you something?"

"Sure." Taking a seat on the end of the bed she looked up at him.

"Why are you really here?"

"You know why. I need you to sign the papers." She shrugged like it was just another day in paradise for her.

"Yeah, but you could've contacted me anytime. Why *now*?"

"I'm ready to move on with my life." She began picking at a piece of invisible lint on her shirt.

"Do you honestly think I'm *that* stupid? After all this time you fly in and have such urgency about this. Something is going on and I need to know what the hell it is." His voice rose as he moved closer to her.

"Nothing is going on!"

"Bull-fucking-shit."

"Even if something *was* going on, it's none of your damn business."

"I'm *making* it my business. If you need help, I'm more than happy to help you, Gracie. But you need to be straight with me. I can't sit here and guess what's going on."

"Like I said, there's *nothing* going on."

"Fine." He grabbed his shoulder holster and swung it around his body. Once he had his Glock secure he turned back to her. "If you change your mind about being honest with me, you know where to find me." Then he walked out of the room.

All signs led to trouble and Cole was determined to figure out what that trouble was. Not only did he have Gracie to worry about, he had Cora too. If they were in some deep shit, he'd go to the ends of the earth to protect them. How fucked up love really was.

Gracie knew Cole was smarter than she'd ever given him credit for. She wouldn't doubt he'd been digging around in her past already. That's just who he was. If that was the case though, she needed to speed things up when it came to him signing the divorce papers. If he uncovered the truth behind why she was so insistent about it, he'd balk and try to fix things for her. She didn't need him rushing in to save the day. If she'd learned anything in the past 13 years, it was the fact that heroes didn't exist. If you wanted something, it was up to you to get it. She'd relied on no one but herself and this predicament was no different. Did she still have feelings for Cole? Of course. They shared so much history and then there was also Cora, their daughter. It was still strange to think of him as a father figure though. Cole never seemed like the type of guy to settle down and take on such a responsibility but here they were trying to figure this thing out together.

"Hi, Gracie," Ava called as she stepped through the doors of the small salon.

"Hey. Where's Cora?" Gracie glanced around the

shop trying to locate her daughter.

"In the back. I put her to work folding towels."

She began to breathe a sigh of relief. When Cora wasn't with her, she would panic. She'd never forgive herself if something happened to her.

"Ava, can I talk to you in private?" Gracie asked and immediately regretted it. She wasn't one for 'girl talk' usually. If there was a problem she found the solution on her own.

"Absolutely. What's on your mind?" Ava motioned to the worn sofa in the waiting area.

Gracie took a seat and began wringing her hand in her lap nervously. "I said something to Cole last night in the," she lowered her voice, "heat of the moment." She looked around to make sure Cora wasn't eavesdropping.

"Oh."

"Yeah. What's crazy is when I said it, it didn't feel as foreign as it probably should have." She let out a sigh and let her shoulders slump slightly.

"The two of you have a past together. Something like that is more than likely familiar."

"I don't doubt that but this will never work. I just don't know how to get that fact through his thick skull."

Ava laughed. "Sorry, you're right. Cole has one of the thickest skulls I've ever seen. Well, besides Luke." Gracie watched the other woman become moony as she spoke of her fiancé. "Cole pretends to be this rough and tough asshole but it's fairly easy to see right through him. But can I tell you something and please don't take offense to this."

"Sure."

"If you don't want to have a future with him, please walk away. He might play a tough guy but that man loves you so much, Gracie. If you string him along, you'll break him."

How was she *not* supposed to take offense to that? "I'm not stringing him along. All I wanted was for him to sign the papers. Had he done that, I could be back in Chicago already."

"I think deep down you know that's a bunch of bullshit. You could've mailed the papers to him. There was no reason to come all the way down here. Not to mention Cora. I also think you somehow wanted her to find out he was her father."

"*What?*" Gracie shot up off the couch at the sound of her daughters' voice.

"Hey, there."

"Mom, what's she talking about?" Cora's eyes began to fill with tears as she wrapped her arms around her midsection.

"Honey, we were just talking." Gracie stepped toward her but Cora began to walk backwards like a wild animal that'd been cornered.

"I heard *everything.*" The tears poured down the teen's face. "Is it true? Is Cole my...*dad?*" She furiously swiped at her face.

"Can we talk about this later?" Gracie tried to reach out and pull the girl in to a hug but she wasn't having any of it.

"No! Is it true? Just tell me, mom!" she screamed, stomping her foot.

Gracie looked back to Ava for support but in all reality she'd dug herself into this hole and it was time to get the hell out of it. She dropped her head—her own eyes welling up with unshed tears. When she finally looked her daughter in the eye once more, she opened her mouth and said, "Yes. He's your father."

"I. Hate. You!" Cora screamed and took off toward the back of the salon.

Gracie knew she needed space but it was hard not running after her. She began to step in that direction but felt a hand on her arm.

"Give her a bit," Ava suggested.

"She'll never forgive me." Gracie shook her head.

"She will. What she needs right now is some space. Let her work this all out in her head, okay?

"I should've never come down here." Gracie plopped down on the sofa once more and buried her tear-covered face in her hands. "This is all my fault."

Ava tried to comfort her but it was no use. As they sat there for a few minutes Ava's head shot up at the sound of a loud bang at the back of the shop.

"What was that?" Gracie stood quickly.

"The back door." Ava began jogging back there with

Gracie hot on her heels. When they arrived in the small back room that held the washing machine and dryer, Gracie glanced at the back door.

"Cora?" she called out.

Ava wrenched open the large steel door and stuck her head out. "Damn it."

"Where is she?" Gracie asked.

"Call Cole. Tell him Cora's ran away." Ava yelled as she headed back into the salon.

Gracie's fingers shook as she worked to find Cole's cell number on the speed dial of her phone. Tears clouded her vision as she scrolled through the numerous numbers and finally found his. She tapped the button and tried to hold her voice steady as she waited painfully through each ring on the other end. What kind of mother was she? She'd just revealed to her daughter that Cole was indeed her father. What was supposed to be a quick trip to get his signature had turned into a cluster fuck of epic proportions.

Cole sat at his desk staring blankly at the monitor on his computer. How could loving someone hurt so badly? How could one moment feel as if you wanted to sing Disney songs while spinning around in a flowered meadow and the next you felt as if someone were driving railroad spikes through your chest? Was this how love was supposed to be? Was it equal parts paradise *and* torture? He'd give anything right now to know how to get through this situation and not be hurt in the end but it didn't appear it would happen anytime soon. Swiping a hand over his face he decided the best course of action was to give Gracie an ultimatum. Either she stayed here in Mississippi and tried to be a family or he would demand that Cora have to live in the same state as him. Was it the asshole thing to do? Of course. But there was no other way for him to be a part of his daughters' life. Clearly Gracie wasn't budging on wanting his signature on those divorce papers so this was the path he'd take.

"You're phone's ringing." Luke tossed an ink pen across the room, it landing on his desk.

Cole picked up his phone and flipped it over to see

Gracie was the one calling. Letting out a sigh he answered it. "Gracie?"

"Cole, I need your help." Her voice was extremely shaky and filled with uneasiness.

"What's wrong?" Cole stood and began to pace the floor around his desk while listening to her explain.

"Cora overheard me talking about you being her father. We were at the salon with Ava and Cora ran away." Sobbing began and he raked a hand through his hair and yanked on the ends.

"Where is she?" he bit out.

"I don't know! She took off out the back door and we've looked everywhere. We can't find her."

"Stay put. I'm on my way." He hung up and looked at Luke. "Cora is missing."

"Let's go." Luke didn't ask questions, for which Cole was thankful.

Fear slid through his veins like ice water as he ran to his truck and hopped in. Luke didn't say much as the tires of the vehicle squealed on the pavement while he pulled the trunk onto the street.

"We'll find her." Luke tried to soothe his worry but right now the only thing that would do that was seeing his daughter's face.

Is this what it was like to be a parent? To be utterly terrified when something happened to your kid? To be filled with so much worry and to dream up the worst case scenario? "Damn right we will." Ignoring the speed limit he drove to Ava's salon and whipped the truck into a parking space near the front door. Gracie was out front with tears streaming down her face.

"Which direction did she go?" Cole—being all business now—asked.

"Out the back door," Gracie tearfully answered.

He ran through the building and out the back door. Looking both ways he panicked when he couldn't decide which direction the kid could've gone. Each moment he stood there felt like hours. "What's that?" Luke came up behind him and pointed toward something about fifty yards away. The sunlight glinted off the object like a flashing neon sign telling them where Cora had run off to.

Cole quickly jogged over and crouched down to pick up the small rectangle. "It's her phone. She must've come this way. Keep Gracie and Ava here just in case she comes back." Nothing else was said as he barked orders and began running down the alley that ran along the back side of the small strip mall. He had to find her. If not for her mom, then at least for him. Even though he'd only found out about Cora being his just recently, he'd go to hell and back to make sure she was found safe and sound. But where the hell could she've gone? She didn't really know the area well and she didn't know anyone except for him, Luke and Ava and her mom. That didn't leave many options since all of those people were at the salon.

Stopping for a moment to think, Cole thought back to the places Cora really loved while she'd been here. The salon. His house… "Fuck." He cursed as he took off running back to the shop. When he busted through the back door all three sets of eyes were on him like laser beams.

"Did you find her?" Gracie asked.

"No, but I think I know where she's headed."

"I'm coming with you." She tried to trail him but he stopped and put his hand up.

"No. You've done enough for one day. Keep your ass here just in case she comes back." Sure it was a harsh thing to say but she wasn't on his list of priorities for the moment. His main concern was to find Cora.

He settled himself in his truck once more and took off down the highway toward Luke and Ava's house. Cora loved it there and if he was a betting man, he'd put all his chips on the fact that the teen was going in that direction. At least he hoped she was.

With the house being around 10 miles from town she'd most likely be about halfway there he estimated in his head. If his phone would stop ringing like crazy he could maybe think for five fucking seconds. Reaching over he grabbed it and hit the button to silence the ringer. Once the device was tossed back into the cup holder he snapped his head up to look at the road. Sure enough he recognized the scrawny teen walking in the direction of Luke's house. Slowing his speed he pulled alongside of her and noticed she was crying. "Need a lift?" he rolled down the passenger side window and asked.

"No."

"Get in the truck, Cora." He tried for his best stern dad voice.

"Just leave me alone."

"Can't do that."

"Why? Because you're my dad?" She finally turned to face him and the heartbreak on her face was gut-wrenching.

"That's probably part of it. Just get in. We need to talk."

"Fine." She huffed and yanked open the door.

"You're as stubborn as your mom." Okay so maybe a little humor would get to her.

"I hate my mom." She crossed her arms over her chest and stared out the window.

"I don't think you mean that. She's been pretty damn good to you."

"She could've told me about you. I had to grow up not knowing about you."

"Same here, kid. I didn't know about you either. But now I do."

"What happens now?" She turned in her seat and looked at him. Yeah, he could see the resemblance to him now. Damn, she looked like a female version of him when he was her age.

"Not really sure. But I do know one thing. Running away isn't the answer. And can I tell you something else?" he asked.

"Sure."

"If you *ever* take off like that again, I will make sure you're grounded until you're 80-years-old. Got it?"

"Okay," she whispered.

"Now, we're gonna go back to the salon. I want you to apologize to everyone for scaring the living shit out of them. Then you and I have some errands to run."

"Like what?"

"Just some stuff." He didn't want to tell her that the errand was actually going shopping for her birthday party this coming weekend just yet. She needed to feel a little bit of guilt for what she'd put everyone thorough first.

Silence stretched until they were almost in the center of town again until Cora finally spoke, "I'm kinda glad it's you."

"What?" he asked.

"If it was gonna be anyone, I'm glad *you're* my dad."

Oh holy hell. Men weren't supposed to break down and cry but right now he wanted to sit there and bawl like a kid who had their candy taken away. Yeah, there were going to be some tough times on the horizon, but he was glad she was his too.

Chapter Twenty-Two

"WHAT ARE WE DOING here?" Cora asked as Cole pulled into the parking lot of the local Party City store.

He shut the engine off and turned to face her. "Shopping for party supplies. Your birthday is this weekend, remember?"

The young girl looked at the front of the store and back to him. "I know. But mom said we would just have a party when we got back home."

"She's more than welcome to do that but I'm having a party for you here too. Come on." He snatched the keys from the ignition and hopped down.

"You really don't have to do this." Cora began

chewing on her thumbnail.

Cole turned around and pinned her with his best '*Dad Stare*'. "I'm new at this crap so I may be off base here. I'd like to throw you a birthday party, would that be okay?" Maybe taking this route with her would cause her to get on board with the party idea.

"You really suck at this parent thing." Cora laughed.

Relief washed over him as her face shone with a smile that was reminiscent of her mother's. "Yeah, I do. How about we keep the shitty parenting thing to ourselves?" All he needed was for Gracie to not trust him with their kid. Then she'd be on a flight back to Chicago and never see his daughter again.

"Deal." She held out her hand for him to shake.

"I have no earthly idea what girls your age like so let's go in here and find some supplies." He reached into his back pocket for his wallet and flipped it open. Thumbing through the bills he then closed it. "I'll give you a $500 limit. Sound good?"

"Wow, that's a lot of money!"

"*Too* much?" He cringed.

"Nope, just enough." She giggled and then took off walking ahead of him.

Gracie was going to have his ass for this little stunt, he'd bet everything in his bank account on it. But he'd be damned if he would let his daughter go without an actual party on her birthday.

"I like the color black." Cora reached for some solid black plates and cups on a nearby shelf.

"Don't you think that's a little morbid for a birthday?" Cole scratched his head. "How about pink?" Grabbing the paper dinnerware from her hands he replaced it with some that was bright fuchsia.

"Uh no. That's not happening." She then tore the items from his hands and threw them back on the shelf.

"Fine." They walked further down the aisle and looked some more.

"I've got it!" she shouted as she stopped in front of some themed supplies. "This!"

"No way, no how. That's *not* happening, Cora."

"It's *my* birthday and you said I could get what I wanted." She crossed her arms over her chest and stared him down. "I want this."

"Well I'm the one with the money and I said no," he countered.

"Then I don't want a stupid party," she said and stomped off.

Cole looked up and blew out a breath. "Please give me strength." Of all the things she could've chosen, she picked *The Walking Dead* theme. What kind of 13-year-old wanted a bloody zombie themed party? "Hey, wait up." He finally caught up to her. "If that's the theme you want, then we'll do it."

"Really?" She acted shocked. "Will you dress up like Daryl?"

"Do I even want to know who or what Daryl is?"

"Trust me, it will be awesome!" She clapped her hands and went back in the direction of the party supplies.

As he followed her, Cole's phone began ringing. "Yeah?" he answered.

"You're a hard man to get ahold of, Mr. Matthews," the man on the other end said.

"Well, you've got me. What can I do for you, Mister?"

"The name's Judge Woodard."

As he stood there, recognition swamped him. This was the federal judge in the case file he'd been handed the other day. Why in the hell was this guy calling? "What's this regarding, Mr. Woodard?" Cole watched Cora toss a bunch of items in the shopping cart while he listened to Judge Woodard.

"Are you familiar with a Damon *'Dash'* Hunter, Mr. Matthews?"

"I've heard of him."

"I'm sure you have since you're married to his sister."

"What does this have to do with me?"

"I'm not into making threats, Mr. Matthews but I believe this situation warrants one."

"Why don't you just cut to the fucking chase instead of hem-hawing around?"

"Sign the divorce papers, Mr. Matthews. Or things will get really bad for Mr. Hunter *and* Ms. Callahan." Then he hung up.

"What the fuck?"

"You're not supposed to say that around kids." Cora laughed as she wheeled a packed cart up to him.

Cole wanted to joke with her but something was going on and his instincts told him it was worse than the scenario he'd planted in his own head. Who the hell was this Woodard guy and why was he making threats like that?

"Got everything you need?" he asked Cora.

"Yep. I'm ready." She pushed past him with the blue cart and went straight for the checkout lanes.

Once he paid the $340 total he grabbed the plastic bags of supplies and led Cora back to the truck. It was time to iron this shit out with Gracie and figure out just why he was now tangled up in this fat fucking mess.

"Hey mom."

Gracie smiled as her daughter bounded out of the truck in front of Cole's house. "Hey, there. Did you guys have fun shopping?" She pulled her in for a bear hug, Cora gasping for air.

"Yeah." The young girl shrugged.

"Here." Cole brought two arm loads of bags to her and sat them at her feet.

"Cole, I said a few things. Not the entire store," she huffed.

He stepped closer and grabbed both sides of her face, "And I told you not to worry about it." Leaning down, he placed a soft kiss on her lips. "Didn't I?"

"Yes, but…"

"No arguing. Let's get this shit inside."

Damn him and his featherlight kisses and suave demeanor. The asshole used it to his advantage way too often. But the strange thing was, Cora was standing right there and saw him kiss her. Why didn't she say something? She at the very least expected her daughter to make some kind of exaggerated gagging noise.

"I've gotta run back to the office for a bit, you two gonna be okay here?" Cole asked.

"Of course we will." Gracie smiled. Why the heck *wouldn't* she be okay there?

"If you need anything, call me. Okay?" Cole had a

worried look on his handsome face.

"Okay." She grabbed the sleeve of his shirt as he headed for the front door. "Is everything okay?"

"Yeah." Cole pulled her to his chest, letting her feel his warmth as she laid her head on his chest. "Just…be careful." Once he released her, he was gone; leaving her wondering what the hell was going on.

She'd known Cole forever and his behavior wasn't exactly normal, even for him. There was one way to figure out what was going on with him and that was to ask Cora. Maybe something happened when they were out. If that was the case, Cora would spill the beans.

Gracie waved goodbye to the broody man and made her way inside the house. Her path through the living room was blocked by a massive amount of packages hidden behind cellophane. Holy shit, it looked like a party store blew up in there. Cora sat amongst the plethora of items, picking each one up and smiling to herself. It'd been a while since she'd seen her daughter so full of joy. What a refreshing thing to witness. Deciding not to approach the subject of Cole just yet, she took a seat on the sofa and just observed. After a few minutes Cora finally looked up and noticed her.

"Mom, you're hovering," she said as she rolled her eyes.

"No, I'm not."

"Uh yeah, you are. You have that look again."

"What look?" Gracie cocked her head to the side in curiosity.

"The one that says you're about to have some sort of heart-to-heart with me." Cora dropped a package of what looked like plastic chain and stood. "What is it?"

"Okay maybe I *do* want to talk." She patted the cushion next to her. "Have a seat."

"Am I in trouble?"

"Well, I'm not happy about you running away today. Cora, something terrible could've happened to you. What if we couldn't find you and you went without your medicine?" The young girl shrugged. "Look, I don't want to sit here and scream at you for what you did, you know it was wrong. But I do need to know how you feel about what you heard." Nervousness took root in her stomach as she waited for her daughter to speak.

"I guess it's okay. I mean, I like him and all."

"I know you're upset with me about keeping it a secret but I was so young and didn't know what to do."

"Mom, I'm not a kid anymore. You don't have to protect me."

"Yes, I do. I'll always want to protect you, you're my daughter."

Cora looked away for a few seconds and then back at her mom. "Are we moving to Mississippi?" she asked quietly.

Gracie blew out a breath, "I don't know." She really did know. There was no way in hell she was moving here. Cole could make some sort of arrangements if he wanted to spend time with his daughter.

"He's not so bad, ya know." Cora smiled a glimmering grin that had Gracie wanting to do backflips.

Wait? Why was it so important that Cora liked him? It wasn't like they would be together in the future. "I'm glad you like him."

"He likes you, too. I'm not stupid; I know you guys

are a thing."

"We are not a thing." Gracie laughed.

"Why not?"

"I don't think this is something I need to discuss with you."

"Ugh, fine." Cora went back to the floor and began riffling through the party supplies again.

"Did something happen while you and Cole were out today?"

"Like what?"

"I don't know. It just seemed like he was upset when you two came home."

She watched her think for a bit while biting her lip. "Some guy called him. He was pretty cranky when he hung up."

"Do you know who called him?"

"Yeah. I heard him say Mr. Woodard."

Gracie's entire body froze as if someone were running ice water through her veins. She'd done everything she could to keep this from happening and yet, it was all falling down around her now. If Spencer Woodard was calling Cole, things were about to get a whole lot worse for Dash.

"Mom?" Cora spoke and pulled her away from her inner turmoil briefly. "You okay?"

Gracie stood and snatched her phone off the end table, "Yeah, everything is fine. I have to make a call. Be back in a few." She headed for the sliding glass doors at the back of the house while scrolling through her contact list on the small touchscreen. Each time she even thought about having to talk to Spencer, bile would rise in her throat and she'd begin feeling more than a little bit ill. She'd done the best she could for her life and Cora's but mistakes were inevitable.

Once she had the glass doors secured, she stepped onto the grass in the back yard and tapped the screen of her phone. Ugh, even looking at his name made her want to lose everything she'd eaten in the last 6 months. Putting the device to her ear she waited for the ringing to begin. When it did, the first ring caused her to damn near jump out of her skin. The second and third weren't as bad, but when Spencer picked up on the forth, she had enough dread weighing her down that it could easily sink her to the bottom of the deepest crevice in the Gulf of Mexico.

"Gracie." His voice was like a cat scratching on a chalkboard.

"Spencer," she replied with minimal confidence in her voice.

"Seems we have a problem, don't we?"

"I told you I'd take care of things. You didn't have to call Cole."

"You're right. I didn't *have* to call him. But I did because you weren't holding up your end of the bargain."

"I've done everything you've asked me to!" she shouted.

"You've done nothing that I've asked. The papers aren't signed, are they?"

"Not yet." Gracie rubbed her forehead with her free hand. The humidity and anxiety were taking a toll on her. "I need more time."

There was silence on the other end for what seemed

like minutes. When in fact, only a few seconds had ticked by. "Listen up, I'm only going to say this once. Your brother is safe, for now, but I can't guarantee how long he'll stay like that. You know how far my reach is, doll face, and I think you know better than to fuck with me. Get that dick wad to sign the fucking divorce papers and I'll make sure Dash comes out of that prison in one piece. But keep trying me and I'll make sure the only way he leaves those gates is in a body bag. Do I make myself clear?"

Tears began to streak down her face as she thought of her brother. She could be the reason he'd take his last breath and that fact killed her inside. "Yes," she whispered into the phone.

"I miss you," Spencer added.

How was she supposed to react to that? She sure as fuck didn't miss him. But once those papers were signed, she'd be spending a lot more time with him. Gracie wasn't sure she was prepared for that yet. Nothing could really prepare you for someone you loathed with every fiber of your being. But this would protect Dash and hopefully help draw down the debt from Cora's medical bills. It wasn't cheap visiting a doctor every few weeks for Cora's diabetes. Sometimes as a mother you had to sacrifice your own happiness to make sure your children were taken care of.

Chapter Twenty-Three

COLE SAT AT HIS DESK staring at his computer monitor. What in the hell did Gracie get herself mixed up in? She was a smart woman so everything he was figuring out didn't seem like something she'd be involved in. Spencer Woodard was a federal judge in Cook County. There were rumors that he was as crooked as a coat hanger but nothing had been proven. There were always those who tended to abuse their power once they'd gotten it. From what Cole had dug up so far, all signs pointed to Woodard's hands being exceptionally dirty. The man had several companies that looked to be a front for something more. What that '*more*' was, Cole couldn't figure out.

"The wheels are turning so quick, I can smell something burning." Luke strode into the office with a coffee cup in hand.

"Not in the mood for your bullshit, Daughtry," he grumbled.

"Whoa, who fucked you in the ass without lube?"

"Ha Ha. Very funny." Cole shot him an annoyed look.

"Damn, you're in a piss ass mood. Anything I can do to ease your bitchy-ness?"

Cole didn't answer him. Sometimes it was necessary to ignore Luke. When you did there was a chance he would go away and stop bothering you.

"Someone needs to get laid." Luke chuckled from across the room.

Cole abruptly stood from his desk and bounded across the room. His strides eating up the tacky ass carpet as he went. Once in front of Luke's desk he slammed his palms down and leaned forward. "Look motherfucker. I told you I wasn't in the mood for your shit. Clearly you don't know what that means. Do I need to beat the meaning into that metro sexual beard you've got going on?"

Luke reached up and ran a hand over his beard. "You don't like my beard?"

Cole stood up straight and blew out a breath. "I swear the next OP we go on, I'm aiming my rifle at you."

Luke placed his hands on his chest. "That hurts my heart, man."

After a few minutes of silence, Cole finally apologized to his partner. "I'm sorry. This shit with Gracie has me so messed up."

"What's going on now?"

Cole motioned him over to his desk and began giving him the run down on the whole Judge Woodard thing. Luke—as usual—stayed stoic throughout the entire thing. He and Cole were quite different when it came to shit like this. Luke was so calm—almost scary calm. But Cole? He was a damn kamikaze in situations such as these. He was a *'shoot first, ask questions later'* kind of guy.

"Not sure how you manage to get yourself covered in so much muck."

"Me neither."

Luke lowered his voice, "you shouldn't be looking into this around here though. If this guy does have his hands in the cookie jar, you don't want it to come back on you."

"I can't exactly access the database from my iPad."

"No, but your little hacker friend can."

"I don't want her taking the fall for shit like this either."

"Then you'd better figure out how to find what you need somewhere else. This really isn't the place to be fucking around the files of a federal judge." Luke shot him a serious look. "And the number one thing you need to do is talk to Gracie. Have you ever come straight out and asked her about any of this? Or did you jump in and play Inspector Gadget from the get-go?"

"I didn't talk to her," he admitted.

"Then do it."

"You're right. I fucking hate when you're right."

"I have many talents. Being right all the time is one of them."

"Yeah, sure. How does Ava feel about you being right all the time?"

"She's still in the *Luke's Always Right Training Program*. But give it time, she'll be on board soon."

Cole pecked around on his keyboard for a few more minutes and then stood. He grabbed his gun and badge from the desk drawer. "Hey, we're having a birthday party for Cora this weekend. Hope you and Ava can make it."

"Wouldn't miss it. Need us to bring anything?"

"Nah, we have the food covered. But she wanted this crazy ass birthday theme…"

"I'm not coming dressed as a fucking Disney Princess."

"No, it's The Walking Dead."

"Really? She's into that shit?"

"Apparently so. She wants me to dress as some dude named Daryl."

Luke began laughing uncontrollably. "That is classic!"

"Whatever. I'm out of here. Just be at my place around four on Saturday."

One of these days he'd get a chance to turn the tables on his partner. But for now, he was at least thankful he *had* a partner.

Pulling his truck in the driveway, Cole turned the key to the off position and sat there staring at his front door. It was strange to be equal parts excited about seeing the people behind that door and filled with trepidation. This thing with Gracie had to be unraveled and soon. If he was going to risk his job for this shit, he wanted full disclosure. If she wasn't willing to give him that, there was nothing he could do to help her. Would he go to bat for her no matter what? More than likely. But there was a difference between choosing a Louisville Slugger, and stepping up to the plate with only a broom handle to swing. He was smart enough to walk into something with both eyes open.

Taking a deep breath, Cole finally flung open the door and began walking up to his house. Lately it didn't seem like just his house though. Gracie and Cora had come in and turned his former bachelor pad into what resembled a *real* family home. That fact didn't scare the shit out of him anymore though. He smiled at the thought of maybe finding something bigger for the three of them. Something with a huge backyard and maybe a dog. Would Gracie want more kids in the future? Hell, he wouldn't mind it. Missing out on Cora's birth set a sour note in his gut, but there was the possibility to start over. Damn. Why the hell was he thinking of a *Leave it to Beaver* lifestyle now? The focus needed to be on resolving the issues with her and laying whatever turmoil she was going through to rest.

It wasn't until he heard her voice that he realized he'd been standing on the stoop gawking at his own front door like a creeper.

"Are you coming in?" she asked.

"Uh, yeah. Sorry." He brushed past her and went directly to the kitchen. "Brain's fried." He yanked open the fridge door and pulled out a beer. After popping off the metal top he chugged back a few swigs and set the brown bottle on the counter.

"Cora wasn't feeling well so she's taking a nap." Gracie picked up the discarded beer cap and tossed it in the garbage.

"She gonna be okay?" Cole heard the concern in his own voice.

"Uh huh. Her little stunt earlier took a lot out of her." He watched her reach into the freezer. "I thought I'd make dinner. You hungry?" She turned around with what looked like some sort of frozen meat in her hands.

"Not really." He threw back the rest of the frothy brew and swallowed. Once the bottle was empty, he tossed it into the trash can—the glass clanking against some other breakable object in there. "Since she's asleep, I think this would be a good time to talk."

"About what?" she asked as she turned her body toward the counter.

"Everything."

"That's a broad spectrum." She chuckled. Damn she had such a sweet laugh.

"Gracie, I'm dead serious here."

She spun around and pinned him with a stare. "Okay

then." After rinsing her hands and drying them she finally placed all of her attention on him.

"Have a seat." Cole motioned to the chair across from him. He couldn't have her sitting right next to him, no, that would only prove to be a massive distraction. What he needed was some distance. Once she was settled in her seat, he began, "I don't know where this thing between us is headed. Do I expect things to go back to the way they were when we were 18? No. But I need some clarity on a few things."

"Like what?"

"For starters, the fact that you told me you loved me the other night. Did you mean it?" Truthfully he didn't want the answer to that question and he was an idiot for even asking it. But this subject needed to be broached. If not, it would be hanging over their heads like a rain cloud getting ready to burst.

"This isn't the time for that."

"Goddamn it, Gracie. When *is* a good time?" He lowered his voice a bit, "Because the way I see it, the only time you want to discuss anything with me is when I'm between your legs."

"Fuck you, Cole!" Gracie shouted and stood. "I don't owe you *any* sort of explanation."

"The hell you don't. At the very least you owe me the fucking truth. Or are you gonna stand there and feed me a bunch of lies again?"

She turned away. "I don't want to do this."

"Do you think I want to sit here and discuss this shit with you? That it's a walk in the park and I'm full of unicorn farts about it? No, I'm not. But it has to be done."

"Why? Why does it even matter?"

"Because we made a kid together, Gracie. She deserves some semblance of order in her life. Or was it your plan all along to fuck me over when it came to seeing her once you two leave here?" Her silence said it all. "Thought so." Running a hand through his hair, Cole then went to the living room and yanked open a small drawer in one of the end tables. He reached in and snatched up the lone manila envelope sitting in there. Going back to the kitchen, he slammed it on the table. "I didn't want to do this; I wanted this to be easy. Somehow you love things being difficult."

"What is that?" She stared at the envelope like it would jump from the table any minute and eat her alive.

"Those are from my lawyer. I'll give you some time to look them over."

"You're planning on taking her away from me aren't you?" Fear clouded her normally sparkling green eyes.

"Just read the damn papers." He shouldn't have stood there and watched as she flipped open the tab and pulled out the small stack of documents, but he couldn't resist anything when it came to Gracie.

"Wait, this isn't a custody order. It's…"

"The divorce papers," he finished her sentence.

"Why did you sign them? I thought…" The look on her face was one of complete confusion.

"You thought I loved you and wanted to stay together?"

"Yeah." Her face now painted with disappointment.

Cole leaned his shoulder against the doorframe. "Gracie, I will always love you but I can't force you to love me. Lord knows I've tried. Even when we were teenagers the only thing I wanted was your happiness. The same applies today. I can't make you to give a damn about me, but when I sit here in turmoil day after day, I have to ask myself if this is really worth it. The only answer I can seem to come up with is, no, this isn't worth it."

"You can't just give up."

"I'm not giving up. I'm giving you what you wanted from the start. All you have to do is sign on that line and this is over and done with. Congrats, Gracie. You'll officially be free of me." Cole pushed off the wall and turned the corner heading to the bathroom. What he needed was a hot shower to hopefully wash the grime of the day away. Just as he stepped through the door and began to close it, Gracie pushed her way through and shut the door. He watched her lock it and stand there with her back to him. "What do you want, Gracie?" No response. "I don't have time for this game. Either say what you need to or get out." He hated how his words sounded so terrible but he was so fucking tired of the games. She'd done a number on his heart already and he wasn't sure he could handle much more. When she finally turned to him, his stomach dropped at the sight of salty tears streaming down her porcelain face.

"I'm not playing games, Cole," she whispered.

"Then what are you doing?"

"That's just it; I don't know what I'm doing. I came down here to have you sign the papers but now that I see your name on that line, I don't know what I feel."

"Just tell me, tell me what the fuck you want from me," he stepped closer, her scent almost drawing him in like a deadly siren song. His fingers reached out to grab a lock of her hair and as he stood there, he twisted the silken strands around his calloused digit.

"I want you," she gently said.

"This can't be the same as it was before. We're not the same people we were back then."

"I know."

"Do you?"

"Yes. I look at you and sure, sometimes I see glimpses of the teenage guy I shared everything with. I'll admit, I've wished for so long he'd come back to me. But that day you picked us up from the airport? I was floored. I never thought you'd turn out to be the amazing man you are now." What the hell was she even doing? Did she think flattery would help her worm her way back into his life full force? Hell, he'd made up his mind earlier today. The plan was to cut her loose and deal with the fallout as it came. He never expected her to be standing here, trying to work things out.

"You've worn me down, Gracie. I've busted my ass to try and make you fall in love with me again but clearly I was going about it all wrong. I can't make you do anything, you have to do it on your own. But I don't think you really love me. I think you've gotten a glimpse of what life could be like and you're scared to go back to Chicago now. Does that sound about right?"

"I have to go back. It doesn't matter if I want to or not," she admitted.

"Why? Why do you have to go back?" She shook her head. "I can't help you if you won't talk to me."

"If I talk to you, he'll find out and Dash will be in danger."

Cole took a seat on the edge of the bathtub and hung his head. "Did you think I wouldn't look into this? Did you honestly think when that fucker called me I wouldn't try to get to the bottom of whatever mess you'd gotten yourself into?"

"I knew you would. I just hoped we'd be out of here by the time you did. I didn't think he'd call you."

"Well, he did. So you can either fill me in about it all, or get on a plane Monday. The choice is yours."

Gracie stood in front of him looking weak—it wasn't a look he'd seen on her before. She was running scared and if she didn't speak up in the next 30 seconds, he would be forced to hold her down and make her talk.

"I'm sure you found out about my brother, Dash. He's in prison for manslaughter right now."

"Yeah, I saw the files on him. Looked to me like he was defending some woman from being assaulted."

"He was. But of course the law didn't see it that way. All they could see was that a man was dead and Dash was the culprit. I hired the best lawyer I could find but it didn't matter. The judge refused to grant any sort of leniency in the case."

"The judge wouldn't happen to have been Spencer Woodard would it?"

"Spencer is a federal court judge. He wasn't supposed to be trying that case. But for some reason, they had him sitting in. I was there for the trial and I guess he saw me."

"Then what?"

"About a year ago, Spencer began to coming into the salon where I worked. He asked me out and I went on a few dates with him. I don't know what I was thinking."

"Did he bribe you, Gracie?" Cole tried to tamp down his anger at the thought of some sleezeball extorting anything from Gracie.

"No, nothing like that," she physically shivered. "In fact, he didn't ask for anything…at first."

"Keep going," Cole prompted.

"We began dating regularly and soon six months passed by. Everything seemed normal but one night at dinner he told me he could get Dash out on parole early. I was excited. Of course I wanted my brother out from behind bars. He shouldn't have been there in the first place."

"What did Woodard want in return?" Cole stood.

Gracie wouldn't look him in the eye as she continued. "He wanted me to marry him."

"What?"

"I thought it was a strange request but after he told me why, I guess I understood. He's going to run for a Senate seat and supposedly voters feel more at ease if you were married with a kid or something."

"And he found a ready-made family."

"Yes. But I couldn't get married.

"Because you're still legally tied to me." Cole sat back down.

"Exactly. When Spencer found out, he was furious. Told me I'd better get my ass down here and get those papers signed or Dash would only leave prison in a body bag."

"Why didn't you go to the authorities?"

"Are you kidding? With his reach he had all kinds of law enforcement in his back pocket. I wasn't about to rat him out."

"What other leverage, besides your brother, does he have over you?" There had to be something else, something she wasn't telling him. Gracie shrugged. "Damn it, I need to know everything." He jumped up and grabbed her by the shoulders.

"Cole, anything I did was to protect my brother and Cora."

"Just tell me."

"He has me on video dealing."

"Dealing what? Cards?" He couldn't imagine she'd be doing anything worse than shuffling decks at a casino.

"Heroine," she whispered as tears began to fall more furiously.

"Jesus Christ. What the fuck were you thinking?"

"I didn't know what was in the packages. Spencer would give them to me a few times a week and I would drop them off at this club downtown. The guy behind the bar would hand me an envelope full of money and I'd take it to Spencer."

"How could you not know what you were doing? Damn it."

"I didn't ask."

"Don't you think that was a pertinent detail?" Cole blew out a frustrated breath as he looked at the scared woman in front of him.

"He offered me extra income to drop off the packages. How could I say no to that? I needed the cash. The doctor bills with Cora were through the roof and we weren't busy enough at the salon to have a steady income. I was desperate."

"How do you know he has video of you?"

"He sent it to my phone about a month ago. He made sure if *he* goes down, I will too. I just wanted to protect my family."

"Please, for the love of God, tell me you never had my daughter with you while you were dropping that shit off."

She shook her head. "No, Jenna kept her for me when I had to make a delivery. I made sure Cora was never connected with any of it directly."

"Thank fuck for that."

"What am I supposed to do? He's dangerous, Cole."

Cole reached up and grabbed both sides of her face—tilting it up so he could look into her eyes. "He fucked with the people I love, which makes *me* 10 times more dangerous than he is."

Chapter Twenty-Four

DID HE JUST SAY '*LOVE*'? Gracie stood there in his bathroom questioning whether the L word even came out of his mouth. With the things he'd said earlier and the fact he'd signed the divorce papers, she'd swear the word love would never fall from his lips again. But the way he looked into her eyes told a different story. They said that he really did care— that he was willing to go through hell and back to protect her and their daughter.

"Stop thinking so hard." She closed her eyes and reveled in the feel of his thumbs moving in a circular pattern over her cheeks.

"Can't help it," she admitted. When it came to him,

she couldn't force her brain to shut off. It was like an overworked computer—trying to figure out this man in front of her.

Soon he was pulling her into his chest, her ear directly over where his heart lay beneath his ribcage. "I need a shower." It felt as if he was pulling her even closer, if that was humanly possible. As she was now, it was like she was molded into him permanently.

"Me, too." She didn't want to leave him, even if that meant stripping down and showering *with* him.

The only sounds in the small space were those of clothing being removed from their bodies. He practically tore his off but took his precious time in relieving her of hers. Gracie didn't mind, not in the least. It could've been due to the fact that his expert hands managed to caress a molten path over each inch he touched. Or maybe it was the way she could hear his breathing increase like this was affecting him as much as it was her. When he knelt on the floor, hooked his fingers in the waistband of her panties, Gracie's breath quickened. He'd soon feel how much this torture was arousing her. But as usual, he took his time with her. One hand began at her ankle and leisurely stroked its way up the length of her leg, stopping just before he hit her sensitive upper thigh. He knew it was one spot she loved touched. It would send her breathing patterns into a hyperventilating state and cause her entire body to quiver. He didn't touch it though; instead, he stood in all his naked glory and turned toward the shower enclosure. As he reached in to turn the knobs, Gracie's mouth began to water at the sight of his sinewy muscles ebbing and flowing about his back. This was how a man was supposed to look. Fit and trim, but with an inner darkness that made you believe he was capable of some really dangerous shit. And he was. Cole was a loaded gun, a dog on a leash. When you pulled the trigger or let go of his harness, he would wreak havoc and mayhem if need be. It partly scared and exhilarated her.

"In you go." He gave her a light push toward the glass doors of the shower. Steam began to pack the room as she opened the door and stepped in among the warm spray. Backing against the tile wall she waited for Cole to join her. He soon did and they stood with the hot liquid pouring over their already hypersensitive bodies. As she stepped away from the wall, he pushed her back toward it, her back sliding a bit from the water running between her and the slick tile. She gave him a questioning look as he pinned her to the surface with his hard body. "Gracie, I'm going to fuck you in this shower. I'm going to make you scream my name." Grabbing both wrists, he lifted them over her head and restrained them against the wall in one hand. Leaning closer, he whispered in her ear, "And when I'm ready to come, the only place I'll be doing it is in here." With his other hand he reached down and ran his fingers through her natural wetness. It shouldn't excite her as much as it did, but Gracie was already on the razor's edge just being this close to him. He somehow did that to her. Some sort of spell was woven where her brain cells melted and entire body turned to mush. In a nutshell, she turned stupid around him. But she needed this, needed to feel him close to her in a way she hadn't felt in so long. If this whole thing ended with her walking away, she at least needed the memory of what it was like to be with the grown-up Cole. The man who turned her world upside down and made her like it that way. Some small part of her wanted his brand of chaos. Or maybe she craved it? Who really knew? The only thing that made sense right here, right now, was the care he placed in preparing her body for his.

"Damn it, Gracie." He halted his motions of stroking her center and grabbed her jaw. "Either you are in this one hundred percent, or I stop. No games. Just you and I doing this." He punctuated his statement with a slight grinding motion of his erection on her stomach. Gracie groaned. "You like that?"

"*Mmmm.*" Words escaped her; she could only manage to make unintelligible noises. He did it again and chuckled as his cock grazed her naked skin. This was going to kill her. It was literally digging her grave and soon she'd be six feet under the earth if he kept this up. "I need you."

"*Do* you?" She nodded. "How bad? Are you aching for me?"

"Yes."

"Hook this leg over my hip." He tapped one of her legs and she did as he said. She was so exposed, so opened up to whatever he wanted to do to her. Even her wrists were still bound above her in his hand. The slight bite of pain from his grip had her eagerness increasing. She was ready, she wanted this. "*Fuck.*" Cole buried his face next to her neck and cursed as he pushed forward and entered her suddenly. Trying to move, Gracie shifted her hips slightly. "Stop," Cole said as he began to kiss his way up her neck and across her face. "Don't get me wrong, I want to come inside you so bad right now but if you keep moving like that, it's going to happen in the next 10 seconds. I'd like to make you come first."

She didn't have an issue with that, and honestly, she was already on the edge. All he had to do was stroke inside of her a few times and her screams would echo off the tile enclosure around them. "I'm so close already," she admitted in a breathy voice.

"I can tell." He tightened his grip on her wrists and began to pull himself from her center.

"More," she whined.

Releasing her wrists, he reached down and hooked her other leg over his trim hip. "Wrap your arms around my neck." When she did, Cole slammed into her, his cock penetrating deeper than it had before. Her spine crashed into the shower wall, but she didn't care. What he was doing felt too damn good to stop. She could deal with the pain as long as the pleasure outweighed it…and it did, tenfold.

Each time he thrust into her, Gracie felt like he was chipping away at something inside her. Something emotional. Something she would never get back and wasn't sure she wanted back. Why did she push this man away all those years ago? Why did she make the decision for him as to whether he would stay in her life or exit it? Why did she tell herself she hated this man? This man that didn't know a thing about being selfish. She'd fucked him over yet he still loved her unconditionally. He had to be some sort of saint for what he'd put up with from her. It was as if she could see herself in a mirror and what she saw disgusted her. No, she couldn't change overnight but she could do the right thing and admit to him what she'd learned.

"Cole, I need to tell you something." This wasn't the opportune time to have a conversation but it had to be said.

"Later," he grunted as he pushed inside her once more.

"Now," she countered.

"This better be life-altering, Gracie." He paused, his hard cock still inside her.

"It is." She let her arms fall from around his neck and placed them on the sides of his face. The 5 o'clock shadow rasping against her soft palms. "I love you."

"Don't." He turned his face away from her.

"No, I need you to hear this, Cole." He faced her once more. "I. Love. You."

With the way he stared into her eyes made her feel like she was under a microscope. What was he thinking? Was he trying to decide how to let her down easy?

"I know you do." His cold eyes began to sparkle with warmth again as a slight smile passed over his face.

"You *do*?"

"Yeah, I do. Wanna know *how* I know?" She nodded. "Because when I gave you those papers, you looked devastated. Like I'd torn your entire world apart."

"You did, Cole."

"I wanted you to see what you've been fighting since the day you pushed me away. I'm not the best man out there, but I'm the one for you. I think you know that now."

"I don't want a divorce." Tears flooded her eyes as emotions swamped her.

"Don't cry, please?" Pulling from her body, Cole tilted her face. "I love you, Gracie. I always have. I never looked for anything better than you because there isn't anyone who can compare. You're everything to me."

"I don't know what to say or do."

"Me neither. But we can start over, together." He reached behind him and shut off the water. "Let's go to bed." Stepping out first, he handed her a towel.

"What about…" Disappointment fell over her.

"Oh, I'm not done with you yet." Kissing her

forehead he pulled her towel tighter and opened the bathroom door. They crept down the hallway and into his bedroom.

"We have to be quiet," she suggested. After all, their daughter was asleep in the bedroom across the hall. That's all they needed was to wake her.

"I can be quiet. You on the other hand," he raised an eyebrow and smiled. "Get your sexy ass under the blanket so I can finish what I started."

～ Chapter Twenty-Five ～

"YOU LOOK absolutely ridiculous!" Luke hooted as he walked into the backyard at Cole's house.

"Shut the hell up." Cole flipped him the bird with his free hand. The other hand was holding a crossbow.

"Oh, stop it, you two," Gracie scolded. "It's all in good fun."

Yeah, he probably did look like an idiot, but Cora wanted a *Walking Dead* themed birthday party and that's what she got. When your daughter wanted you to dress up as Daryl, you fucking dressed up like Daryl. Even if that meant wearing a greasy looking wig and carrying around a crossbow. If he wanted to admit it, this was fun in a way. Cora was having a blast and even she'd dressed up. Of course she was a zombie, but it worked.

"You were supposed to dress up, too," Cole mentioned to Luke.

"I did."

"No you didn't. You look like the same asshole you are every other day."

"Okay, I guess were gonna have to split these two up." Ava walked over and gave Luke a dirty look. "How did you guys end up being partners anyway? You can't seem to get along more than three minutes."

"Luck of the draw I guess," Cole said. He gave Luke a lot of shit, but it was all in good fun. Honestly he knew Luke had his back and would take a bullet for him. Not that he'd taken any as of yet—Cole seemed to be the metal magnet when out in the field. Luke was more careful, he wasn't as much a kamikaze as Cole.

"Can we open presents yet?" Zombie Cora asked.

"Sure." Cole ran inside the house and grabbed the giant wrapped box. It wasn't very pretty but it did the job. He only hoped she like what was inside. He knew it was a risk but something told him she *and* her mom might like this one.

Cole struggled to carry the huge box out the sliding glass doors but finally made it. Cora's eyes were huge as he sat the massive object on the patio table.

"Wow!" The now 13-year-old exclaimed.

"Here ya go." He motioned to the package giving her the go ahead to rip into it.

He watched her tear into the paper—most of it being picked up by the slight breeze and carried across the small backyard. Once she had the outside done, she pulled open the flaps and peeked inside. Her brow furrowed as she then began to pull hunks of tissue paper from it. Several minutes went by until she finally removed all the white material. Pulling out another, smaller box, she gave him a quizzical look.

"Open it." He nodded.

God, he really hoped he wouldn't disappoint her with this gift. He'd put so much thought into it and if she didn't like it, he'd be screwed in more ways than one. Standing there on pins and needles he waited until she had the smaller box open. When she pulled the item from it she looked over at him again.

"It's a picture of a house," she stated.

"Do you like it?" he asked.

Cora shrugged. "I guess. It's kind of a weird present though."

Cole stepped closer to her and spoke, "I know how much you like Luke and Ava's house out in the country, I thought you'd like to live in a place like that too."

"Oh my God, *Cole*?" Gracie stepped over to him and their daughter and grabbed the picture frame from Cora's hands. "Did you *buy* this house?"

For some reason embarrassment struck him as he opened his mouth to answer her. "Yeah, I did," he admitted.

"But, why?"

He grabbed her hands and held them in his. "I want the two of you to stay here in Biloxi. I want to be a family. This was the first step in making that happen."

He watched her facial expressions as she stared at the picture behind the glass. When she finally looked up to him, he didn't expect her to say, "I want that too." At least that was one of the two who went for his idea, now to see if Cora was on board.

"Are you okay with this?" he turned to his daughter and asked.

She stayed silent for what seemed like forever but finally spoke up. "Sounds good to me."

Damn, that was just awesome in his book. What more was there to do except to pull both of them into the tightest hug he could muster? "Thank you," he told them as he pretty much squeezed the life from them.

When he let them go, Gracie was wiping tears from her eyes. "Sorry, I seem to be a basket case lately."

He kissed her lightly on the lips. "Doesn't matter, you're beautiful no matter what you do."

Cora opened a few more gifts from Luke and Ava and soon she sat next to him pecking away on her phone. "Ready for cake?" he asked her.

"I guess so." She didn't look him in the eyes.

"What's wrong?"

"I won't have any friends here."

"You'll make new ones. You're a cool kid, others will flock to you."

"I hope so. I just want my mom to be happy. Please don't hurt her." The teen finally looked him in the eye.

"I'm not planning on it. I've loved your mom since the day I saw her in math class in high school."

"Please don't tell me all the gross details." She began making a gagging sound.

Cole erupted in a fit of laughter. "I'll save those for your next birthday."

"Cora, why don't you run inside and grab the cake," Gracie suggested.

"Okay. I've gotta use the bathroom anyway."

He watched her stand and walk into the house, closing the sliding glass door as she made it through.

Once they had the situation in Chicago taken care of, he'd move them to Mississippi and they could all start over. He didnt' want the same thing he had with Gracie all those years ago because, hell, they'd both changed so much. What he did want was a fresh start. They could all be a family and learn about each other, together.

"She's been in there for a while." Gracie looked to him and then to the door behind them.

"I'll go check on her." He placed his beer bottle down and headed for the back door.

Walking into the kitchen Cole stopped, something didn't feel quite right. He began to call out for Cora. She didn't answer. Where the hell was she? Rounding the kitchen table he glanced down at the floor to discover the birthday cake on the floor. It appeared to have been dropped. Why would she drop her own cake on the floor? It didn't make sense. Taking long strides he made his way through the house calling her name as he opened each bedroom door and the one to the bathroom. She still didn't answer. Panic rose in his gut as he imagined the worst case scenario. Did she run away again? She'd seemed happy about moving to Biloxi, surely she didn't run away because of that. Traveling back through to the kitchen his phone began ringing. He pulled it from his back pocket and saw 'Blocked Number' on the screen.

"Yeah?" he gruffly answered.

"I don't think you took me seriously, Mr. Matthews."

Recognizing the voice on the line he said, "Judge Woodard. What can I do for you?"

"There're quite a few things you can do for me, but the first would probably be to stop making plans with Ms. Callahan and her daughter."

"How the fuck do you know what I'm up to?" Cole bit out.

"My reach goes beyond Chicago, way beyond actually."

"I don't doubt that. You're a crooked motherfucker, I'm sure your filthy hands are in every cookie jar."

The other man laughed. "I'd be a bit kinder if I were you, Mr. Matthews."

"Yeah? And why the fuck is that?" Cole was beyond irritated.

"Because I have something you want."

"Trust me you don't have a damn thing I want."

"I beg to differ." Silence drafted over the line and soon Cole's blood ran cold when he heard a new voice on the line. "I'm sorry about the cake," Cora began crying.

"See?" Judge Woodard said.

"You fucking bastard!" Cole roared.

"Here's what I want. Tomorrow at noon, you'll bring Gracie and the divorce papers with you to this address," he rattled it off and Cole quickly jotted it down. "Once they're in my custody, you'll walk the fuck away and never speak to, or contact them again."

"What makes you think I'd do that?" Cole reached up and yanked the wig off his head, tossing it to the kitchen floor.

"Because if you don't, I will make your daughter disappear, for good."

"If you harm one hair on her head, I will make for damn sure you feel the worst pain you've ever fucking felt," Cole warned.

"Then I suppose I will just have to see you tomorrow." Woodard hung up.

"Goddamn it!" He chucked his phone on the table.

"What's going on?" Gracie popped in the back door. "What happened to the cake?" She knelt to assess the damage. "Where's Cora?" she stood and asked. Cole couldn't frame a thought or sentence right now. He was already in combat mode, thinking of how the hell he was going to make this asshole pay for taking his daughter. "Hey, where is she?" Gracie asked again. She must've seen the look on his face because her soft features turned hard as hell. "Where the fuck is she, Cole?" she screamed.

"I'll get her back."

"What you mean you'll get her back? Who has her?"

"Judge Woodard." Cole tried to pull her into him but she wouldn't have it. She shoved at his chest instead.

"No!" she yelled.

"Hey, what the hell is going on in here?" Luke stepped through the door and asked.

"I need your help." Cole said to his partner.

"With what?"

"Getting my daughter back and making this motherfucker pay for taking her." Cole took off toward his bedroom, shucking his costume as he went.

Luke followed him. "You know this will come back on us, right? This guy is at a federal level."

"Do you think I give a fuck about my job right now?"

"I think you're being irrational about this. We need to formulate a plan instead of getting emotional."

"Did this fuck bag take *your* kid? No! He took mine. Emotions or not, I want to see him in tiny little pieces scattered in the Gulf."

As he pulled on his tactical pants and a black t-shirt he waited for Luke to say something.

"Fine. What do you need from me?"

"Still have your AR-15 with the suppressor?"

"Of course."

"Bring it." Cole reached under the bed and pulled out a black handled box. He tossed it on the bed and popped it open. "He fucked with the wrong man this time."

∽ Chapter Twenty-Six ∽

GRACIE SAT ON THE END of the bed later that night wondering why she'd let this get so out of hand. She knew Spencer was watching her but she made stupid decisions anyway. She was only trying to protect Dash and her daughter, but now? Cora was gone and Cole was about to do something really stupid to get her back.

"There has to be another way to do this," she said to Cole as he began assembling pieces of a gun.

"Then *tell* me another way. Because from where I stand, this is the *only* way."

"What if he hurts her?" Gracie became emotional thinking about what could happen to Cora.

Cole stepped closer to her. "There's no guarantee he

won't. Just let me do what I do best and hopefully by tomorrow evening she will be right here with us."

"I shouldn't have come down here."

"Stop it. The fact of the matter is this asshole can't keep doing this to people, he has to be stopped."

"But you don't have to risk your career to stop him."

"There is one thing I value above all else in my life. Family. I don't turn my back on my family and I sure as fuck don't run from danger when they need me."

"Let's just call the police. They could help."

"If he has law enforcement in his back pocket in Chicago, don't you think he has them here too? Be smart about this. We're going to take him down and put an end to this shit."

She didn't know what to say to that. Cole was in combat mode and nothing she said would sway him from the decision he'd already made. No, this whole thing wouldn't end with Spencer in handcuffs. It would end with a bullet lodged somewhere in his body. Cole wasn't in the mood to play nice—she could see the anger written on his face like a poem of despair. Gracie hated

Spencer for what he'd done but never in a million years would she've thought to kill the man for it. Maybe it was her softer female sensibilities shining through but there really had to be a cleaner way than bloodshed to end this.

She was terrified at the thought something could happen to Cora but in a way, she knew Cole would go to any lengths to make sure she was safe. That showed in his focus while gathering his stuff.

"Where're the divorce papers I signed?" Cole asked as he put the last piece of his gun together.

She went over to the dresser and pulled the envelope from the top drawer. Handing it to Cole she had a puzzled look on her face. "Why do you need them?"

"I need you to sign them."

"No. I'm not signing anything."

"Gracie, you have to."

"Why?"

"Because he wants the papers signed and you to go back to Illinois with him."

"But I'm *not* going back there."

"Yes, you are. Just fucking sign the damn thing."

"Are you *kidding* me? After all we decided and you buying a house? You're giving in that easily?" She tossed her hands in the air not believing this was even happening.

"You can't stay here and be safe. As long as you're around me, he's going to be a danger to you and Cora."

"So, that's it. This thing is over?"

"Yes."

"I don't believe you!" she shouted.

"Well, believe it. I can't sit here knowing you guys are in some sort of danger because of me. Sign the papers, go back to Chicago and things will work themselves out."

"No, they won't. I love you, Cole. Why are you doing this?" She couldn't help the tears that escaped from her eyes while on this subject. Was he really pushing her away that easily?

"I love you too but they're some things in life that even love can't fix."

Cole hated himself for talking to her like that. But he

needed even Gracie to believe she was leaving. If that bastard, Spencer, saw through his plan, he'd do something they would all regret. If *she* believed it, so would the cock-sucker who had his daughter.

She hadn't signed the divorce papers yet and he needed her to hop to it. "Here." He handed her a pen from the nightstand drawer. "Sign them." She snatched the pen and papers from his hands, not saying a word as she scribbled her name on the lines indicated by yellow tabs. Once she was finished, she plopped down on the end of the bed. "I'll be at Luke's. Be ready and packed by 11:30 tomorrow." He grabbed his duffle bag and left the room.

When he was in his truck, Cole started it up and pulled out of the driveway. He'd told Gracie he was on his way to Luke's house, but again, he might've lied. If they were gonna get a jump on Woodard, he needed to get the lay of the land where the meet would happen.

Cole grabbed his phone from the front console, scrolled through his recent calls and found Luke's number. It rang a few times before the other man picked up. "You on your way?" Cole asked.

"Yep. ETA is five minutes."

"Good, we'll get there about the same time."

"Sure you want to do this? It's not too late to back out." Luke tried once more to persuade his decision.

"Not changing my mind so stop asking."

"It was worth a shot. I'll back you no matter what though."

That's what he wanted to hear. "Glad to hear it. See you in a bit." He hung up and continued down the road. He'd never been to the botanical garden where Spencer wanted to meet so it was necessary to get in there and see what they had to work with.

"Damn, there's a lot of shit in here." Luke commented as he looked around the dome-shaped enclosure of the botanical garden. "I'm not sure how we're gonna pull this off."

"No way we're gonna get a shot inside here from the outside." Cole looked around at the glass enclosure. "Not really any place to conceal anyone either."

"*Fuck,*" Cole cursed.

They stood there for a few more minutes trying to come up with a plan. On their way in they learned the building would be open to the public tomorrow at the same time Spencer set up the meet. Bringing civilians into this bloody mess would only cause more problems than they were prepared for. The plan was to get in, take care of Spencer, grab Cora and get the fuck out of there. But with people milling about looking at rose bushes, it would complicate things.

"I might have an idea," Luke spoke up. He began laying out a plan that just might work. They'd have to be careful but if it all fell into place this could turn out in their favor.

After surveilling the location once more, the two men finalized their plan and headed toward the entrance. Cole knew he couldn't go home with Gracie being there so he instead followed Luke home. Right now all he wanted was to fall into her arms and hold her but he had to focus on the task at hand. And that was making sure

Spencer didn't fuck with anyone ever again.

Chapter Twenty-Seven

 **GRACIE SAT ON THE FRONT** steps of Cole's house, waiting for him to pick her up. As usual, he pulled in early. Nothing was said as he grabbed her and Cora's bags and hefted them into the bed of the truck. When she climbed in, she looked over at him sitting there all stoic and rigid. Wow, this was one *focused* man.

"Please talk to me." She turned in her seat to face him.

"There's nothing to say."

"Of course there is, Cole. I can't go back with Spencer."

"You don't have a choice right now."

"I *always* have a choice."

He didn't respond to that. What he didn't know wouldn't hurt him either. She'd devised her own little plan for when she saw Spencer. There was no way she'd let Cole lose his career over her stupid mistakes. She could take care of herself and she was ready to show that to him.

The meeting place was only a few miles from Cole's house and as soon as they pulled in the parking lot of the botanical gardens, Gracie was swamped with nerves. What if this all went south and Cora got hurt?

"Shit," she bit out.

Cole put the truck in park and turned to her. "What?"

"Cora's been without her medicine for almost 24 hours."

"What happens if she doesn't take it?" Concern laced his features.

"She could go into a diabetic coma." Fear struck her so hard she froze.

"Does Woodard know about that?"

"Yes. We talked about it."

"We'll figure it out." Cole then flung open his door

and hopped down from the truck.

She noticed he wasn't carrying a gun or any sort of weapon. Why was he going in unarmed? Surely he had something on him to use on Spencer, right? Gracie patted her purse and kept it close to her body. At least *she* had something in there that would help out in a pinch. She only hoped Cole wouldn't be pissed that she took it from his top dresser drawer. If so, he'd just have to deal with it. There was no way in hell she'd let anyone hurt her daughter.

"You ready?" He pulled open the door to the building and ushered her through.

"Yeah." As she walked in, an overwhelming floral scent hit her in the face. After this she'd never look at rose bushes the same way again.

"I'm sorry, Gracie," she heard him say from behind her. But she didn't reply. Her main concern was getting her daughter back.

They set off on the concrete path that twisted and turned throughout the building. The entire thing was set underneath a glass dome of sorts, housing plants from what seemed like every corner of the earth. The bright hues of the flora should've made her smile, but the only thing on her mind was seeing her daughter. Once that was done, then maybe she could breathe a sigh of relief.

Further along the path they went, passing a couple of stragglers who were checking out the vegetation around them. When they turned a corner, it all opened up to some sort of sitting area with small picnic tables and a few patio chairs scattered about. A bubbling fountain with a koi pond was the centerpiece for it all. As she glanced around the area her eyes landed on Cora who sat beside Spencer in one of the wrought iron chairs.

"Punctual as always. That's something I love about you." Spencer's voice was like steel wool on a chalk surface.

"I'm here, now what?" she bit out.

"Divorce papers?" He reached out his hand.

Gracie looked over to Cole who held the large envelope. "Here." He handed it to her and in turn she passed it to Spencer.

Sliding open the flap, he pulled the pages out and

began to look them over. "Good." He then turned to Cora, "Come along. We have a flight to catch."

"We're not going anywhere with you." Gracie put her hand up to stop Cora.

"Gracie, don't," Cole said from behind her.

"No. You have terrorized us long enough with your sick games." She reached inside her purse and felt the cold steel under her fingertips. Just as she went to yank it out, Cole grabbed her and pulled her into him.

"Leave it. This will all be over soon, I promise," he whispered in her ear.

Gracie pulled away just as she heard a familiar laugh. Her brow crinkled as Ava walked by chatting and giggling into her phone. Just as she passed Spencer, she stumbled a bit causing him to grab ahold of her to steady her body. "Holy cow! You'd think I just learned how to walk." She laughed. "Thanks for being so kind and catching me." Ava flipped her hair over her shoulder and continued to walk away. What the hell was her role in all of this? Gracie was stumped.

"Time to go," Spencer grabbed Gracie's arm and

wrenched her away from Cole.

"Let go of me!" She reared back and slapped him across one cheek. "Fuck you, Spencer!" Tears began trailing down her face at the thought of leaving this building with him. She just couldn't do that. He didn't seem to give a damn though as he grabbed her once more and tried to leave.

"Wait." Cole spoke up and the other man turned his attention toward him. "I think you might want to reconsider taking them with you," Cole said in a semi-jolly tone. What the hell was his problem? This wasn't a happy occasion.

"And why not, Mr. Matthews?"

"Because in about 15 minutes, you'll be dead." Cole crossed his arms over his chest.

Spencer erupted in a fit of laughter at Cole's statement. "Funny."

"Is it?" Cole's head cocked to the side leaving Gracie wondering what was happening.

"It really is. You see, when that woman…her name is Ava, by the way. When she bumped into you, you more than likely didn't feel the tiny needle prick when she injected something into your skin. But she did. Right there underneath your arm." Cole stepped closer to Spencer. "You're probably feeling it now, actually."

"What the hell did she do?" Spencer began to rub an area on his side.

"My partner and I have extensive knowledge of poison. Arsenic, cyanide...pretty much any poison known to man, we know about it. We know what it does to a human when they come in contact with it too."

"What the fuck," Spencer began to gasp for air, grabbing his chest.

"We got our hands on a tiny amount of one called polonium."

"You son of a bitch!" Spencer roared.

"Oh wait, you know all about Polonium *don't* you? Isn't that what you laced cocaine with when a competing dealer was doing business on your turf?"

"Those people deserved to die, if you're stupid enough to buy coke off the streets, you're stupid enough to get ahold of some that's cut with poison! That crackhead was in my region, I sell drugs there, nobody else!" Spencer reached around his back while still gasping for precious air. When he brought his hand around front, he held a shiny black pistol—pointing it at Gracie.

"I wouldn't do that if I were you," Cole warned.

"Fuck you! I'll kill every single one of you, including that blonde bitch."

"That wasn't a good thing to say. Her fiancé is hiding nearby camouflaged in a gilly suit. See that red dot bouncing around near your heart?" Spencer looked down. "That's his rifle aimed right at you. He's probably more than a bit upset that you threatened the woman he plans to spend the rest of his life with. Can't say I blame him."

Spencer grabbed his chest with his free hand and dropped to his knees. "Fu…ck…yo…u!" he tried to say.

Gracie watched Cole walk right up to him and kick the gun out of his hand. He then leaned down and spoke right to Spencer's face. "No, fuck you." Gracie cringed as Cole reared back and slammed his fist into the other man's nose.

"Time to go." Cole grabbed her and Cora by the arms and led them toward the exit.

"What about him?" she asked, looking back at the man gasping for air on the ground.

"He's allergic to peanuts. Ava injected him with peanut oil. He's in anaphylactic shock but once the paramedics get here, he'll be fine."

"But you said…"

"I lied." Cole chuckled.

Gracie stopped just as they made it to the parking lot. "I thought you were going to kill him."

"I thought about it. But I changed my mind."

"And Luke?"

"He was hiding in the bushes but all he had was one of those laser pointers that you aggravate cats with."

Cole continued to walk to his truck, Gracie and Cora hot on his heels. "But he's still going to be out there!" She grabbed his arms and tried to twist him around to face her.

"Gracie, calm down."

"How am I supposed to be calm right now?"

Cole reached into his pocket and pulled out a small rectangular object. "I have his confession on tape. He'll be going away for a very long time."

"He still has me on video though." She wrapped her arms around her midsection.

"Not anymore. I have a hacker friend who remotely wiped every device he has. She backed up most of it and is sending it anonymously to the FBI field office in D.C. Minus the video with you on it, of course."

"Wow, so you're like James Bond?" Cora spoke up.

"Not really." Cole chuckled. "I'm Matthews...Cole. Matthews."

"I don't know what to say. I can't believe you did this for us," Gracie said tearfully.

"Haven't you figured out that I'd fly up to the moon and break off a chunk for you?" he reached out and pulled her to his chest. "I would do anything for you, if only you'd let me."

"But you said love couldn't fix everything." She sobbed into his black shirt.

He reached down and gently placed his hands on both sides of her face, "I lied. It can fix everything."

How the hell had she gone without this man for so many years? He was the one person who completed her puzzle. Yeah, he was that pain in the ass corner piece that kept slipping under the table, but he was still there when she needed him. Now they could fit their pieces together and start fresh. If life were like a strand of hair, they'd be the split ends that were finally mended.

THE END

Read on for a taste of *'Torn Ends'*

TORN *Ends*

MAGNOLIA SERIES: BOOK THREE
Content for Torn Ends is not yet edited and is subject to change

Damon *'Dash'* Hunter glanced around as the tall metal gate in front of him took its time sliding open. *Freedom.* That's what he'd have in just a few minutes. It seemed as if the gate's leisurely pace was due to the fact it didn't want him to leave the place that'd been his home for the past three years. To hell with that. He *was* leaving. He'd done his time and thankfully his sister had his back on the outside. Every single day he was in his tiny cell, he'd thought about the events that'd led him to be incarcerated in such a place. No, he didn't mean to *kill* the guy—*that* was an accident. But he'd lost control and that wasn't something Dash never did. He'd learned his lesson. How could you not with endless hours to sit and dwell on the events of the past? If there was one thing he had planned now that he could taste his freedom, it was from now on, everything he did would be on the straight and narrow.

"You look like shit," he heard the familiar voice say.

"Fuck you, too." He laughed and pulled his best

friend in for a hug.

"It's been *too* long, Dash."

"Don't get all weepy on me, Lucky."

"I don't go by that name anymore. It's just Liam now." Liam pulled away from Dash and smiled.

"Got out of the life, huh?"

"Trying to."

"It's been too damn long." Dash ran a hand through his shaggy hair and looked up at the sky. He then glanced back at the facility that'd been his home for far longer than he wanted it to be. "Just glad to be out of there."

"You got the raw end of the deal. I'm sorry man." Liam shook his head.

"I'm ready to get things back on track."

"You sticking around here?"

"Thinking about heading down to Mississippi. My sister lives there now. Says it's real nice."

Hell, anywhere but here would be a good place right now. He'd spent too much time hating himself for what he'd done but all that was behind him now.

"Yeah, I've been contemplating heading west. You know, where this all began."

"Ah, Tacoma."

"Not that I want any part of it, just wanna see where the *Sons of Destiny* took root."

"Not me, man. I'll stick with somewhere I can hold down a job and keep my life straight."

"Good luck with that." Liam laughed. "Well, come on. Let's get you as far away from this place as we possibly can."

Dash followed his friend to what looked like a brand new Camaro. Once it was unlocked, Dash slid in and reveled in the feeling of the buttery leather under his ass. All he'd been sitting on lately was steely cold metal and the lumpy mattress in his cell. Three fucking years he'd been in that place for a crime he never meant to commit. Sure, the other man lost his life, but Dash was only trying to protect a woman from being assaulted in a bar parking lot. His club brothers were supposed to have his back but as soon as the cops showed up, they fucking split. So much for the *'code'*. He'd always love riding his Harley but from now on, the leather on his back would be blank. Never again would he sport the patch of any club. There was only one person you could count on and that was yourself.

"Did Whitney come visit while you were on the inside?" Liam asked as he drove them away from the prison.

"Not a damn day." Dash wasn't surprised. It wasn't like she was his old lady or anything. They'd pretty much had a sexual relationship and that was it.

"That's rough."

"Yeah. I'm sure she shacked up with one of the other guys." He looked over at his driver.

"Don't look at me. You know I wouldn't try to get on your turf." Liam laughed.

The further the car traveled away from the iron bars of prison the more anxious Dash became. How the hell was he supposed to start his life again after three damn years? It wasn't possible to just pick up where you left off.

"You need any money?" Liam asked.

"You know I wouldn't ask you for cash."

"You didn't ask, I'm offering. How much you need?"

Dash thought for a minute. "Hell, I don't know. Enough to get me and my bike to Mississippi."

"Done. Just let me know when you want to go and I'll get it taken care of."

"The sooner the better. I'm already sick of looking at this place."

Dash reached inside his bag and grabbed a pony tail holder. His hair was short when he'd been incarcerated but for some reason he'd grown the mop out. But with the summer sun blazing through the car window, he was sweating like crazy. Time to tie it back.

Liam drove a few more miles before they ended up at the storage lot he'd rented. Wasn't much you could do with your shit while you were in the pen so he'd had his best friend rent this space and toss his junk in it. Including his Hog. Damn he couldn't wait to see her again.

"Here's the key." Liam tossed the silver key into his lap.

"Thanks, man." As soon as the car was parked, Dash got out and walked to the steel door of the storage space. He crouched down and grabbed the padlock—sticking the matching key inside. With a slight turn, it popped open. Once the key was in his pocket, he grabbed the handle at the bottom and yanked upward. When it was cleared completely, he stepped inside to see all of his worldly possessions. *Damn*, it was crazy to see your entire life stuffed in a small space like that. But he could give two shits less about most of it. The one thing he needed was sitting right in front of him. Fucking hell he missed her.

Brushing the specks of dust off the tank, Dash took stock of the sexy Harley in front of him. He could already feel the air of the open road as he cruised down to Mississippi.

"Need help getting this stuff out of here?" Liam asked, stepping into the locker.

Dash looked around. "Nah, donate it all to charity. This is all I want." He patted the black leather seat of his bike.

"Alright. When you heading out?"

Dash grabbed his nearby helmet and popped it on his head. In a few more seconds he had her fired up and rumbling the entire row of storage spaces. "I guess now's as good a time as any!" he yelled over the grumble of the engine.

"I don't care, mom."

"Brandi! Don't walk away while I'm talking to you!"

"Look. I don't care about some stupid garden party or the fact that your wrinkled friends want to set me up with some banker. This isn't the 40s."

"Young lady. You will not speak to me in that manner!"

Brandi already had her fill of her mom for the day. She'd pushed and pushed until she was about to snap in half. Why couldn't the woman get over the fact she didn't give a damn about meeting some nice guy or even about showing up in the society pages? All Brandi wanted to do was work her job at the local newspaper and live her life.

"I wish you would listen to me, just this once," her mom lowered her voice.

"I *am* listening. But I'm also telling you that I don't give a flying fuck about anything you're saying." She headed for the front door of the Civil War era plantation home. She'd grown up here with all the house staff and rules. She was 28 now, she could make her own decisions—good or bad—and be happy about them.

"I cannot believe you'd use that foul language toward me." Damn, her mom sure did lay on the thick southern accent when she wanted to. "I have a right mind to tell your father."

Brandi rolled her eyes and grabbed the door knob. "Go ahead. Maybe he'll *ground* me." She laughed as she slipped outside.

Why the hell had she even come by here? Oh that's right, she'd accidentally left her phone here when they'd come back from a European vacation the other day. It was the second damn vacation she'd taken with them in less than 6 months. How many trips did one person need? To Brandi a nice vacation was driving over to Georgia and sitting on Tybee Island for a weekend. She didn't need the fancy restaurants or expensive shops to make her happy. Clearly she was adopted, she thought. She didn't act like her mom *or* her dad. Hell, he wasn't around most of the time while she was growing up. His deep water oil drilling business kept him away for the better part of the time. And when he was home, he didn't care to spend any quality time with her. It was more than likely the reason Brandi tried to find comfort in the arms of the guys she tended to date. All of them had one thing in common. They were bad boys. She knew damn well they weren't relationship material, well, one she thought could've been but he was happily married to a gorgeous redhead and they had a 13-year-old daughter. So much for thinking he was the one for her. But for all the men who passed through her life and bed, Brandi never really felt like she'd been in love. In lust? Sure. But love, not really. She'd crushed on a few of them at one time or another but that was as far as it went.

"Why am I even *thinking* about this shit?" she asked

herself as she climbed into her beat up Toyota. Her car wasn't even up to her mother's standards. Oh well. As usual she rolled the windows down, cranked up the radio and gunned it out of the driveway. What she needed right now was a stiff drink and about 30 miles between her and her overbearing mother.

As she traveled down the two lane highway toward the city, Brandi cranked the song on the radio and began to belt out the lyrics loudly *"I'm gonna pop some tags! Only got $20 in my pocket!"* She stopped singing and took a drink from her water bottle. Then began again, *"This is fucking awe-some!"* Just then she felt her car begin wobbling. Slowing her speed she pulled onto the shoulder. Just great, something was wrong with her car and here she was on this stretch of highway that hardly anyone traveled. After the car was in park, she shut the engine off and got out. She rounded her door and saw the drivers' side tire completely flat. "This is *NOT* fucking awesome," she said aloud. Grabbing her phone from the console, she unlocked it and sighed when she saw the 'no service' tag at the top of the touch screen.

"*Seriously*? This day just keeps getting better." She tossed the device on the seat and slammed the door. Should she take off walking, or stay here and hope someone would pass by and help her? The fact of the matter was she didn't know a thing about changing a tire. It wasn't like she thought she was too good for it, she just never had to do it before. "Guess I'll hang out here for a bit," she said. At least she still had access to Candy Crush on her phone, which would pass a little time. Well, as much time as it took her to use the 5 lives she had saved up. After they were gone, she'd have to let nature entertain her. Oh boy. That sounded like more fun than a barrel full of dildos. She snickered at the thought of a barrel full of dildos. Where would one even find something like that? She knew you could order a bag of dicks online—she'd sent one to co-worker at the newspaper. But a *barrel* of dildos? That might prove difficult to track down. As she sat on the hood of her car contemplating barrels of sex toys, Brandi heard something off in the distance. It was either a super loud car, or a motorcycle. As the sound came closer, she realized it was in fact a motorcycle.

"I'm saved!" She slid off the hood and stood by the driver side door. As the motorcycle came closer she began to wave to stop the rider. They slowed down and pulled in front of her car. Once the rider shut he engine off and dismounted he began walking toward her. He reached up and plucked his helmet off and Brandi damn near fell on her ass.

"Car trouble?" he asked.

"My tit…I mean, tire is flat." Her cheeks became hot at her flub.

The man smiled and bent down to assess the situation. Just so happened she was *assessing* a situation as well. One that involved his ass in those leather pants.

"There a spare in the trunk?" he asked.

"Should be." On shaky legs she popped the trunk. "Shit!" She slammed it back and stepped away.

"Everything okay?" He walked closer.

"Uh, yeah. No. There's just something in there that I don't want anyone to see."

"Trust me, Peaches, I've seen it all."

"Maybe not…" she cringed.

"How about you pop the trunk, I'll grab the tire and won't look at anything else in there?" Damn he was sweet. But why was he calling her *'Peaches'*?

"Well, okay." She reached in the car and pulled the lever again. She stood back and waited for his reaction.

"Holy Fuck," Dash whispered as he lifted the trunk lid of this woman's car. Now this threw him for a loop. He leaned out a bit to look at her again. Nope, she didn't seem like the type to be into this shit. So much for judging a book by its cover.

"Found the tire yet?" she yelled back to him.

"Uh, yeah, I found it." What the hell was he supposed to say? This was some hardcore shit. Trying to be the gentleman, Dash dug out the spare and slammed the trunk. When he rounded the car he chanced a look at her and as he suspected, her cheeks were a deep pink.

"That's not my stuff," she blurted out.

"None of my business." He shoved the small jack

under the car and began to crank it.

"Really, it's not mine."

"And really, it's none of my business." He continued to work on changing the tire. When he was finished he motioned for her to open the trunk again. He put the flat in and slammed it shut.

"You probably think I'm some kind of freak for having all that in there," she said with her head down.

"I'm not here to pass judgement on you, Peaches."

"Thanks." The poor thing looked mortified.

"Get that to a tire shop and get it patched. Shouldn't need a new one." He walked a few feet past her and turned back around. "Can I just say something?"

"I guess."

Dash's boots crunched the gravel loudly as he walked up and stood toe-to-toe with her. "Deny it all you want, but that *is* your shit in there. And if you were mine, I'd use that crop on your tight little ass for lying about it."

Thanks for reading a sample of '*Torn Ends*'

 Social Media

Find Taylor Dawn@

Website & Blog: http://www.taylordawn-author.com/

Facebook:
https://www.facebook.com/AuthorTaylorDawn/?fref=ts

Twitter:
@TAYLORDAWNBOOKS

About The Author

Taylor Dawn (formerly writing as C.D. Taylor) began writing as an item to check off her bucket list. She resides in the southernmost part of Illinois, right on the mighty Mississippi river. She enjoys the quiet country life with her husband, son and the many farm animals that make up the rest of the family. Deciding that farm life was just a little too mundane, Taylor began writing roamcne and fantasy to liven things up, so far so good. Before starting her writing career, Taylor entered the field of cosmetology. When she isn't writing, she can usually be found sitting around a table making people laugh. She has always wanted to be a standup comic. She loves pulling practical jokes, dresses up in a costume every Halloween and believes that dancing is the key to a happy life (even if you aren't a good dancer). She believes that life shouldn't be taken too seriously, we will never get out alive anyway. More than anything, she is a kid at heart, she doesn't believe in bedtimes, eating everything on her plate, or having ice cream only for dessert. Her favorite quote is by Dr. Seuss..."Why fit in, when you were born to stand out."

Great Reads by Taylor Dawn

Our Second Chance (Chances Are: Book 1)

Left to Chance (Chances Are: Book 2)

A Fighting Chance (Chances Are: Book 3)

Saving London

Loose Ends (Magnolia Series: Book 1)

73803171R00227

Made in the USA
Columbia, SC
23 July 2017